REVENGE
OF THE
BEETLE
QUEEN

M. G. LEONARD

REVENGE OF THE BEETLE QUEEN

Chicken House

Scholastic Inc. / New York

Text copyright © 2018 by M. G. Leonard Ltd
Illustrations by Júlia Sardà copyright © 2018 by Scholastic Inc.

All rights reserved. Published by Chicken House, an imprint of Scholastic Inc.,
Publishers since 1920. SCHOLASTIC, CHICKEN HOUSE, and associated logos are
trademarks and/or registered trademarks of Scholastic Inc.

First published in the United Kingdom in 2017 as *Beetle Queen* by
Chicken House, 2 Palmer Street, Frome, Somerset BA11 1DS.

Library of Congress Cataloging-in-Publication Data available
ISBN 978-0-545-85348-4

10 9 8 7 6 5 4 3 2 1   18 19 20 21 22

Printed in the U.S.A   23

First edition, March 2018

Book design by Baily Crawford

Also by M. G. Leonard

For Sam, Sebastian,
& Arthur

We can judge the heart of a man by his treatment of animals.

—IMMANUEL KANT

CHAPTER ONE

Snow White

*T*here was a gentle tap on the door.

"Madame?"

Lucretia Cutter turned her head, her lidless eyes glistening like two inky cysts. Her four black chitinous legs clung effortlessly to the white ceiling, the fabric of her purple skirt tumbling toward the floor. "Yes, Gerard?" she replied.

"The American actress Ruby Hisolo Jr. has arrived for her dress fitting," the French butler said through the door. He was forbidden from entering the White Room unless invited.

"You can bring her down."

"As you wish, Madame."

She listened as the discreet footsteps of the butler retreated up the hallway. It was thrilling to be able to detect the slightest movement in the space around her. Her new body and heightened senses made her powerful. She hungered for the moment when she could show the world who she really was. And it was coming. Soon.

She reached out with her human forearms and crawled to the wall beside the door, descending at alarming speed, reaching the floor and flipping up onto her hind legs. She folded her middle legs into special pockets in the lining of her skirt as she walked across the room, zipping up the split and hiding away her beetle body. She picked up the black wig that lay lifeless on her glass desk and pulled it on, then lifted her white lab coat from the back of the Plexiglas chair. Sliding her hands into the sleeves, she shrugged it onto her shoulders, then whipped out a pair of oversize sunglasses from a pocket and pushed them onto her nose, covering her compound eyes.

She pivoted to check herself in the mirror, grabbing the ebony walking stick that was propped up against the desk. She didn't need the stick, but it encouraged people to believe that she'd had a car accident, and the accident had provided a plausible cover story while she'd metamorphosed within her pupation chamber.

Her senses twitched. She felt vibrations from silent footsteps, those belonging to her personal bodyguard.

Ling Ling was a Kunoichi, a female ninja, trained by Toshitsugu Takamatsu, the bodyguard of Pu Yi, the last Chinese emperor. She had been the youngest principal dancer in the New York City Ballet, but her career ended during a performance of *Swan Lake*, when her ankle shattered as she executed the Black Swan's legendary thirty-two fouettés at a record-breaking speed. Ling Ling had hung up her pointe shoes to take up the ninjato sword, and she was deadly.

Lucretia Cutter opened the door. Ling Ling was waiting outside, dressed in her customary black suit.

"Any sign of those wretched beetles?"

Ling Ling shook her head. "Craven and Dankish are still looking."

"Imbeciles," Lucretia Cutter muttered. "Send out the yellow lady-bugs. I need eyes all over the city. Those blasted beetles could ruin everything for me. I want them found, and I want them destroyed."

Ling Ling gave a curt nod.

The battle with the Emporium beetles had been unexpected, and Lucretia Cutter wasn't in the habit of losing a fight. She wanted the beetles obliterated, not only because they were evidence of her secret work farming transgenic insects, but because they had publicly humiliated her. She'd had to bribe a lot of people to stay out of prison and keep the images of her new eyes off the front pages of the newspapers. Those beetles had cost her time and money, and she wouldn't be happy until they were ground into dust.

"And, Ling Ling, to accompany our spies, send out the venomous Coccinellidae—the eleven-spotted yellow ladybugs. If there's anybody else out there poking their nose into my business, I want them elimi-nated." She raised her index finger. "Although they're not to touch Bartholomew Cuttle. Understood? He's mine."

Ling Ling bowed and padded away.

Lucretia Cutter closed the door. Bartholomew's escape had upset her, but he'd be back. He wouldn't be able to help himself. Tapping her forefinger against her top lip, she contemplated the renegade beetles.

Really, she should be commending herself on their abilities—they'd come from *her* laboratories, after all.

She smiled. Who'd have thought splicing Bartholomew Cuttle's DNA with beetle DNA would have had such impressive results? Coleoptera that thought for themselves and demonstrated free will? That was new. She'd never seen a mix of beetle species cooperating to fight an enemy. It was exciting—although, she'd noticed, they lacked a killer instinct. She sneered. They probably inherited Bartholomew's soft heart. Her new beetles were part German shepherd: trainable, able to fight and carry out orders. She'd bred an army of obedient slaves, and right now, that was all she needed.

Walking over to the two-way mirror behind her desk, she pulled a lipstick from her lab-coat pocket, applying the shimmering gold paint and smacking her lips together. She could throttle that Crips boy for freeing the Cuttle beetles. He'd set her work back years.

A knock on the door and the sound of a well-known husky giggle made her turn around.

"Come in." She fixed a polite smile on her face.

Gerard opened the door and a sultry blond girl in a pink sweater and white pleated skirt tottered in.

"Ruby, darling, so good to see you," Lucretia said, crossing the room.

Ruby Hisolo Jr. flicked her blond curls over her shoulder and looked critically around the sparsely decorated room.

"Wow! Who's your interior designer?" She lifted her hand. "No. Don't say. Whoever it is, fire them. It's like some kinda science lab in here." She grimaced. "It's creepy." She jabbed a perfectly manicured finger at Lucretia Cutter. "You're taking the pharmacy-chic thing way too far. What this room needs is a splash of color"—she flicked her finger at random areas of the room—"apricot or peach. And cushions. Everybody loves cushions. I know a great guy if you need help"—she giggled—"which I think we both know you do."

Lucretia Cutter didn't reply, her expression remaining a polite smile throughout the awkward silence that followed.

"Just tryin' to help," Ruby sighed, unconcerned. She fluttered her eyelashes at Gerard. "I'm thirsty. Got any bubbles?"

The butler went to a fridge under the lab bench, taking out a frosted glass and a dark green bottle. He opened the bottle, filled the champagne flute, and handed the glass to the waiting actress.

Lucretia Cutter clapped her hands together. "So, are we going to steal the hearts of the world at the Film Awards?"

"Of course I am." Ruby emptied her glass in one gulp, handed it back to the butler, and wiped her mouth on her sleeve. "Why else would I be here?"

"Good." Lucretia Cutter smiled through gritted teeth and reminded herself that this fitting was important. "Gerard, bring in *Snow White*."

"Snow White? Who's Snow White?" Ruby frowned. "I thought this was *my* fitting? I told your people on the phone. I'm a big star now, and I ain't gonna . . ."

Gerard wheeled in a dark slender trunk that was as tall as he was.

"I call my creation *Snow White* because it is made from the purest white substance to be found in the natural world," said Lucretia Cutter.

Gerard flicked the catches and the door of the trunk swung open. The inside of the box glowed with light radiating from a delicate dress that hung on a gold hanger.

"Oh my!" Ruby's manicured fingertips brushed against her red lips as she gasped in awe. "It's a dress made of fairy dust!" She stepped toward the trunk, stretching out her hand to touch it.

"Actually, it's made of beetles."

"It's *what*?" Ruby snatched back her hand.

"The *Cyphochilus* beetle, to be precise," Lucretia continued, "an Asian beetle. The extreme whiteness comes from a thin layer of reflective photonic solid on its scales. These scales are whiter than any paper or material mankind has produced. There is a complex molecular geometry to their scales, which are able to scatter light with supreme efficiency."

Ruby was peering at the dress with horror. "You're telling me that dress is made from bugs? They're dead, right?"

"To produce such perfect white scales, *Cyphochilus* beetles must deflect all colors with equal strength," Lucretia Cutter said. "This is a miracle rarely found in nature. But to use these perfect white scales in a garment designed for a ceremony filled with light, cameras with flashbulbs, spotlights—well, that has *never* been done." She looked Ruby Hisolo Jr. in the eye. "The wearer of this dress will dazzle everyone who looks upon her. She will truly *be* a star."

Ruby's eyes flickered back to the dress in the box.

"Would you like to try it on?" Lucretia Cutter whispered, coming closer to the actress. "I've tailored it perfectly for your figure."

Ruby nodded her head slowly. "Mm-hmm. Okay."

Lucretia Cutter signaled for Gerard to take the dress out of the trunk and hang it on the white modesty screen standing on the other side of the room. "Go behind the screen and slip it on. Gerard will get out the mirror for you."

Ruby eyed the dress cautiously. "They're just bugs, right?"

"Precisely." Lucretia Cutter nodded, her smile fixed firmly on her face as she watched the actress walk hesitantly across the room and go behind the screen. "Just bugs."

"Aww, man." Ruby sighed as she slid the dress over her head. "This dress feels unbelievable."

The American actress came out, barefoot, wearing *Snow White*, and the polite smile on Lucretia Cutter's face relaxed into a real one. The dress was dazzling, cut like a 1920s flapper dress, but instead of sequins or beads, it was covered in tiny white beetle elytra, shimmering and reflecting light with every movement of the actress's body.

Gerard folded out the lid and sides of the trunk to reveal three full-length mirrors that allowed Ruby to see herself from all angles. She turned her back to the mirrors and looked over her shoulder, pouting at herself.

"Oh YES!" She jumped up and down in excitement. "I look out of this world!"

"As radiant as a goddess." Lucretia Cutter nodded.

"Yeah. Look at me. I'm a total goddess." Ruby put her hands on her hips and leaned into the mirror, showing off her ample bosom. "I gotta have this dress." She shimmied, and the beetles gave a satisfying rattle. "No other girl at the Film Awards is gonna have a dress like this."

"Other dresses will look like dirty rags next to this one," Lucretia Cutter said. "And when the flashbulbs pop, as you glide down that red carpet, every one of these beetle scales will reflect the light perfectly, giving you the aura of an angel."

"As long as I look better than Stella Manning." Ruby paraded toward the mirror and then away again. "That old witch is yesterday's news. This year, I want all eyes on me. It's gonna be me giving the tearful speeches and getting the Film Award."

"I can promise, no one will be able to take their eyes off you. This dress will go down in history. It will never be forgotten."

"Who knew beetles could be pretty?" Ruby threw up her hands dramatically. "I'll just die if anyone else wears it!"

"I'm honored that an actress of your caliber will be wearing my creation to the Film Awards."

"My stylist said you were a genius, Letitia—"

"Lucretia—"

"—mm-hmm, Letitia, whatever," Ruby said, still marveling at her own reflection, "and I didn't believe her. But how wrong was I?"

"You're too kind." Lucretia Cutter's patience was wearing thin. "However, I must tell you that if you want to wear this dress to the Film Awards, there are some rules that you must agree to."

"Rules?" Ruby frowned. "What kinda rules?"

"You will not see the dress again until the morning of the ceremony, when a member of my staff will come and do the fitting, then drive you to the awards in one of my cars. You are allowed to tell the press that you are wearing a Cutter Couture creation, but you must not describe the dress to anyone. It is to be a secret."

"A secret?" Ruby arched an eyebrow. "I *love* that!" She clapped. "I'll surprise the world when I step out of the limo onto the red carpet. Yes!" She held out her hand to Lucretia Cutter. "Lulu, you got a deal."

"Then the dress is yours," Lucretia Cutter said, ignoring the actress's outstretched hand.

"Sweet." Ruby shrugged, taking one last look at herself in the mirror before skipping behind the screen and, a second later, handing the dress to Gerard. She came out, pulling her pink sweater over her blond curls and slipping her white stilettos back on. "It's been a pleasure doing business with you, Lulu." Ruby stopped to check her makeup in the mirror.

"Oh no," Lucretia Cutter replied, "the pleasure will be entirely mine." She gestured to the door. "Gerard will show you out."

After the door had closed behind them, Lucretia Cutter turned to *Snow White*, admiring her creation. She tilted her head back, and from deep within her throat she made a ghastly clicking sound.

The dress, hanging in the open trunk, shimmered and vibrated like it was coming apart, suddenly exploding into a whirlwind of movement as thousands of specially bred *Cyphochilus* beetles flew out of their fastenings and swarmed around Lucretia Cutter's head like a sparkling tornado.

Lucretia laughed. This was going to be so easy.

CHAPTER TWO

Pop-Pop Pie

*D*r. Bartholomew Cuttle carefully set down two plates on the table in Uncle Max's kitchen, each piled with steaming hot minced lamb in gravy, mashed potatoes, cubed carrots, and a pool of peas.

"Thank you, Dr. Cuttle, sir," Bertolt Roberts said in a polite squeak, pushing his oversize spectacles up his nose.

"It's my pleasure, Bertolt." Bartholomew Cuttle wiped his hands on his jeans as he turned back to the kitchen worktop. "I'm not much of a chef"—he picked up another two plates—"but this is something I *can* cook. It's a family recipe, passed down from father to son."

"Mmmmm." Virginia Wallace breathed in the smell of the food as she reached for her cutlery. Quick as a shot, Bertolt slapped the back of her hand. Virginia scowled at him but returned her hands to her lap.

"It's basically the ingredients of a shepherd's pie"—he put a plate of food in front of Darkus—"just *not* in a pie." He chuckled as he sat down beside his son. Darkus loved the way the skin around his dad's blue eyes crinkled when he smiled, spreading happiness to the edges of his face. "My father made this for me when I was young, and now I make it for my son." He gave Darkus an affectionate look and ruffled his brush of dark hair. "It's your favorite, isn't it, Darkus? *Pop-Pop pie*, he calls it, after my father."

"Dad!" Darkus pulled a face, but felt a warm glow in his chest and a smile tweaking the edges of his mouth. Only a few weeks ago, he'd desperately wished for his dad to be joking around like this, and now, here he was. Uncle Max said that, as he was just out of the hospital, they had to take care not to let him exhaust himself, but Dad got stronger every day. Soon things would be back to normal and they would go home.

He looked across the table. He was going to miss seeing Bertolt and Virginia every day. They were the best friends he'd ever had.

"Tuck in, everyone," his dad said.

"Pop-Pop pie?" Virginia snorted, grabbing her fork, mixing the peas, meat, and carrots into the potato, and shoveling it into her mouth as if she hadn't eaten in a week.

"It's delicious, Dr. Cuttle, sir," Bertolt said, before he'd taken a bite.

"Please, Bertolt, you've got to stop calling me sir. Mr. Cuttle is fine. Or, if you like, call me Barty—everyone else does."

"I couldn't possibly . . ." Bertolt spluttered, his ghostly complexion flushing pink. "I mean, you're the director of science at the Natural History Museum, and—"

"We mostly call you Darkus's dad," Virginia butted in, her mouth so full her brown cheeks were puffed out like a squirrel's. She swallowed. "It's only when you're around that Bertolt gets all weird and calls you sir."

Bertolt stared down at his dinner, eating it like it was a complicated puzzle in need of solving. He was blushing so hard that Darkus could see his scalp through his frizz of white curls.

The day that Dad had got out of the hospital, and Bertolt had met him for the first time, he'd bowed. Bertolt's own father wasn't around, and Darkus suspected that sometimes his shy friend wished for a dad like his.

"Well, you can definitely call me that. I'm proud to be Darkus's dad." He looked at Darkus, his expression suddenly serious. "After all, he saved my life."

"Excuse me," Virginia protested, cocking her head. "I think you'll find we helped."

Bartholomew Cuttle laughed. "Of course, Virginia, and I suspect you're never going to let me forget that, are you?"

"Nope." Virginia shook her head, her black braids flying out, brightly colored beads clattering together. She'd taken to braiding her hair since meeting Marvin, the frog-legged leaf beetle. He found the plaits easier to cling to.

There was silence as they ate, and Darkus became aware that Virginia and Bertolt were waiting for him to speak.

It was time. They'd planned what he was going to say, even rehearsed it, but now he found that he couldn't make the words come out. He filled his mouth with peas and mashed potato, not daring to look up in case he saw Virginia's face telling him to get on with it.

Virginia lifted her empty plate and licked the last of the gravy, causing Bertolt to tut loudly.

There was a slam and a clatter from downstairs.

"It's the prof!" Virginia said, looking at Darkus with meaning.

Two minutes later the kitchen door swung open and Uncle Max blundered into the room, all smiles and friendly greetings.

"There's dinner on the stove, Max, if you're hungry," Barty said to his brother.

"Great!" Uncle Max went over to the cooktop and clapped his hands together. "Pop-Pop pie!" he exclaimed happily, taking out a plate from the cupboard overhead and emptying each of the pans onto it. "I haven't had this in eons."

Virginia's face fell as she realized there'd be no seconds.

Uncle Max removed his safari hat and pulled up a chair. "So?" He looked at Darkus as he picked up his fork. "Did you tell him?" He turned to his brother. "Amazing, isn't it? I wouldn't believe it myself if I hadn't seen them with my own eyes."

Barty frowned. "Believe what?"

Uncle Max made a choking noise, and Darkus suddenly found everyone staring at him.

"Darkus?" His father looked confused. "What's amazing?"

This was it, the moment he'd been waiting for. So why was he nervous?

He stood up, his chair scraping on the floor. "I've got something to show you."

Barty looked at Uncle Max, who nodded enthusiastically. "You're going to love this," he said, picking up his safari hat and popping it back on his head as he filled his mouth with Pop-Pop pie.

"Well then, you'd better show me what it is. I'm intrigued."

Virginia and Bertolt jumped up, speaking to each other with looks as they followed Darkus out of the kitchen.

"We need to go outside"—Darkus looked over his shoulder at his dad—"and climb down a ladder. Are you strong enough to do that?"

"I think I can manage a ladder." Barty nodded.

"It's a big ladder."

"I'm fine, Darkus, really."

Darkus led them out of Uncle Max's flat and down into the street. It was a little past six o'clock. The December night had descended and the streetlights were on. The Laundromat was open and the lights shone in Mr. Patel's newsstand, but the other shops on the parade—Mother Earth, the health food shop, and the tattoo parlor—were dark.

Darkus thought about the morning they'd beaten Lucretia Cutter, and the sound of the gunshot that had ripped through his shoulder as he hurled himself into his father, knocking him to the ground and saving his life. It was the only thing Dad remembered about the rescue. Uncle Max had decided that until he was well again, it would be best if the children kept the mountain of beetles in the sewer, and their role in his rescue, a secret.

It had turned out to be a hard secret to keep. Dad repeatedly asked how they'd got him out of Towering Heights, and Uncle Max would tap his nose, wink at Darkus, and reply: "All in good time, Barty. Darkus and I don't want to embarrass you with how easy it all was."

The worst thing was having to hide Baxter. The rhinoceros beetle had gone underground, back to Beetle Mountain. Darkus hated being separated from his friend. He missed having the large black beetle on his shoulder. He kept talking to his collarbone, expecting Baxter to be hunkered down there, listening, and then stopping midsentence when he remembered he was alone. He longed for the moment when he could introduce his father to Baxter, and tell him the amazing story of how he, Bertolt, and Virginia had saved Beetle Mountain and rescued him from Lucretia Cutter.

And now that moment had arrived.

Barty came to stand behind Darkus, facing the ruins of the Emporium. The shop door had been screwed back on, a piece of graffitied corrugated iron bolted over it. Strips of tape barked CAUTION and POLICE LINE DO NOT CROSS. A yellow triangle filled with an exclamation mark warned BUILDING UNSAFE.

Darkus stepped up to the door, pulling at a leather shoelace tied around his neck and taking out a key.

"What are you doing?" Barty's eyes flicked anxiously to Uncle Max.

"It's all right," Darkus said, opening the door. "We don't normally go in this way, but it's perfectly safe."

Uncle Max nodded cheerfully at his brother.

Darkus took his dad's hand and led him into the Emporium. "Come on, you'll see."

CHAPTER THREE
Beetle Ball

Led by Darkus, they picked their way through the mess of rubble and brick dust, over and between fallen floorboards and lintels, and through the arch into the kitchenette at the back of the shop, where the ceiling was still intact. The room was covered with shattered glass and plaster dust. An old floral apron hung off the back of a cupboard door.

Darkus pulled his dad toward the small bathroom beyond. In the middle of the floor was an open manhole. Virginia disappeared down the hole, followed by Bertolt.

"I'll go next, shall I?" Uncle Max looked at Darkus, who nodded.

"Righty-ho. See you down there." He clambered down, his safari hat the last thing to disappear.

"There's a ladder of metal rungs in the bricks," Darkus explained.

"And this thing you want to show me"—his dad looked at him, puzzled—"it's down there?"

Darkus nodded. "Go on. I'll follow you." He smiled as his dad climbed onto the ladder. "Trust me, you're going to love it."

Darkus scrambled to the edge of the manhole, the back of his neck tingling with excitement. His feet knew where to find the rungs. Descending into the dark, damp climate of the sewer, he heard Uncle Max.

"Barty, I'm going to cover your eyes."

"I can barely see a thing as it is," Darkus's dad grumbled.

"Nearly there now."

Darkus dropped to the ground, darting along the white path around his father and Uncle Max, and stepping onto the Human Zone—a white rectangle, the size of a Ping-Pong table, painted on the floor. In it were three seats from old cars and a coffee table. The white path and rectangle were for the children, and the beetles understood that they had to stay off this part of the floor to avoid getting accidentally crushed.

On the coffee table, a flickering oil lamp filled the chamber with moving shadows, and beside it waited Virginia and Bertolt. Darkus felt a thrill of excitement racing up his arms, his heart beating faster.

Uncle Max led Dad to the larger of the car seats. "Right, put your hands out. That's it. Feel that? It's the back of a chair. Now sit yourself down. Whoops, to the left, yes! Marvelous." He looked at Darkus, his hands still over Barty's eyes.

Darkus took up his position between Virginia and Bertolt, their backs to Beetle Mountain. He nodded, and Uncle Max took his hands away from Barty's face.

Barty blinked and looked around the dark cavern. "I don't understand . . ."

"I've got something to show you," Darkus said, his blood pounding in his ears. "You wanted to know how I got you out of Towering Heights? This is how." He lifted his chin and sucked air through his back teeth, making a high screeching sound. Out of the darkness came the rattling sound of beating wings, and a giant black rhinoceros beetle, almost invisible in the shadowy chamber, landed on Darkus's shoulder. It reared up, waggling its front legs at Darkus's dad.

"This is my friend Baxter," Darkus said. "He helped me rescue you."

His father leaned forward. "It's a *Chalcosoma caucasus*," he whispered, his eyes wide.

"And this is Marvin," Virginia said as a cherry-red metallic bobble wrapped around the end of one of her plaits unfurled, revealing itself to be a frog-legged leaf beetle. The beetle hung upside down for a moment, then dropped onto Virginia's shoulder.

"And this," Bertolt said as his white puffball of hair lit up, "is Newton." A firefly the size of a golf ball rose up above Bertolt's head, his abdomen aglow.

"And these," Darkus threw his arms wide, making a series of rhythmic clicking sounds, "are all the beetles that saved you."

The silent mound behind him exploded with light as the bioluminescent spots on the thorax of hundreds of fire beetles flashed into view. Up in the cavernous roof of the chamber, the fireflies switched on their belly lanterns, light rippling across the ceiling like the northern lights.

Virginia stamped her foot, clapping her hands against her sides in a rhythmic beat that got steadily louder as a high-pitched noise, like the string section of an orchestra, answered her. One eerie note split into two, then three harmonizing sounds. Like a miniature conductor, Marvin rose up on his chunky back legs and pointed at an invisible percussion section tapping out a melody on upturned teacups. A gaggle of dung beetles pushed a series of preprepared sewage balls off the back of the mountain into a giant puddle, making a plopping sound in time with the beat. A faintly recognizable tune rose out of the insect orchestra, and Virginia's shoulders bopped up and down in time to the strange music.

"Is that . . . ?" Bartholomew Cuttle looked at his brother in wonder. "Are they playing Marvin Gaye's 'Grapevine'?"

Uncle Max grinned and nodded, clapping and bobbing his head to the beetle music as a shower of black-and-white tumbling flower beetles back-flipped down the mountain and a chain of red-and-black giraffe-necked weevils did the conga around the base.

The fireflies swarmed together, forming a giant spinning disco ball. Pairs of Hercules and rhinoceros beetles leapt off the branches of the butterfly tree that sprouted from the center of Beetle Mountain, linking horns and helicoptering in circles as a loveliness of ladybugs soared up, grabbing onto the dangling legs of the rhinoceros and Hercules beetles, forming red ribbons that undulated as the beetles spun.

Bartholomew Cuttle's mouth fell open as he watched a troupe of jewel beetles strut out of their teacups, flicking and flaunting their pretty green elytra. Catching hold of a ladybug ribbon, they swung up, somersaulting from one hovering pair of hanging forelegs to another, their iridescent wings reflecting the light of the fireflies.

As the music crescendoed, Darkus gave the signal, and a flood of flying beetles swarmed out of the mountain, grabbing onto his clothing with their clawed legs and slowly lifting him off the floor until he was hovering a foot above his dad's head. "These beetles carried you out of Towering Heights, Dad!" he called out. "Just like this! They saved you."

Baxter zoomed toward Bartholomew Cuttle, dancing around in the air in front of his face, waggling his front legs in time to the music.

"NO!" Bartholomew Cuttle was suddenly on his feet, waving his arms. "STOP! STOP THIS RIGHT NOW!" He knocked the rhinoceros beetle to the ground.

"Baxter!" Darkus cried out.

The beetles holding him aloft became confused, and the insect music descended into an alarming cacophony as the startled fireflies scattered and the dizzy spinning beetles retreated into their mountain of teacups. Darkus found himself dumped on the floor. He scrambled over to his beetle friend, scooping him up in his hands and cradling him to his chest.

"Are you okay, Baxter?" he whispered.

The rhinoceros beetle nodded his horn.

"What did you do that for?" Darkus shouted angrily at his dad. "You could have hurt him!"

Bartholomew Cuttle turned on his brother, his eyes manically wide. "What have you done?"

"Not me, Barty," Uncle Max said, putting his hand gently on his brother's shoulder. "This is not my work. It's yours. These beetles are the result of *your* experiments, *your* research."

"NO!"

"If you meddle with the fabric of a creature, do you think you get a say in how it evolves?" Uncle Max patted his brother. "As it happens, I think you've done a good job."

"No." Bartholomew Cuttle staggered back, shaking his head. "I never achieved results like these. Look at them! They can dance! They're cognizant!" He shook his head and pointed at Beetle Mountain, his eyes growing wide. "This is . . . this is dangerous. We have to get rid of it."

"Dad! No!" Darkus shouted. "These beetles saved you! They saved me!" He hugged Baxter to his chest. "They're my friends!"

Virginia and Bertolt scurried over to Darkus, helping him to his feet.

"You don't understand," Darkus pleaded. "These beetles are amazing. They're special. Spend some time with them, and you'll see."

"No, son, *you* don't understand," Bartholomew Cuttle said. "Nothing good can come of this."

"I thought you loved beetles!" Darkus cried.

Dr. Bartholomew Cuttle fixed his eyes on his son, his shoulders straight and his forehead lifted. "These are not beetles, Darkus. These are Lucretia Cutter's creatures."

CHAPTER FOUR

Base Camp Blues

"*I*t was *me* that saved *him*, and now he expects me to pretend none of it ever happened!" Darkus kicked the sofa, immediately regretting it as his toes burnt hot with pain. He grabbed his foot, collapsing down onto the olive-green cushions, careful not to knock Baxter off his shoulder. "He's treating me like a kid," he added, staring gloomily up at the tarpaulin ceiling of their den, Base Camp.

"He's trying to protect you, Darkus," Bertolt said calmly from his workbench. He was screwing bulldog clips to a metal pole to make a pinching stick while they waited for Virginia to arrive. Newton bobbed happily above his pom-pom of white hair, bioluminescent abdomen flickering. "And you *are* a kid."

"I don't need protecting." Darkus sat up. "*I* didn't go and get myself kidnapped, did I?"

"No, but you did get shot," Bertolt reminded him, looking over his large glasses at Darkus's bandaged shoulder.

"It's just a flesh wound. I'm fine now—look." Darkus slapped his bandage, then gasped as a bolt of pain eclipsed his throbbing toes.

"Right. Yes, you're fine. I can see that." Bertolt sighed. "You shouldn't be angry with him. He's just trying to be a good dad."

"I know, I know." Darkus rubbed his palms against his temples. His head ached and his stomach was twisted with worry.

Dad had been behaving oddly ever since they'd shown him the beetles, and Lucretia Cutter was still somewhere out there. At night, in his dreams, Darkus's dad heard the scratch of her clawed feet coming after him, chasing him into a dark nightmare of two-way mirrors and angry stag beetles.

"Nothing is the way I thought it was going to be," he said, lifting Baxter off his shoulder and scratching at the bandage that held the dressing over his bullet wound. It was wrapped around his torso several times, gathering uncomfortably under his armpit. He put the rhinoceros beetle on his knee and gently rubbed the insect's chin. "You should see the way Dad stares at Baxter. It's like he wants to do experiments on him."

"He wouldn't." Bertolt put his screwdriver down.

"No, I don't think so." Darkus shook his head. "But after we got back from the sewer yesterday, he set up a microscope in Uncle Max's bedroom. From the look of him, he didn't sleep last night. And this morning"—Darkus paused—"he *shaved off his beard*! In my whole life, I've never seen him without a beard. He looks like . . . well, not my dad. He's so thin now, and without his beard, it's like he's a stranger."

"He's been through a lot," Bertolt said. "You both have."

"Yeah." Darkus sighed. "But he won't talk to me about it."

"What about your uncle Max?"

"He's acting like everything is brilliant, which is how I know it definitely isn't. He's worried, too. Last night, when they thought I was sleeping, I heard them arguing." He shook his head. "This morning, I tried to talk to Dad, but he kept changing the subject, asking me about school and—get this—girls!"

"Girls!" Bertolt laughed.

"He asked me if I thought Virginia was pretty!" Darkus couldn't hide his outrage. "I mean, c'mon!"

"Of course she's pretty."

Darkus felt his face going purple. "That's not what I meant. Something serious is going on, Bertolt—something to do with Lucretia Cutter—and Dad won't let me help. We don't know what she's going to do next."

"Maybe she won't do anything," Bertolt said hopefully. "After all, she's a fashion designer."

"She's more than a fashion designer. You know that." Darkus clenched his teeth. "If she isn't up to anything, why did she kidnap Dad in the first place?"

"Calm down, Darkus. We got your dad back, didn't we? And the beetles are safe. No one knows they're hiding in the sewer. It's all going to be okay."

"You don't understand. I thought everything would go back to being normal when Dad came home, but it's not. I thought he'd love the beetles, but he hates them."

Bertolt blinked at him. "It'll be okay. You've got a good dad."

"He's different." Darkus struggled with his words. "He changed when we showed him Beetle Mountain. He has this look in his eyes all the time, like there's something he's thinking about." Darkus bowed his head. "It's like when Mum died. If I walk into a room, he doesn't notice I'm there. Even if I'm standing right in front of him." His voice wobbled. "I thought I'd got him back, but I haven't." He punched a sofa cushion. "*And* he's made me promise not to go any-where near Lucretia Cutter, or have anything to do with her. Do you know, he *lies* when people ask where he was all those weeks when he was missing? He says he was doing research. And he's lying to me too. He knows what Lucretia Cutter's doing, and he won't tell me."

"You can't know that," Bertolt said, gently.

"I *do* know it." Darkus looked away. "I know it like I know my mum is dead." He punched the cushion again.

There was a loud clatter on the other side of the Base Camp door, and Virginia stormed in.

"It's snowing!" she said, her brown eyes shining. "Come outside and see."

"Is it?" Bertolt turned to look at her. "That's the first snow this winter."

"I know! Just in time for Christmas! Come on." Virginia spun around and ran back out of the door. Bertolt looked at Darkus, concerned.

"I'm fine," Darkus said.

Bertolt gestured to the door. "Are you coming?"

"Are you kidding? Of course I'm coming." Darkus gave his friend a weak smile. "It's snowing!"

Bertolt smiled with relief and followed Virginia out of the door.

Darkus lifted Baxter from his knee and stood up. He held the beetle against his cheek and gently leaned his head toward him. "I won't ever let anyone hurt you, Baxter," he whispered, lifting his hand so that he and the beetle were looking at each other, "and I won't let Dad separate us, either. Not ever."

Baxter rubbed the tip of his horn against Darkus's nose.

Moving his hand to rest against his collarbone, Darkus waited as the rhinoceros beetle clambered onto his shoulder, and they headed out of Base Camp together.

They scrambled through the warren of tunnels constructed from the bric-a-brac furniture in the yard. A Grand Archway made of bicycles strapped together with cable ties offered a choice of tunnels, signposted as Weevil Way, Tok-Tokkie Tunnel, and Dung Ball Avenue. Scurrying into Weevil Way, careful not to trigger Bertolt's booby trap, Darkus ran in a crouch, bursting out from under the folding table to find Virginia dancing around in circles with her arms up, trying to grab the fat flakes of snow that fell from the mushroom-colored sky.

Bertolt stuck out his tongue and caught a snowflake, which promptly melted. Newton dodged a series of flakes and took cover in his hair.

"The moment there's enough snow to make a snowball, you're dead meat." Virginia grinned at him.

"I'm a pretty good shot," Darkus replied with a wry smile.

"Nah," Virginia shook her head, "you're going down. You can even have Bertolt on your side and I'll have you both begging for mercy in minutes."

"Hey!" Bertolt protested halfheartedly.

She pushed up her coat sleeve and whirled her arm around to demonstrate her snowball-hurling deadliness. Darkus laughed. You couldn't be angry when snow was falling from the sky—it made hard surfaces soft, covered up problems, and transformed the world into a giant playground.

CHAPTER FIVE

Turning Rogue

Novak sat on the edge of her pink marshmallow of a bed, nervously swinging her legs. She stared at the tower of cases and trunks beside the door, hope and anxiety churning her insides. It felt odd to be leaving Towering Heights. She'd always lived here, but today she was traveling to a private school in Copenhagen. She'd never been to a school before. She hoped the girls there would like her.

She was wearing her smartest traveling outfit, a candy-floss-pink dress and matching bolero jacket, with thick white tights and ballet pumps. The scabs from the assassin bug bites were beginning to fade, but she still wanted her body covered. She knew she was different from other girls, and she didn't want anyone to see the bites and ask difficult questions. Mothers weren't supposed to lock their daughters in prison cells and send assassin bugs in to hurt them.

Mater hadn't guessed that Novak had helped Darkus rescue his dad, but she'd been severely punished for distracting Mawling when he should have been guarding the cells. Mater had thrown her in a cell for a whole week, and released the assassin bugs to feed on her. For the first few hours, she could brush off the bugs, but eventually Novak had gotten up, and she had danced. She'd filled her head with the music from the ballet *Giselle* and danced all the parts in the story about the peasant girl who fell in love with a faithless prince. Dancing made it harder for the bugs to climb onto her. She'd killed countless numbers of them as she leapt and spun, but finally she was unable to dance any longer, and fell to her knees. Every bite hurt. There were so many of them. She'd imagined Darkus kneeling beside her, holding her hand, telling her to be brave. Mater was his enemy, and now she was Novak's enemy, too.

A knock startled her from her thoughts. It must be the car. She jumped to her feet.

"Mademoiselle." Gerard stood in her bedroom doorway. "Your mother wishes to see you."

Novak blinked, surprised. "I need a minute."

Gerard nodded. "You are to go to her rooms immediately." He bowed his head. "I'll wait outside."

Novak hadn't seen Mater since she'd ordered Craven to throw her in the cell. Did she want to say good-bye? Novak gently lifted off the headband that was holding back her long silver-blond hair. The band had a corsage of dusty-pink silk roses that sat prettily on the side of her head. Nestled in the corsage, almost invisible, was a jewel beetle, her body shimmering all the colors of the rainbow.

"You can't come with me, Hepburn. It's not safe," Novak whispered. "Not to Mater's rooms."

The pretty jewel beetle flicked her antennae huffily as she clambered up out of the silk flowers.

"I know, I know, but I'll be back soon, and then you and I are getting out of here—forever." Novak stroked Hepburn's thorax with her little finger. "I'm going to put you in my handbag."

She opened her pink leather shoulder bag. It was packed for the journey to Copenhagen. She carefully wedged the headband between two books so that Hepburn's hiding place wouldn't get crushed. "You'll be safe in here." She blew the beetle a kiss and closed the bag. "I'm ready," she called, opening the bedroom door.

Gerard walked ahead of her in measured strides. Halfway down the hallway he stopped and turned his head. "It is good Mademoiselle is leaving here." He faltered and swallowed. "I cannot protect you."

Novak took his white-gloved hand and gave it a squeeze. They walked along the corridor and down the stairs in silence, hand in hand. When they reached the third floor Gerard let go.

"*Sois courageuse,*" he whispered. "Be brave." He knocked on the door.

"Come," Lucretia Cutter called out.

Novak commanded her heart to beat slowly and regularly, arranging her face into a blank mask before pushing the door open.

Mater was sitting at her dressing table, her back to the door. Her chambers had cathedral-height ceilings constructed of arches and were an artist's exercise in shades of black. Black walls, black doors, black glass, black lace . . . and everything was edged with gold. Novak had always found the rooms terrifying, but it was the faint lingering smell of pear drops—or was it rotting bananas?—that most unnerved her.

She stepped into the room. "Good morning, Mater." She dropped into a curtsey, her eyes locked on the black floorboards. Lucretia Cutter slowly turned around in her ebony chair, and Novak braced herself to receive the critical gaze of her mother.

She was wearing a floor-length black kimono with gold embroidery that matched her lips. The fringe of her black bobbed wig brushed the top of her trademark sunglasses.

"You wanted to see me?" Novak kept her eyes on the floor.

"Oh yes. So I did."

There was a long silence, and Novak's hands began to shake as her mother scrutinized her. "I'm going to school today," she said, to break the silence.

Mater turned back to her dressing-table mirror. "No, you're not."

"What?" Novak flicked her gaze up, her heart jumping when she saw her mother staring at her in the mirror.

"I've changed my mind."

"But I've packed, I . . ."

"I'm shutting up the house. We will be flying to LA in a few days."

"LA?"

"Yes, I've got to prepare for the Film Awards."

"Film Awards?" Novak stuttered. "But you don't like awards ceremonies . . ."

"I'm going to like this one a lot." A smile twisted her mouth. "And you have been nominated for an award."

"I have?" Novak's mouth dropped open.

"Yes, in the Best Actress category." She laughed. "Isn't that hilarious?"

"Best actress?" Novak couldn't believe what she was hearing. It was her dream to win a Film Award. Only the truly great actresses won a Film Award.

Novak felt a draft on the back of her neck, and suddenly Ling Ling was there, standing at her shoulder.

"Ah, Ling Ling, do you have news for me?"

Ling Ling didn't answer, but looked pointedly at Novak.

"Go away." Lucretia Cutter shooed Novak out of the room with a hand weighed down with diamond-encrusted rings.

"Yes, Mater." Novak curtsied again and backed away.

Outside, she stood for a minute trying to work out what had just happened. Her mother hated awards ceremonies. She never attended them, even when she won things, so why would she want to go to the biggest award ceremony in the whole world when it was Novak who was nominated?

Imagine if I won, Novak thought, and a thrill of excitement made her heart swell. A thousand sparkling fireflies seemed to be darting about inside her chest. She sighed and leaned her head against the door, hoping to hear a bit more about the Film Awards.

"What's the news on those revolting cousins, the owners of the Emporium?" she heard Mater ask Ling Ling.

"Humphrey Gamble and Pickering Risk are still in prison, but without evidence to support the charge that they shot Darkus Cuttle, the police will have to release them eventually."

Novak went cold, goose bumps rising on her arms. *Darkus, shot?*

"Forget those morons. They're so unbelievably stupid, they're hardly a threat." She laughed, and, after a pause, sighed. "If only that boy hadn't leapt in front of his father, there wouldn't be all this fuss. It's made it impossible to stay in London. Just when I think I've paid off everyone, a new witness appears. I can't risk the media attention. I wasn't shooting to kill Bartholomew Cuttle, just put him out of action. I should have let you do it. Did you take care of that obnoxious journalist?"

"Emma Lamb won't be reporting any more news stories," Ling Ling replied. "No one will hire her now."

"Good."

Novak crept backward, away from the door, and then ran down the hall. Gerard was waiting by the stairs.

"The car is here, Mademoiselle."

"I'm not going," Novak gasped. "She's changed her mind."

She ran up the stairs two at a time. Her heart was breaking apart; her only friend in the whole world had been shot, by her own mother. Darkus was dead.

CHAPTER SIX

Migrating Jailbirds

*H*umphrey Gamble was lying on his back in his bunk. He stared at the gray foam mattress above him, following the diamond shapes cut out by the wire bed base, trying to ignore his cousin's endless babbling. Out of the corner of his eye he saw a wood louse trundle along the whitewashed wall toward his chubby elbow. He pinched it between his thumb and forefinger, popping it into his mouth. There wasn't enough food in prison.

Wood lice aren't very tasty, he thought as he chewed the tiny ball with his front teeth. *Beetles are better. More meat on 'em.*

Pickering was still jabbering on in the bunk above him.

"The big question, Humpty, is what do we do first?"

"I've told you not to call me that," Humphrey growled.

Pickering's giggle was a quacking hiss of spittle. His sallow head peered down from above. "What do you think we should do when we get out of here?" His scraggly eyebrows were raised, and his yellow, ratlike teeth jutted out of his partially open mouth. His elbow of a chin was clothed in salt-and-pepper stubble, and his thin, wiry hair hung down like unraveling string.

"Whatever," Humphrey grunted, rolling away from Pickering's bloodshot eyes to face the wall.

"But I'm asking *you*," Pickering persevered. "C'mon, Humpty, we're partners now. Do we find the boy first? Or do we visit Lucretia Cutter? She owes us half a million pounds, remember?" He poked Humphrey's back with a bony finger. "We gave the beetles to her, it's not our fault the nasty beasties fought back."

"The moment they let me out of here I am going to a kebab shop." Humphrey rubbed his empty belly. "And then I'm going to find that boy and hammer him into the ground."

"Yes!" Pickering shrieked. "We'll get the boy first!" He clapped excitedly, then stopped. "But wait, what will you buy your kebabs with?" He shook his head. "No, we must visit Lucretia Cutter first and get what's rightfully ours. Once we've got our money, you can have a bathtub of kebabs!"

Humphrey harrumphed, but nodded. He could see the sense in this, and he definitely liked the idea of a bathtub filled with kebabs.

"And *then*"—Pickering flapped his hands—"WE'LL KILL THE BOY!"

"Shhhhhhhhhh!" Humphrey hissed. "They'll never let us out of here if they think the first thing we're going to do is kill a kid."

"Oh yes!" Pickering whispered. "We must keep it a secret, Humpty. Shhhhhhhh!" He giggled.

Humphrey shook his head. Something had happened to Pickering when their home above the Emporium had collapsed into a heap of rubble. It was as if a tightly coiled spring inside him had been twisted too far, and now it bulged and bounced in unpredictable directions. Pickering used to care about stuff . . . like his appearance. He was scrupulously clean, always with neatly trimmed nails and nose hair. But since the beetles had fired an arsenal of poo at him, he'd stopped washing. Everything that used to matter, like his precious antiques and the shop, had melted away, leaving only three things that interested him: the money, that boy, and Lucretia Cutter. His crush on the billionairess who'd offered to buy their beetles seemed to have only grown more intense with rejection. He'd tied knots in Muckminder, his comfort blanket, until it resembled a doll, and at night, when he thought Humphrey was sleeping, he called it Lucretia and kissed it.

Humphrey had gone over and over the events that had led to his and Pickering's arrest, but couldn't work it out. Someone had planted bombs in his house and shot the kid, Darkus Cuttle. They'd been charged with both crimes, though neither of them owned a gun, nor had any reason for blowing up their own home.

Humphrey was not happy about the possibility of a lifetime in prison. He didn't mind the place itself: It was clean, which is more than could be said about his bedroom, and he'd never lived in luxury.

The people inside were no different from the people outside. Humphrey believed everyone would rob you given half a chance—he knew *he* would. The main thing that upset him about prison was the food, or severe lack of it. He missed his meat pies with cranberry sauce. His pendulous gut was greatly reduced after a month of prison food; his skin hung off his bones like melting wax. He nursed a permanent bellyache, and the more his stomach hurt, the more murderous his thoughts became.

The sound of footsteps approaching made him turn toward the barred wall of their cell. Pickering swung up into a sitting position, his hairy feet dangling down in front of Humphrey's face. He *really* needed to clip his toenails.

A guard in uniform, with a peaked hat and a large bundle of keys, stood on the other side of the bars.

"It's your lucky day, gentleman. It would seem Her Majesty's Prison Service no longer wants to provide you with accommodation."

"What?" Pickering leapt down to the ground, gibbering with excitement.

"We're free to go?" Humphrey rolled himself onto the floor and sat up on his knees.

"It would appear that way," the prison officer replied.

"I don't understand." Humphrey frowned.

"The charges against you have been dropped. Lack of evidence. You can pick up your clothes and possessions on the way out. Follow me, please."

"But . . ." Humphrey pulled himself to his feet, astonished. Pickering was already dancing through the cell door after the guard.

Humphrey lumbered behind them, his belly roaring like an angry lion as he realized he was finally going to get a decent meal.

Pickering dropped back and linked his sticklike arm through Humphrey's. "The money first," he whispered, winking. "And then we go get that nasty boy."

Humphrey gave a silent, solid nod. Once he'd filled his belly, he was going to enjoy taking that boy apart.

CHAPTER SEVEN

What Happened to Spencer Crips?

King Ethelred Hall School hummed like a drowsy beehive. A jangling bell sounded and the building exploded as children clad in black-and-purple uniforms zoomed out of doors and gates like angry hornets. Darkus waited for Virginia and Bertolt by the main gate.

"What are you doing now?" Virginia asked as the three of them set off up the road together.

"Don't know." Darkus shrugged. "Dad's at home being weird. I caught him yesterday coming out of the Emporium with a sample jar of beetles."

Bertolt stopped dead, a look of alarm on his face. "He wouldn't hurt them?"

"No." Darkus shook his head. "All my life he's taught me not to kill or hurt living things. I think he's studying them. His desk is piled high with books, and he only comes out of his room to go to the bathroom."

"What's he doing in there?" Virginia wondered.

"I think he's trying to work out what Lucretia Cutter's done to them," Darkus said. "I tried to tell him that I understand the beetles, that I'd been inside Towering Heights and could help, but he said I wasn't objective, that I wasn't being scientific."

"Scientific!" Virginia scoffed. "What does that even mean?"

Bertolt started to reply. "I think what he means is—"

"Okay, Einstein." Virginia put her hands on her hips, cocking her head in mock despair. "I know what he means. I just think . . ." Her face froze.

"What?" Bertolt frowned. "What is it?"

Virginia looked into Bertolt's eyes, her face deathly serious, and silently mouthed the words "Don't move!" She leapt toward him, grabbing his shoulder. Bertolt yelped but held still, looking terrified.

"What is it? What is it?"

"Darkus!" Virginia shouted. "Get me a box, a container, anything! *Quick!*"

Darkus searched his pockets in a panic and pulled out a clear plastic Tic Tac box, a few brightly colored sweets left at the bottom.

"Pull the lid off," Virginia instructed, her hands cupped together as she carefully pulled them away from Bertolt. "Empty it."

Darkus quickly did as he was told and held out the empty container.

"Wow! This thing's going mental trying to get out," Virginia said, not taking her eyes off her cupped hands. "Ow! It bit me!"

"What bit you?" Bertolt asked.

"The ladybug."

Bertolt was shocked. "Ladybugs don't bite."

"Well, this one does."

"Actually, some ladybugs are cannibals," Darkus said.

"Cannibals?" Bertolt's eyebrows shot up. "They eat each other?"

"Darkus, I'm going to open a tiny gap between my index and forefinger." She nodded at the two fingers of her right hand. "Hold the box over the gap."

Darkus nodded as he placed the clear plastic box over Virginia's fingers.

"Here goes." Virginia's face was so concentrated her eyebrows were touching. She carefully opened up a gap—just a chink—under the plastic container. A black-and-yellow shape shot into the box. "Got you!" she crowed, flipping the box upside down, turning the beetle on its back, and flattening her hand over the top. "Quick, give me the lid."

Darkus handed the white plastic lid to Virginia and she sealed the container, holding it up so they could all see it.

"It's a yellow ladybug!" Bertolt said.

"A big one." Virginia looked at Darkus.

The six-spotted ladybug was angrily throwing itself at the wall of the container, trying to get out.

"She's watching us!" Darkus hissed.

"Who is?" Bertolt looked from Darkus to Virginia in alarm.

"Lucretia Cutter." Darkus swallowed, his mouth suddenly dry.

"The yellow ladybugs are her spies. Remember, there was one in the entomology vault in the Natural History Museum, when I was looking for Dad?"

Virginia nodded. "From now on, we need to keep our eyes peeled."

"It was on *me?*" Bertolt squealed. "Why was it on me?"

"I thought I saw one the other day," Virginia said to Darkus, "outside the Emporium, but when I looked a second time it had gone."

"We should stick together," Bertolt said, clearly shaken, "at all times."

"Agreed." Darkus nodded. "I need to get back to Base Camp, make sure Baxter is all right."

Darkus had been banned from bringing his rhinoceros beetle into school after Baxter had crawled out of his blazer pocket during domestic science and nibbled the bananas laid out to make banana cream pie. When she saw him, the teacher, Mrs. Pavlova, had screamed. Robby, the class bully, had chanted loudly, "Beetle Boy FREAK! Beetle Boy FREAK!" and the other children—the ones who weren't screaming—had joined in. After that, Darkus had left Baxter in his tank in Base Camp when he went to school.

"Well, I need to go to the library later," Virginia said, carefully putting the Tic Tac box in her backpack and zipping the pocket closed, "but we should take the ladybug to Base Camp. Keep it there. You can get Baxter at the same time."

"Why the library?" Darkus asked.

"Benson's history homework, finding a primary and secondary source of evidence from a real event. I figure the library's the best place to go. I thought I'd use a newspaper article about Lucretia Cutter." She grinned. "Doing detective work and homework at the same time."

"That's a good idea." Darkus nodded.

"We can go to the library together." Bertolt looked hopefully at his friends. "We've all got to do Mr. Benson's assignment, after all."

"Yeah"—Virginia slung the backpack over her shoulder—"but I'm the one doing Lucretia Cutter. You can't copy my idea."

"I've found something on the old microfilm viewing thingy, come and see." Virginia waved her hand in front of the boys' faces.

Darkus and Bertolt got up from the library computer where they'd been searching the newspaper archive for stories about Lucretia Cutter. The computer archive went back only three years, because the bulk of the historical archive was stored on microfilm and had to be viewed on a special machine, which Virginia had claimed as soon as they'd walked through the doors of the library. The microfilm machine had a large monitor, and below it was Virginia's chosen microfilm tape, which looked like a ribbon of photograph negatives. As she pressed a red button, the tape was fed underneath a lens and an image appeared on the screen.

Virginia jabbed her finger at it. "Listen to this," she said. *"Spencer Crips, a sixteen-year-old boy from east London, who works as a laboratory assistant at* Cutter Laboratories"—Virginia paused, flinging them a look loaded with meaning—"*is thought to have tragically drowned in the Camden canal. Police were unable to recover his body, which was swept away into the sewer system, but a pair of his shoes and a watch were discovered on the bank of the waterway. He leaves behind a devastated mother, Mrs. Iris Crips, who asked that we print this statement: 'Spencer is my life. I don't believe he has drowned. He's a good swimmer. Please, if you see him, contact the police.'* Chief Superintendent Suborn said that Mrs. Crips was grief-stricken and, unfortunately, they were certain Spencer Crips had drowned."

"I don't understand. What's that got to do with anything?" Darkus frowned at Virginia. "Other than Spencer What's-His-Name working for Lucretia Cutter, it's got nothing to do with the beetles."

"Don't you think it sounds a bit odd?" Virginia said. "A pair of shoes, a watch, but no dead body?"

"Maybe he went for a swim in the canal and got dragged under," Bertolt said.

"Are you kidding me? Have you seen how shallow the canal is? Shopping carts stick up out of it." Virginia pointed to the screen again. "And look, this article is dated five years ago."

"So?" Darkus prompted.

"So . . ." Virginia rolled her eyes impatiently. "Haven't you ever wondered how long the beetles have been living in their mountain? We know they were born with their special abilities in Lucretia Cutter's laboratories, but when? And how did they get out of there? Something must have happened for them to end up in the Emporium."

"Yeah." Darkus nodded. "That's true."

"I think this is it." Virginia pointed at the picture beside the article. A boy with a friendly crab-apple face, topped by a clump of unkempt fair hair, smiled at them from behind rectangular glasses. "Spencer Crips."

"What makes you think Spencer Crips has anything to do with the beetles?" Bertolt asked.

"Because I'm a genius." She tipped her head to one side and smiled. "And I worked out how long the beetles have lived in the mountain."

"How?" Darkus asked.

"Marvin told me." She held her hand underneath the hair braid Marvin was clinging to, and the cherry-red beetle dropped down onto his giant black legs. "He doesn't understand time, so I explained what Christmas is. I showed him the colored lights that are being strung up in our street, and the decorated trees in people's windows, and he told me he's seen four Christmases before."

"He *told* you that, did he?" Darkus snorted.

"No, smart aleck, obviously not. Marvin can't talk, he's a beetle. But he can tap his leg on the table, and that's how he tells me numbers. He tapped his leg four times—that means Marvin has seen four Christmases. It's December now, so this will be his fifth Christmas." She narrowed her eyes and pursed her lips, daring either of them to doubt her.

"That's pretty clever," Bertolt said, looking at Darkus.

"Yeah, that's good," Darkus admitted.

"I know!" Virginia crowed. "I was looking for something that happened about five years ago that might explain it, but that's not all . . . Marvin recognizes him."

"What!?" Darkus spluttered.

"He got excited when he saw this picture. He dropped onto the screen, and—I swear—he stroked Spencer Crips's face."

"Weird," Bertolt whispered, his eyes wide.

Darkus put his face close to the glass of the screen, leaning his shoulder in so Baxter could see the picture. "Baxter. Do you recognize him? Do you know Spencer Crips?"

The rhinoceros beetle nodded his head.

"See!" Virginia said. "They all know him."

Darkus looked at Virginia. "But what does this mean?"

"It means we need to visit Mrs. Crips and ask her what she thinks really happened to her son." Virginia jumped to her feet. "Because I have a hunch that he might still be alive."

"No!" Bertolt looked horrified. "We can't ask a stranger about whether her son is dead or not!"

"I can't go anyway," Darkus said flatly. "Dad's forbidden me from doing any detective work to do with Lucretia Cutter."

"But you're here looking through articles to do with her." Virginia put her hands on her hips.

"Yeah, but this is homework for Benson, in the library." Darkus shrugged, feeling uncomfortable. "It's safe, and Dad isn't going to know what articles I was looking at. Going and talking to someone about Lucretia Cutter, that's definitely forbidden."

"Oh, come on," Virginia protested, "this may not have anything to do with Lucretia Cutter, in which case it'll be fine, and if it does . . . well, don't you want to know?"

"Of course I do, but I'm supposed to sit around doing nothing," Darkus said miserably, "not getting into trouble, or in the way."

"Doing nothing is the same as helping Lucretia Cutter," Virginia said. "And what about the yellow ladybug? She's watching us."

"Yeah, I know," Darkus agreed, "which Dad would say was even more of a reason to keep out of trouble."

"You know what I think?" Virginia said, crossing her arms. "I think this"—she waved a hand at the newspaper article—"is similar to stories I read a couple of months ago, about a scientist who disappeared from a locked vault in the Natural History Museum. The police and the papers said he'd run away or killed himself, and they didn't want to investigate. They did nothing."

Darkus's eyebrows shot up.

"What if this is the same, Darkus?" Virginia said. "What if this is like when your dad disappeared? What if Spencer Crips is alive somewhere? What about Mrs. Crips?"

"But . . ." Darkus looked at the ground. "I promised Dad."

"We won't be going anywhere near Towering Heights. Mrs. Crips lives in Hackney."

"How do you know that?" Bertolt asked.

"I looked her up in the phone book. Twenty-seven Elton Road." Virginia grinned, holding up a large blue book that was on the table beside the microfilm viewer. "C'mon, Darkus," she pleaded. "Your dad couldn't mind us going to talk to an old lady who's probably never even met Lucretia Cutter."

"We could ask him," Bertolt said helpfully.

Virginia slapped his arm. "No, we couldn't."

Darkus thought about all the rules he'd had to obey since his dad had got out of the hospital. He wouldn't actually be disobeying any of them directly. "I suppose it's not really to do with Lucretia Cutter . . ."

"We may not even find out anything," Virginia coaxed.

"Oh, all right!" Darkus threw his hands up. "I'm sick of sitting around and waiting for someone to tell me what's going on. Let's do it."

"Yes!" Virginia punched the air. "I say we visit Mrs. Crips now. We can take the bus—it's about twenty minutes away."

"If we find out anything important," Darkus said, feeling a surge of excitement, "we can tell Dad and Uncle Max and show them the yellow ladybug." He smiled. "Then Dad will see that I *can* help."

CHAPTER EIGHT
Scud

Number 27 Elton Road stood out from its neighbors like a rotten incisor in a line of pearly-white teeth. The cracked paving in the tiny front garden was choked with ivy and dandelions, and the path up to the front door was clogged with chip bags and sweet wrappers. Darkus noticed the curtains were drawn.

"This building looks sad," Bertolt whispered.

"Baxter, you're going to have to hide," Darkus told the rhinoceros beetle. "You too, Marvin, and you, Newton."

Baxter crawled into the neck of Darkus's green sweater, Newton disappeared into Bertolt's thicket of white hair, and Marvin curled himself up around the end of one of Virginia's braids.

"C'mon." Virginia knocked on the door loudly and pushed Bertolt forward. They had decided that, as Bertolt was the neatest and least frightening, he should do the talking.

They waited for Mrs. Crips to open the door.

"Shall I knock again?" Virginia whispered, and then a click sounded, and the door opened a sliver.

An eye and a nose, framed by curly gray hair, peeped through the gap. The eye blinked. "Yes? Who is it?"

Virginia poked Bertolt in the back.

"Good day, Mrs. Crips. We are sorry to bother you," Bertolt said politely. "My name's Bertolt, this is Virginia, and this is Darkus. We know it's a terrible imposition to ask, but we were wondering if we could talk to you about Spencer?"

Mrs. Crips opened the door a little wider. She was a small woman, shrunken by a stooped back and rounded shoulders. She wore a black dress, and her springy gray curls were tangled and uncared-for, but she had a kind face, and its deep lines suggested she had smiled a lot in her past.

Her scraggly eyebrows rose as Bertolt haltingly explained that they were detectives and had come across Spencer's story in the library, that they felt his case hadn't been properly investigated by the police, and that—with her permission—they'd like to do a bit of investigating of their own.

"Of course," Bertolt added, blinking, "if you'd rather not talk about it we'd quite understand—"

"You see," Virginia interrupted, "we think Spencer may still be alive."

Mrs. Crips's face brightened and she let the door swing open. "You've no idea how long I've waited for someone to say those words. Come in, come in."

The square hallway opened out into a dingy living room. Beyond it, Darkus could see a beige kitchen and cork-tile flooring. Along the long left wall of the living room was a thin shelf that stepped up over an old electric fireplace to become a mantelpiece and stepped down again on the other side, becoming the top of a bookshelf. The shelf was stuffed with framed photographs, as were the side tables that hovered beside the two armchairs sitting on either side of a grubby circular rug. The pictures were all of Spencer: Spencer building a sandcastle, Spencer's school photos, Spencer straddling a bicycle. In one picture Spencer was a happy-toothed toddler holding his mother's hand. Mrs. Crips was young and smiling, a homely woman in a flowery dress, her unruly hair pinned up, one caramel-colored curl flying free in the wind.

Standing in the darkened room, Darkus could feel how desperately Mrs. Crips missed her son. He sat down on one of the arms of the big chairs, suddenly feeling the weight of how much he missed his own mother.

"Look." Virginia elbowed him and pointed at a picture hanging on the wall above the fireplace. A skinny teenage Spencer in a white lab coat, his hands balled up in his trouser pockets, was looking adoringly through rectangular spectacles at an enormous dung beetle sitting on his shoulder.

Darkus gasped.

In the kitchen, Mrs. Crips filled her kettle and took out porcelain teacups. "I had a packet of biscuits in here somewhere," she said, opening and closing cupboards.

"Don't worry," Bertolt said. "We'll manage just fine without them."

"Oh no, I insist. It's not every day I have visitors who want to talk about Spencer."

Once the kettle had boiled, Bertolt lifted it and poured water into the waiting teapot. "We really don't want to be any trouble."

"No, no, no trouble at all," Mrs. Crips said, her head inside a cupboard. "My Spencer loves to dunk a biscuit in a cup of tea. Here we are now." She turned around with a packet in her hand. "I knew I had some."

"I'll carry it," Bertolt insisted as she loaded the teacups onto a floral tea tray.

Mrs. Crips pulled a small side table between the two armchairs. "Set it down here—Bertolt, is it?—thank you."

Mrs. Crips sat down opposite Darkus with a happy sigh. "I can't remember the last time I had a conversation with anyone other than the postman," she said, looking at the three children. "Now, why don't you tell me what it is that you want to know about my Spencer?"

"I read in the paper, Mrs. Crips"—Virginia paused, and Darkus wondered what was going to come out of her mouth—"that you think Spencer . . . um, that perhaps he didn't drown like the police said?"

"No. Spencer would never drown," Mrs. Crips replied with certainty. "He was a good swimmer and the canal is shallow."

"But what about the shoes and his watch?" Virginia asked.

"Pooh!" Mrs. Crips's face scrunched up like she had smelled something bad. "I don't know why that appeared in the papers." She shook her head. "It's rubbish."

"So what do you think did happen?" Darkus asked.

"All I know is that Spencer didn't come home from work one day," Mrs. Crips said. "The shoes and the watch weren't his. The shoes must have belonged to some other unfortunate soul, but my Spencer is a size nine and those shoes were a size eleven. He wore scruffy trainers, and those were smart brogues. I told the police all of this, but would they listen?"

"No," Darkus replied. "I'll bet they didn't investigate any of it."

"Spencer was kidnapped," Mrs. Crips said. "I'm sure of it."

"How can you be sure?" Bertolt asked.

"What other explanation is there? My Spencer is a caring, happy boy who would never do anything to worry me. Wherever he is, he's being held against his will and can't contact me. That's kidnapping."

"Do you have any idea who did it?" Virginia leaned forward. "Or why?"

Darkus's eyes flickered up to the photograph of Spencer and the dung beetle. He had a horrible feeling he knew what had happened.

"The day that Spencer went missing, before the police came and told me all that rot about him drowning, a woman came here and took Scud."

"Scud?"

Mrs. Crips pointed at the photo. "Spencer had a pet dung beetle called Scud."

Bertolt glanced at Darkus, who looked at Virginia. She nodded in reply to their silent question.

"Did the woman who took him have a walking stick and big sunglasses?" Virginia asked.

Mrs. Crips shook her head. "No, it was an Asian woman in a black suit with a chauffeur's cap. She said Spencer had stolen property belonging to Cutter Laboratories. She barged right in here, searching the place until she found Scud's kettle in Spencer's room—Scud slept in an old copper kettle filled with damp soil, you see—and took him, without so much as a by-your-leave."

"That sounds like Lucretia Cutter's chauffeur." Bertolt looked up at Darkus.

"I told the police about her, but they laughed at me." Mrs. Crips shook her head. "They even asked me if it was true that Spencer was a thief."

"Mrs. Crips . . ." Darkus leaned forward. "We believe every word you are saying." He hesitated. "Scud, was he . . . clever?"

Mrs. Crips gripped the arms of her chair and stared at Darkus. "How could you know that?"

Darkus looked at Virginia and Bertolt. The three of them got to their feet.

Baxter crawled out from his hiding place under Darkus's sweater. Marvin leapt down from Virginia's braid as Newton rose out of Bertolt's hair, glowing.

"Because we have beetles like Scud," Darkus replied. "This is Baxter"—he pointed to each beetle in turn—"and this is Marvin and this is Newton. Our beetles understand humans, too."

Mrs. Crips's eyes were wide and her mouth open as she looked at the three beetles.

"Oh, my dears, if this is true," she whispered, "then you are in terrible danger."

"We know." Darkus nodded. "That's why we need you to tell us as much as you can about what happened before Spencer disappeared. It might help."

Mrs. Crips's eyes darted from side to side, her shoulders dropped, and she sighed.

"Shall I pour the tea?" Bertolt asked, lifting the teapot. "It'll be ruined if it's left much longer." Newton danced about him, flashing, happy to be out of hiding.

"Spencer wanted more than anything to be a vet," Mrs. Crips said as Darkus and Virginia returned to their seats. "But he didn't get on with school. He was bullied. He dropped out and got a job working for a cleaning company, doing night shifts in big offices, vacuuming carpets and wiping down desks. One of those offices was Cutter Laboratories in Wapping.

"One morning he comes home from work saying he's seen a job posted up on a notice board, to be a laboratory assistant looking after beetle farms. He was so excited about getting to work with living creatures that he applied, and he got the job. I was so proud. And Spencer loved it. I've never seen him so happy. He was working in a laboratory in the East End and learning new things every day. He'd come home and tell me about different species, and the work he did feeding them jelly and recording their behavior on special charts. He was good at his job, so they promoted him. That's when the strange things started to happen. They made him sign a legal document promising not to tell anyone about his work. He couldn't say anything, but something about this new work troubled him. Spencer's dinner conversations became about how animals deserved to roam free, in their natural habitat, especially ones clever enough to know they were living in a cage.

"The day before he disappeared . . ." She paused. "Spencer came home from work in a state. He wouldn't tell me what had happened, but his behavior worried me and I badgered it out of him. He said that if he got caught he'd be fired, but that it was a small price to pay for the beetles' freedom."

"What had he done?" Darkus asked.

Mrs. Crips bit her lip. "Spencer was monitoring a special selection of beetles called the Bartholomew Cuttle Strain."

Virginia grabbed Darkus's arm.

"These were beetles intelligent enough to understand their surroundings. Experiments were being carried out on these beetles, and Spencer had to record their behavior in the hours and days after each experiment." She shook her head. "Spencer had a big heart. He grew attached to the beetles, a dung beetle in particular who he called Scud. Some of the experiments were cruel, and Spencer hated to see the insects in distress.

"One day, one of the normal dung beetles—the ones they bred in the farm tanks—died. Those beetles were used as control tests and weren't tightly monitored, so Spencer put the dead beetle into Scud's tank and smuggled Scud out of the laboratory in his lunch box. He wrote on the chart that Scud had died. No one in the laboratory realized that the dead beetle wasn't Scud, and no one was interested in the ordinary farmed insects. Weeks passed. No one noticed the missing dung beetle, but the other beetles knew what had happened, and they clamored for Spencer to free them, too. Their unhappiness in the laboratory made him feel terrible, and so he came up with a plan. He made a careful note of each species of beetle, and measured each individual beetle's size. Then he collected matching samples from the farm tanks, and once he had a group of beetles that mirrored the Bartholomew Cuttle Strain, he stayed late. When no one was about, he smuggled the special beetles into a cake tin, replacing them with the ordinary beetles, and then he left the laboratory"—Mrs. Crips looked at the children—"and he set the beetles free."

Virginia sucked in her breath and looked up at the picture of Spencer on the wall. "That was brave."

"Mrs. Crips," Darkus said, "our beetles—they're Spencer's beetles, or descendants of them. What he did was heroic. I wish you could see them all. There's this amazing place called Beetle Mountain and all Spencer's beetles live there, free and happy. He did a good thing."

"I'd swap ten mountains of happy beetles to have my son back," Mrs. Crips said.

There was an uncomfortable silence.

"We'll find him, Mrs. Crips. You'll see," Bertolt said.

"So Lucretia Cutter's making beetles, in these insect-farm things—but why?" Virginia asked on the way back to the bus stop. "And why would she kidnap Spencer?"

"Bet Dad knows what's going on," Darkus said. "I wonder why the beetles are called the Bartholomew Cuttle Strain?"

"Maybe she's repeating the same experiments she did with your dad," Virginia said, "on the Fabre Project."

"Maybe." Darkus frowned.

"We need to find out more about the work they did when they were part of the Fabre Project," Bertolt said.

"Dad's not going to tell me anything," Darkus sighed, "and we can't ask Lucretia Cutter . . ."

"What about Novak?" Bertolt said. "She helped you before."

Darkus frowned. He hadn't heard from Novak since the morning she helped him rescue his father. "I don't want to get her into more trouble than she's already in."

"Is there no one else we can talk to?" Virginia said.

"I can't think of anyone." Darkus frowned. "Wait a minute! I'm being an idiot. Of course there is: Professor Andrew Appleyard."

CHAPTER NINE

Entomophagy

*I*t was five o'clock, and getting dark when they left Mrs. Crip's house. Darkus, Virgina, and Bertolt hopped on a number 73 bus to Angel tube station, where they scrambled through the barrier and onto a train, switching from the Northern line at Monument to the District line and getting off at South Kensington. A short walk from the Natural History Museum, Darkus came to a halt in front of a five-story redbrick building with a pair of white pillars on either side of the front door and black wrought iron balconies below the windows.

When the buzzer sounded, Darkus pushed the giant door, entering a churchlike vestibule with a mosaic floor and a grand, sweeping staircase.

"This place is posh," Virginia said, looking up at the ornate cornices on the ceiling. "Is Professor Appleyard rich?"

"I don't think so," Darkus said. "He's just lived here a really long time, from before things got expensive. He's pretty old—he worked with my dad at the Natural History Museum before he retired."

As he reached the top of the staircase, Darkus saw the door to apartment number 15 was open, and a thin, elderly gentleman, dressed in a powder-blue pajamalike robe, was standing in the doorway. He blinked at the children through half-glasses propped on the end of his nose.

"Is that Bartholomew's son?" he said, his forehead wrinkling as his eyebrows rose. "My, you've grown up quickly. What are you doing here?"

"Hello, Professor. We wanted to talk to you about something," Darkus replied. "It's really quite urgent."

"Well then, come in, come in." He waved the children through the door and into his home. "I must say, I was relieved to hear that Barty had reappeared. He had me worried for a moment there. It was very naughty of him to disappear off on a research sabbatical and not tell anyone about it. He gave us all a terrible fright."

Darkus grimaced. The research sabbatical was the story Dad was telling everyone, and he was shocked by how readily people accepted the lie. When they asked about the locked room, his father would calmly explain that he'd never gone in there, that it was a mistake blown up by the newspapers into a big mystery. People would nod knowingly and reply, "You can't trust what you read in the papers."

"Aren't you going to introduce me to your friends?" Professor Appleyard asked.

"Sorry." Darkus pointed. "This is Virginia, and this is Bertolt."

"Nice to meet you, Virginia," Professor Appleyard said, shaking her hand, "and you too, Bertolt."

"The pleasure is all mine, Professor," Bertolt said.

"Here we go." Virginia rolled her eyes and Bertolt scowled at her.

"Now, young Cuttle, have you come with a message from your father?"

"Kind of," Darkus said, distracted by the walls of the professor's hallway, which were built from glass terrariums. Each one was lit with white, green, or red lights, and furnished with earth, greenery, and a species of invertebrate. He saw locusts, crickets, and a variety of beetles, including longhorns and June beetles.

"Whoa! Tarantulas!" Virginia pushed her nose up against one of the tanks. "Pink ones!"

"Yes." Professor Appleyard chuckled. "Now, can I interest you children in a bite to eat? I was about to make myself supper."

"I'm starving," Virginia replied.

"Marvelous, but first, why don't you bring out your *Chalcosoma caucasus*"—he pointed at Darkus—"your *Lampyridae,* and your *Sagra buqueti*?" He smiled at Bertolt and Virginia.

The three children stared at Professor Appleyard.

"How did you know we had beetles?" Darkus asked as he lifted Baxter out from the neck of his sweater.

Professor Appleyard clapped his hands together with delight as the three beetles leapt and landed on their humans' outstretched hands.

"I've spent my life observing beetle habitats and watching insects. I can spot twitching antennae from thirty paces, although I must admit this is the first time I've discovered the habitat to be children. The *Sagra buqueti* was in plain view. I saw him before you walked through my door. The Lampyridae was peeping over Bertolt's ear, and as for your *Chalcosoma caucasus*, Darkus, his horn was poking through your sweater. The size, shape, and color of the horn is a dead giveaway as to the species of a beetle, you know."

"His name is Baxter," Darkus said.

"He's unusually large; where did you get him?"

The children looked at each other.

"Actually, that's what we came to see you about," Darkus replied.

"Well, I hope you don't mind, but I'm going to ask you to put your coleopteran friends in this empty tank, to keep them safe." He lifted the lid of a tank carpeted with brown mulch. "There are other insects that roam free in my home, and some of them are predatory."

Darkus placed Baxter in the terrarium and Newton flew in to join him, but Marvin wasn't so keen. "Let go!" Virginia held her hand over the tank and shook it, but the metallic red beetle clung on stubbornly. "C'mon, Marvin. It's only for a little while."

Marvin reluctantly let go, one leg at a time, dropping onto Baxter's elytra. The frog-legged leaf beetle kicked his hind leg, spurring Baxter forward.

"Ha! Look!" Virginia pressed her nose to the glass. "Marvin's riding

Baxter." Marvin waved his forelegs at Virginia. "See you later, little dude."

Professor Appleyard's brow furrowed as he stared hard at the beetles. "This way to the kitchen."

The children followed him to the end of the hallway of tanks and into a wooden-floored kitchen with a sink, work surfaces, and cupboards along one wall and a low rectangular table in the middle of the space, surrounded by floor cushions. The professor opened the fridge and lifted out two plates, setting them down on the low table.

"Please do sit down." He turned and grabbed a ramekin of thick brown liquid from the side. "Mustn't forget the satay sauce." The children sat cross-legged on the cushions, and Bertolt peered at the plates. "Now, what did you children want to talk to me about?" the professor said, joining them.

"Um, excuse me, Professor," Virginia asked, "is that octopus or squid?" She poked one of the crispy black shapes.

"Neither! It's tarantula tempura. High in protein, low in fat, and surprisingly tasty."

"You eat spiders?" Bertolt whispered, aghast.

"And those?" Virginia's eyes were bulging out of her face.

"Cricket satay," Professor Appleyard replied, with a smile. "My favorite."

"This is your supper?" Darkus asked, astonished.

"Yes, I'm rather into entomophagy."

"Ento-moph-agy?" Darkus sounded the word out.

"Insect eating." The professor chuckled. "Although strictly speaking, a tarantula is an arachnid." Darkus grimaced. "Come now,

Darkus, eating an invertebrate is no different from eating any other kind of creature. Birds feed on them and you eat birds. Your digestive system is probably full of tiny creatures you haven't realized you've swallowed."

Darkus stared at the spiders. "But the hairs . . ."

"Singed off before they were dipped in batter." Professor Appleyard offered the children chopsticks. "Would you like to try one?"

Bertolt shook his head. "No thank you."

Virginia bent down, her nose almost touching the rim of the plate. "You really eat them?"

Professor Appleyard picked up a tarantula with his chopsticks, dashed soy sauce over it from a bottle on the table, dusted it in cayenne pepper, and bit into it.

Bertolt squealed and covered his eyes.

Darkus was transfixed. He'd never seen anyone eat a spider.

"It's not that different from seafood or vegetable tempura," the professor said after he'd swallowed.

"But why . . . ?" Darkus struggled to word his question without sounding rude.

"A personal project, really." He lifted a skewer of grilled crickets and dipped it in the peanut sauce. "I've been a vegetarian most of my life. I don't eat meat because I don't wish to be a part of the aggressive factory farming that the demand for animal meat has created. It's not sustainable and it's damaging the planet."

"But I like burgers," Virginia said, "and bacon sandwiches!"

"Oh yes, me too, Virginia, me too, they are delicious," Professor Appleyard agreed, "but the human race is growing at such a fierce rate that even if we chop every forest to the ground to raise cattle, there won't be enough meat to feed the world's population in a few years."

"We mustn't chop the rain forests down!" Bertolt said, distressed.

"I agree." Professor Appleyard nodded. "But if there is not enough meat to feed the people on this planet, then what will they eat?"

"Vegetables?" Virginia suggested, looking at the fried spiders.

"If you live in a wealthy country you can buy a rich mix of vegetables, but not elsewhere. However, there *is* a way to farm animals that are high in protein but don't require masses of land and feed."

"Insect meat?" Darkus guessed, although he'd never thought of insects as being meaty.

"Insect protein." Professor Appleyard nodded, taking a cricket between his teeth, sliding it off the skewer, and munching on it happily. "In the West we have a strange relationship with insects. We'd never think of eating them, but one day we may have no choice. Although in some of the fanciest restaurants they are an expensive delicacy."

Virginia snorted out a laugh. "That can't be true!"

"It is! There's a lovely restaurant in Denmark that serves ants, and they taste of peppermint."

"Those tanks in the hall?" Darkus looked over his shoulder.

"My own miniature insect farm. I rear my own food. I like to keep everything alive and fresh for as long as possible before it's cooked, and then they are killed humanely by freezing them. All my insects are bred for food—well, apart from the ones in the meditation room—and I'm working on an insect cookbook," Professor Appleyard said proudly. "It's my retirement project."

"No one's going to buy an insect cookbook!" Virginia scoffed.

"I'm trying to invent recipes that make insects as tasty as possible," Professor Appleyard said, smiling politely at Virginia. "You'd be doing me a great service if you'd try these and let me know what you think."

"Yeah, Darkus." Virginia's eyes lit up. "Try one."

"*You* try one," he shot back.

"I'll eat one if you do," Virginia dared him.

"Spider or cricket?" Darkus asked.

"Spider."

"*I* don't have to eat one, do I?" Bertolt whispered, looking a little green.

"You've got to eat the whole thing and swallow it," Darkus said to Virginia, grabbing the smallest spider he could see on the plate.

"Deal." Virginia picked up a crispy arachnid between her thumb and forefinger.

They looked at each other and bit into their spiders at the same time.

Darkus pushed the whole spider into his mouth at once, and he tried to make a noise like he was enjoying it, but it came out like a groan. Virginia bit off a leg, her face contorting as she struggled to control her disgust. Bertolt giggled, clamping both hands over his mouth. Darkus tried to blank his mind and focus on the taste, but he kept picturing a big, fat, hairy spider in his mouth.

Professor Appleyard leaned forward. "How does it taste?" he asked. "Is it nutty?"

Bertolt exploded into peals of laughter as Darkus and Virginia frantically chewed and swallowed.

"Wasn't so bad," Darkus said, his face twisted with disgust.

Virginia was holding half a spider away from her face as if it smelled bad. "If you don't stop laughing I'll shove this down your throat." She waggled it at Bertolt, who shrieked.

"Now, now, you're making an awful fuss. They really don't taste bad at all." Using chopsticks, the professor lifted another tarantula, seasoned it, and popped it into his mouth. "Perhaps you should have dipped yours in the satay sauce."

"Perhaps." Darkus wasn't so sure satay sauce would make eating a spider any nicer.

"Think of it this way," Professor Appleyard said. "You don't have problems eating a hamburger, do you?"

Darkus shook his head.

"Isn't it as peculiar a concept to eat a cow as it is to eat a spider?"

"But a hamburger doesn't look like a cow!" Virginia held up her half-eaten tarantula. "This looks like a spider."

"Maybe if it didn't look like a spider it wouldn't be so bad," Darkus agreed.

"Perhaps that's the trick." Professor Appleyard nodded. "For us, eating is about what it looks, smells, and tastes like, but in some places eating is about not starving."

Darkus thought about what the professor was saying. He tried to imagine being really hungry, the kind of hungry you get at the end of the school day when you are on your way home and you know that dinner is hours away. He picked up a skewer of crickets, dipped it in the peanut sauce, and slid one off with his teeth, copying the professor.

"Actually, the crickets aren't that bad," he said to Virginia and Bertolt.

"Such noble beasts," Professor Appleyard said. "Your father's love affair is with the beetle, but mine is with the cricket. I find their singing to be one of the most calming sounds."

"Singing?"

"Yes." The professor slid back from the table and walked to a door on the far side of the room, opening it a sliver. "Come and listen."

An orchestra of chirps throbbed away inside the room.

"This is my meditation room," Professor Appleyard replied, letting the door swing open as the children gathered around him. It was a box room with a curtain of white linen covering the window, and the wooden floor was clear except for a blue mat. Large bleached branches the size of saplings leaned against the walls, and sitting on the branches were hundreds of crickets, singing a melancholy song.

Darkus ran his tongue over his teeth, feeling guilty about having eaten one.

"I come here to clear my mind and meditate on life." The professor smiled.

"You have a room especially for thinking?" Virginia asked.

"Thinking is as important as eating and washing and sleeping. There are rooms for all those things."

"We have a place like this," Bertolt said. "It's filled with beetles and we go there to try and work things out. We call it Base Camp."

Darkus smiled at Bertolt, and then remembered why they were here. "Professor, we need to talk to you about our beetles."

"Of course, how can I help you?" he said.

"Our beetles are transgenic," Darkus said, "made by Lucretia Cutter. We know she's breeding beetles, but we don't know why."

"Transgenic?" Professor Appleyard leaned against the wall and exhaled. "Lucretia Cutter's breeding beetles?" He looked at Darkus, his eyes wide. "Are you sure?"

Darkus nodded.

"We think it's something to do with the Fabre Project," Virginia added. "That was your project, wasn't it?"

Professor Appleyard covered his face with his hands and took a deep breath before answering. "It was your father who persuaded me to invite Lucy Johnstone onto the Fabre Project," he said. "She was truly brilliant. A different girl back then. Barty had got her all excited about beetles." He shook his head. "Of course, it was your mother's joining the team that really shook things up. Once Bartholomew set his eyes on Esme, he could think of little else." He looked at Darkus. "Your mother used to make the most incredible insect paella, you know. I wish I had that recipe."

"Mum ate bugs?"

"Of course! She was an ecologist. She was very interested in the relationship between humans and their food."

Darkus's insides lurched. It felt wrong when other people talked knowledgeably about his mother.

"Do you know why Lucretia Cutter would want to breed lots of transgenic beetles?" Bertolt asked, wringing his hands as he waited for the answer.

"She could have many reasons," the professor replied. "In a balanced ecosystem beetles are not a threat, but if an aggressive species is introduced in large numbers, they can wreak havoc." He stood up straight, and it was as if he was talking to himself. "An invasive species of wood-boring beetle can reduce a forest to a graveyard of dead trees in less than a week."

"Why would she go to the effort of making lots of beetles to destroy a forest?" Virginia frowned. "That doesn't make any sense."

"In World War II, the Germans believed that the Russians had bombed them with potato weevil larvae"—Professor Appleyard took off his glasses and polished them with the corner of his linen shirt—"to destroy the potato crop, starve the people, and break morale." He put his glasses back on. "In the diary of the Russian entomologist Alexander Konstantinovich Mordvilko, there are references to the weevil bomb . . ."

"It was real?" Bertolt asked.

"Beetles used as weapons?" Darkus had never heard of that before.

Professor Appleyard nodded. "Invisible weapons that no one takes seriously until they are starving."

"How many beetles would you need to breed to make a weapon?" Bertolt asked.

"Gazillions." Virginia looked at Darkus. "Lucretia Cutter can't make a gazillion beetles in Towering Heights. She must be doing it somewhere else."

"In her laboratory in the East End—where Spencer Crips worked," Darkus said.

"But why would she want that kind of weapon?" Bertolt asked.

"Money, maybe?" Professor Appleyard frowned. "Perhaps she's developing a technology she hopes to sell."

"But she's already wealthy," Bertolt pointed out.

"For some people, what they have is never enough, no matter how great." Professor Appleyard stared into a time gone by and shook his head. "The world would not be enough for that woman."

"Dad said something like that when he was in the hospital." Darkus looked at Virginia and Bertolt. "He said, 'Lucretia Cutter will not stop until she has the world at her feet.'"

"One of the fundamental flaws of the Fabre Project was that, in our hope to achieve something truly great, we failed to consider the risks." Professor Appleyard shook his head.

"Risks?" Darkus echoed.

"A small change in an ecosystem can cause a massive shift. No matter how you try and control the impact of changes you make to a species, there's no insurance against nature taking control, of evolution powering forward and making decisions you might not have wanted. A biological beetle weapon could be disastrous for the human race." His voice petered out into a whisper.

Darkus looked at Virginia and Bertolt. "That sounds bad."

"I'm sorry." Professor Appleyard shook his head. "What am I thinking? You mustn't listen to a word I'm saying." He ushered them out into the hall, to the tank containing their beetles. "I'm scaring you unnecessarily. Don't listen to me." He patted Darkus's back. "I'm afraid you must be on your way now—I've got things I need to do. I'm very busy." He lifted the lid, and they each reached in and picked up their arthropod. "You mustn't worry about Lucretia Cutter. She really isn't your concern. I'll talk to your father about it. Thank you for your visit—it's always lovely to see a Cuttle." The professor smiled brightly, pushing the children out into the hall and closing the door on them before they could even say good-bye.

Once the door was closed, Professor Appleyard shuffled back through his flat, his hand over his hammering heart. If Lucretia Cutter was breeding transgenic beetles, he was going to have to do something about it. He went to his meditation room and sat down cross-legged on the blue mat, breathing in slowly through his nose, closing his eyes, and breathing out through his mouth.

Behind him, a lemon-yellow ladybug with eleven black spots on its elytra clambered in through the open window.

CHAPTER TEN
Daedalus Complex

*W*HERE HAVE YOU BEEN?"

The force of the anger in his father's voice shocked Darkus. He halted in the living-room doorway, Virginia bumping into his back.

Bartholomew Cuttle was standing in front of Uncle Max's sofa, his fists clenched by his sides. Frown lines were visible at the corners of his mouth. The absence of a beard made him look thinner and younger.

"I—I mean, we, er . . ." Darkus stammered, unable to hold his father's stare.

"Virginia, Bertolt, you're to go home immediately," his father said. "Your parents are waiting for you. Darkus is grounded."

"Oh dear," Bertolt said, blinking frantically.

"From tomorrow, you are forbidden from seeing him."

"What! Why? That's not fair!" Virginia's hands jumped to her hips. "We haven't done anything wrong!"

"Sir, whatever your reasoning," Bertolt gabbled, breathlessly, "I'm sure we—"

"You still haven't answered my question." Bartholomew Cuttle looked back at Darkus, cutting off Bertolt. "Where have you been?"

Darkus looked at Uncle Max, who was standing in front of the mantelpiece, his shoulders stooped and head bowed.

"Nowhere, um, we . . ." Darkus had never seen his dad like this. It frightened him.

"Never mind. I don't want you to lie to me. I *know* where you've been." Bartholomew Cuttle sank down onto the sofa. "The police called. The three of you were seen leaving Andrew's home."

"The police?" Bertolt gasped.

Darkus looked at his dad, goose bumps springing up all over his body as he tried to read his expression. "What's happened?"

His father rubbed the heels of his hands into his eye sockets. "Andrew's in the hospital, in a coma. He's in critical condition." He looked at Darkus. "They don't expect him to wake up."

"What! How?" Darkus felt his stomach spasm with fear. His father's face was as gray as old chewing gum.

"They think it might have been some kind of insect bite."

"Insect bite?" Darkus thought of the yellow ladybug in the Tic Tac box back at Base Camp. It had bitten Virginia.

"It's her!" Bertolt looked at Virginia, his eyes wide. "She did it."

Virginia's hands fell from her waist, slack with shock. "But . . . but he was fine! He was making us eat spiders and telling us all about—" She glanced at Darkus.

"What was he telling you?" His father's steely voice made Darkus's heart skip anxiously.

Virginia's bottom lip trembled.

"He was telling us about his bug cookbook," Darkus said, feeling a surge of anger, "and how Mum used to make a delicious insect paella."

A strangled noise came from his father's throat.

Bertolt took Virginia's hand and tugged her backward. "Come on," he whispered. "I think we should go home."

Virginia locked eyes with Darkus. He could see she didn't want to leave him.

"I'll see you at school," he said, with a nod to reassure her.

She nodded back and left with Bertolt. Uncle Max followed them, to see them out. Darkus heard the front door close and Uncle Max's footsteps retreat to the kitchen.

"You won't be going back to King Ethelred Hall School," his father said.

Darkus frowned. "What?"

"You've been through a lot, Darkus. A break will do you good. Uncle Max can tutor you so you don't fall behind, and then, when we're able to return home, you can go back to your old school in Crystal Palace."

"When we're *able* to go home? What does that mean?"

"Darkus, listen to me, please. I need you to do as I ask. You need to be somewhere safe."

"What's wrong with here?" Darkus stuck out his chin.

"Darkus, we are living above a mountain of Lucretia Cutter's beetles, and she's looking for them. Do you think she won't come for them? Because she will." The hard look in his eyes softened and he shook his head. "I've racked my brains. I can't think of anywhere that would take them. They will have to fend for themselves, but it's too risky for you to stay."

"We could all move away?" Darkus suggested. "Together."

"No, I want you away from the beetles." Bartholomew Cuttle looked at Baxter, who sat unmoving on Darkus's shoulder. "All of them."

"NO!" Darkus looked at his dad with horror. "You can't do that!"

"Darkus . . . Lucretia Cutter, she's going to do something terrible." A desperate look sent his father's blue eyes darting about the room.

"Then we'll stop her," Darkus said, stepping toward his dad. "Together. Us and the beetles, they can help, they can—"

"No." His father's face hardened. "Darkus, you're to stay out of this. You're my son, it's my job to protect you. I will not let Lucretia Cutter harm you again."

"Can't you tell someone? The army? Or the government? There must be *someone* who can help!"

"Don't you think I've tried?" He gave an exasperated sigh. "Lucretia Cutter is powerful."

"I will never leave Baxter, ever." Darkus folded his arms across his chest. "If the beetles aren't coming with us, then I'm staying right here."

"Darkus, that's enough. You have no say in this."

"I'm not going." Darkus stamped his foot. "You can't make me."

"Darkus, please. This is not a game. I'm trying to do what's best for you."

"How do you know what's best for me?"

"You disobeyed me," his dad replied sternly. "You purposely went to Andrew to find out about Lucretia Cutter, after I expressly asked you not to, and look what's happened!" He threw his hands in the air. "You and your friends think this is some sort of childish detective game, but it isn't."

Darkus swallowed; he was scared by what had happened to Professor Appleyard. Was it a yellow ladybug that had bitten him? Virginia had been bitten, but she hadn't gotten sick. What if *they* had led the lady-bugs to the professor? What if it was his fault that Professor Appleyard was in the hospital?

"I didn't mean for the professor to get hurt," he mumbled.

"Darkus, that wasn't your fault. How can it have been?" His dad leaned forward. "But don't you see? It could've been *you* in that hospital bed!" Darkus shook his head, certain in the knowledge that Baxter would never let one of Lucretia Cutter's creatures near his skin. "That's why I'm sending you away."

"You're treating me like a child, but I know what Lucretia Cutter is. I've seen her! I've fought her! Remember?" Darkus clenched his fists, anger lifting his chest. "It was ME who rescued YOU! You can't protect me—you can't even protect yourself! *You're* the one she kidnapped and put in a prison cell, and *you won't even tell me why.* We need to work together. It's only together that we can beat her."

"Darkus, that's in the past. It's over. You must forget about it."

"FORGET ABOUT IT? She tried to kill you . . ."

"And she shot *you*!" His dad moved toward him and grabbed his shoulders. "Lucretia Cutter kidnapped me because she wanted to force me to help her do something, but I refused. That's why she tortured me. But all the time I was in that cell, I knew that if she'd known that I had a son, she would have taken you, and then she could've made me do anything."

"What did she want you to do?"

"Darkus, I don't want you involved. If anything happened to you . . . I would fall down and never be able to get up."

"And what about if something happens to *you*?" Darkus shouted, stepping back and wrenching his shoulders out of his dad's hands. "You don't know what it was like, not knowing where you were . . . what had happened to you . . ." A surge of emotion cut off his words.

"Darkus, listen . . ."

"NO!" His body was shaking uncontrollably. "*You* listen! Why have you shaved off your beard?" He glared accusingly at his dad. "Why are you wearing fancy new clothes? What are you doing in that room with the microscope and *my* beetles? You're pretending everything is normal, but it's *not*."

"Darkus, those beetles, I know you care about them, but . . ."

"YES! They're my *friends*. They were there when you weren't. They helped me when I needed them, and those beetles fought and beat Lucretia Cutter. They're on our side. We *need* them. This isn't just about us, you know? There's a boy, called Spencer Crips, Lucretia Cutter's got him. His mum hasn't seen him in five years!"

"Darkus, calm down. Please. You're gibbering."

"I WILL NOT CALM DOWN." Darkus stared fiercely at his father. "I'm not stupid. I *know* you're up to something."

"Darkus, I'm not going to argue with you about this anymore. If I find out that you've been poking around anywhere near Lucretia Cutter . . ."

"You'll do what?" Darkus stuck out his chin.

"I'll call in the exterminators." His father's face was stony.

Darkus stared. "You wouldn't! You don't believe in killing things."

"Those beetles will bring Lucretia Cutter. If you won't go somewhere safe, then I will have to get rid of them."

Darkus felt like his stomach was being sucked into a black hole as he stared into his father's flinty eyes. He wanted to shout at him, but he had no words. Instead, he spun on his heel and stormed out. He pounded up the stairs, slowing at the top of the second flight as a sob erupted from his chest. He stumbled forward onto all fours, crawling up the last steps to the landing outside his bedroom. He hammered the floor with his fist, sucking in air as the bullet wound in his shoulder made him wince, hot tears blurring his vision.

Baxter hopped down from his shoulder to the ground, rearing up onto his back legs and waggling his forelegs with concern. Darkus wiped his eyes and rolled over onto his back, glaring at the ceiling.

"Why is Dad being like this, Baxter? If he could just see the power of the beetles, he'd see that together we're more than a match for Lucretia Cutter. We should be fighting her, not running away."

Baxter's elytra flipped up, his soft amber wings unfolding as he leapt, flying onto Darkus's chest. The rhinoceros beetle settled down in the pit between his ribs, folding his serrated legs under his abdomen and resting his head on Darkus's chest.

Darkus lifted his hands, placing them protectively around the beetle. "I don't care what he says, Baxter. I won't ever let him separate us. If he tries, then I'll run away and never come back." He thought about what his dad had said about the beetles being *her* creatures. "Dad's making a terrible mistake, you know, Baxter? Without the beetles, we don't have a chance against Lucretia Cutter."

After a while he sat up, putting Baxter back onto his shoulder. Opposite him was the tower of cardboard boxes that he and Uncle Max had moved out of his bedroom the day that he'd come to stay, all those months ago. His eyes flickered down the pile, stopping at the box second from the bottom. It had a ripped corner. He remembered clumsily dragging it backward out of the room and tearing the box. The teeth of Nefertiti had spilled out onto the floor, together with a load of folders.

Suddenly he was on his knees. *The folders!* He remembered that they had each had the words *Fabre Project* on them.

He listened to the muffled voices of his dad and Uncle Max in the living room as he silently and carefully brought down the boxes, to get to the one with the ripped corner. He hadn't known what the Fabre Project was back then, but he did now. If Dad wasn't going to tell him what was going on, then he'd find out for himself.

He reached the ripped box and pushed back the cardboard flaps. There they were, two piles of faded red and yellow folders, all marked *Fabre Project*. He lifted them out and put them on the floor.

Downstairs, the door to the front room opened, and he froze.

"I won't be back late," he heard his dad say. "Visiting hours at the hospital are till nine."

Darkus looked about in panic—the landing was a mess of boxes and his father's folders.

"I hope the old boy pulls through," Uncle Max replied. "Don't worry about us. I'll keep an eye on Darkus."

"I've got a bad feeling about all of this, Max."

"Don't jump to conclusions," Uncle Max reassured him. "Andrew is an old man. I know the doctors say it looks like an insect bite, but it could have been a stroke or a heart attack."

"That's why I have to go, to be sure, and poor Andrew has no one."

"You can take my car."

Darkus closed his eyes tight, dreading the sound of his father coming up the stairs to say good-bye, but a second later he heard the front door slam.

Darkus grabbed up the folders, running on tiptoe into his room, and dumped them on the floor. He returned to the hall and hastily restacked the boxes. He was scrambling back into his room when he heard Uncle Max's footsteps on the stairs. He threw an armful of clothes over the folders, then dropped cross-legged onto the floor, grabbing the nearest book.

There was a knock. "Come in," Darkus said, trying to calm his breathing.

"I thought you might be hungry," Uncle Max said, pushing the door open. He was carrying a plate of ham sandwiches and a banana in one hand, and a glass of milk in the other.

"I'm starving," Darkus admitted.

"Good book?" Uncle Max's eyebrows waggled. Darkus looked down and realized he was holding *An Intellectual History of Cannibalism* upside down.

"I wasn't really reading," he admitted.

"Shame." Uncle Max grinned. "That's the best book about eating people I've ever read."

Darkus smiled, sitting forward as his uncle put the plate and glass on the makeshift cardboard-box table. He lifted Baxter off his shoulder, placing him beside the plate. He peeled the banana and broke off a chunk for the rhinoceros beetle.

"Thanks, Uncle Max." He took a bite of the sandwich.

"Right, well, I'll be downstairs if you need me . . . you know, if you want to talk things through, or"—Uncle Max shrugged—"anything."

"Are we really going to leave?" Darkus asked.

"I'm afraid I think we have to."

"But I can bring Baxter, can't I?"

"Um, well, I'm, er . . ." Uncle Max looked at Baxter. "Your father's got strong opinions about our little friend."

"Dad's wrong," Darkus said, "about the beetles."

"Possibly." Uncle Max nodded. "But he's your father. He knows more about these things than either of us. We should support him."

"I just want him to listen to me, to let me show him what the beetles can do. Will you talk to him, Uncle Max?"

"I'll try." Uncle Max looked like he was going to say something more, but then changed his mind. "Just shout if you need me," he said, and closed the door behind him.

Darkus looked at the heap of clothes, listening to Uncle Max's retreating footsteps. He slid over and uncovered the folders, taking the top one and pulling out the paper inside. Grabbing his sandwich, he ate as he systematically worked his way through pages and pages of notes, skimming over Latin words, drawings—some of beetles—graphs, diagrams, and streams of numbers. His heart sank. He couldn't understand any of it.

He took another folder. It was full of similar pages. He took a third, flicking through the papers without taking them out. His fingertips found two photographs. One, the larger of the two photographs, he'd seen before, on Lucretia Cutter's desk: It was of the Fabre Project team.

He stroked his finger across his mother's face. Her smile was wide and warm, and her thick black hair fell down past her shoulders. She was wearing a dark collared shirt under a white lab coat, her hands folded in her lap. On the back of the photo were names written in his father's handwriting. He set it aside and looked at the second photograph, a small square image of his father as a young man, clean-shaven with thick framed rectangular spectacles, looking into the camera with a smile of wonder as he held in his hands a giant Goliath beetle.

CHAPTER ELEVEN
Warning Flare

From her bedroom window, Novak watched the steady stream of yellow ladybugs coming in and out of Towering Heights. Mater was looking for something or someone. Her heart clenched in her chest; it wouldn't be Darkus, since he was gone.

Her eyes filled with tears. It had been two days since she'd learned her friend was dead, and the tiniest thoughts of him made her cry. Not even Hepburn could console her, and each time she broke down in sobs, her heart hardened a little more toward Mater.

Through a blur of tears she saw another ladybug zip in through the third-floor window to Mater's rooms. Fed up with watching, Novak decided to find out what was going on. She slipped out of her room and crept about the house, listening at doorways, sauntering past adults in conversation, and then, as Novak was passing the security room, her spying finally paid off. She overheard an agitated Craven shouting at Dankish.

"Get a move on, man. Those blasted ladybugs have beaten us to it. We look like ruddy idiots. The boss'll sack us and replace us with beetles if we're not careful."

Dankish's reply was a muffled grunt.

"NO! Give it here. You put the gas into the tank with the funnel."

"I don't want to go in the sewers," Dankish grumbled. "It smells bad down there, and there are rats."

"*You* smell bad most of the time, but you don't see me complaining," Craven snapped back. "As soon as we've fueled up the flamethrowers, we'll chuck them in the van and drive to the sewage works, get into the tunnels from there. I for one can't wait to find that rotting heap of beetles and incinerate the lot of them!"

Novak felt the blood drain from her face. They were going to burn Darkus's beetles! First Mater had murdered Darkus, and now she wanted to kill his beetles!

Novak ran, her feet clattering against the stone floor. She slid to a stop outside the servants' lift and dragged back the gate, hopping in and pulling it shut. As the lift ascended to the fifth floor, she felt tears roll down her cheeks. She wiped them away angrily. A panicked sense of helplessness drove her forward. Darkus loved those beetles, and they were Hepburn's family. She had to save them—but how? She was trapped in Towering Heights. Maybe she could get a message to someone—but who?

She thought about Darkus's father, but he'd be grief-stricken from losing his son. He wouldn't want to help the daughter of the woman who'd killed Darkus. She thought of Bertolt and Virginia, the boy and girl Darkus had called his friends, but she didn't even know their last names. How would she find them?

She had to warn someone. Craven and Dankish couldn't be allowed to destroy Darkus's beetles.

As the elevator pinged, Novak remembered Darkus's uncle, the man that had punched Gerard. Maximilian Cuttle, Mater had called him. He might be able to help, and she knew where he lived: on Nelson Parade.

Novak wrenched the gate back and sprinted along the corridor into her bedroom. Her luggage, all that was left of her dream of going to school, was still packed, destined to come with them to LA now. Gerard had told her that Towering Heights was being closed and they wouldn't be returning.

Novak threw herself onto her bed and pulled a lavender stationery set from a drawer in her bedside table. "Oh, Hepburn, something awful is happening!" she said to the vase of hydrangeas beside her bed.

Hepburn emerged from underneath a blue flower, a rainbow of colors reflecting off her elytra as she clambered up to Novak's eyeline.

"Craven and Dankish know where your mountain of teacups is. They're going to burn it!"

Hepburn stood up on her hind legs in alarm, waggling her forelegs, almost falling off the bouquet.

"We've got to get help." Novak slid out a piece of paper, picked a purple pen from her pen pot, and started to write.

The white telephone beside her bed rang. Novak picked up the receiver without taking her eyes from her letter to Maximilian Cuttle. "Hello, Millie."

"Hello, dear. I've just been instructed that you're going to the Empress Hotel this evening."

"Tonight? But it's late!"

"Yes. You fly to LA in the morning, early. I was just wondering if you wanted me to make you anything, a snack or drink to take with you?"

"Oh!" Novak felt a flutter of panic. Time was running out. "Could I have some melon for the journey?"

"Of course, dear, I'll bring it up."

"Thank you."

She replaced the receiver, then hastily finished the letter, folded it, and slipped it into a lavender envelope. "We need to get ready to go," she said to Hepburn, sealing the envelope and writing *Maximilian Cuttle* on the front. Hepburn flipped up her colorful wing cases and fluttered over to Novak's arm.

"I'll get the bracelet," Novak said to the beetle, crossing the room to her handbag and pulling out a wide silver bangle with a chunky setting containing a semiprecious green stone. She flipped a catch and the green stone sprang back on hinges to reveal a hidden pill pot. Novak pulled a few petals from the blue hydrangea and lined the silver chamber, then dipped her finger into the vase and drew out a drop of water, dripping it onto the petals. Hepburn strutted along her wrist and clambered in, wriggling to make herself comfortable on her hydrangea bed.

There was a knock on the door and Millie bustled into the room with a small Tupperware container of sliced watermelon. "Come on, dear—you must put on your coat and shoes."

Novak carefully closed the secret compartment. "Millie," she said, taking a deep breath, "I need you to do something for me. It's very important."

"Nothing's more important than making sure you're ready for when that car arrives." Millie blinked furiously. "You know how the mistress gets if you're late."

"This *is* more important, Millie." Novak held out the letter. "I need you to deliver this."

"What is it?" Millie looked at the envelope suspiciously.

"It's urgent. It needs to go to Nelson Parade immediately. Can you find out where that is? Maximilian Cuttle lives in the building next to the shop that blew up. I don't know the number."

Millie gasped and stepped back, her hands raised, shaking her head with alarm. "Oh no, dear, you mustn't get mixed up in all of that. It was bad enough, that day, when you . . . I mean, if the mistress found out . . ."

"Listen, Millie, she didn't find out about that and she won't find out about this, either. Mater and I will be on a plane on our way to LA tomorrow morning. Please, Millie, I wouldn't ask if it wasn't important." Novak could hear her own heart beating. *"Please."*

Millie took the letter reluctantly, nodding imperceptibly as she slipped it into the big wide pocket of her white apron.

"Thank you," Novak whispered, her eyes filling with grateful tears. Darkus was gone, and she couldn't bring him back, but at least she could save his beetles.

CHAPTER TWELVE
The Cavalry

*D*arkus woke up and blinked. Something was tickling his ear. He turned and saw Baxter on the pillow beside his head, mouth open, smiling up at him.

"Hey, Baxter," he whispered, sitting up in his hammock. The two black-and-white photographs he'd fallen asleep clutching fell from his chest onto his lap. "Is everything okay?"

Baxter flicked up his elytra and pointed a front leg up to the sky-light. The night sky was a deep, star-speckled black, but a particularly yellow star seemed to be growing and flashing.

"Newton?" Darkus rose to his knees, careful not to rock the hammock, and pulled the window open. The firefly zoomed in.

"Hello!" Darkus held out his hand and the beetle landed on his palm, folding his soft wings away under his copper-colored elytra. "Where's Bertolt?"

Flash, flick, flick, flick, dark, flick, flash, dark, flick, flick, flick, dark, flick.

"Calm down. Why all the flashing?" Darkus looked closely at the lozenge-shaped beetle. "Are you trying to tell me something? Is there a pattern to your light?"

The firefly started flickering and flashing again, in exactly the same pattern as before.

"Is that Morse code? Are you using Morse code?"

Newton nodded proudly.

"No way!" Darkus leaned out of his hammock and grabbed a pencil and paper from the top of the filing cabinets. "Do it again. *Flash, flick, flick, flick, dark.* That's a B!" Darkus watched the firefly intensely. "That's an A, an S, an E . . . B-A-S-E . . . it's Base Camp! Bertolt's in Base Camp?"

Newton looped the loop in delight at being understood.

Darkus scrambled out of his hammock. "When did you learn Morse code?" He pulled his favorite green sweater over his pajamas and shoved the rolled-up photographs into his trouser pocket. "Did Bertolt teach you?"

Flash, flick, flash, flash, dark, flick, dark, flick, flick, flick, dark.

"Y-E-S, yes!" Darkus laughed. "Of course he did. He kept that quiet."

His heart was suddenly light at the thought of his friend being close by. He held out his hand and Baxter clambered on, racing up his arm to his shoulder. "Is Virginia there, too?" Baxter nodded at him and Darkus grinned. Virginia never did as she was told, and Bertolt always ended up doing what she wanted, even if he disapproved.

He grabbed the small flashlight, strapped to wide elastic, that hung from the brass hook at the foot of his hammock, pulled it over his head, and switched it on. Clambering back onto the filing cabinets, he reached his arms up out of the skylight and grabbed onto the wooden window frame, jumping up through the hole and sitting on the roof tiles to the left of the window. He often came up here with Baxter. He liked to look out across the neighboring streets and watch everything coming and going around Nelson Parade. People rarely looked up, which Darkus thought was a pity, because the sky was always more interesting than the pavement.

Careful to avoid the loose tiles, he slid down the roof, stopping before the slumped section that hung over the ruin of the Emporium and picked his way toward the gutter. Peering over the edge of the rooftop, he saw the black wrought iron fire escape. It was a seven-foot drop to its top platform, but if he let himself hang from the gutter, dangling his legs down, it would only be a couple of feet.

He closed his eyes and hoped no one was in the kitchen, before securing his grip on the ironwork that strapped the gutter to the roof and sliding off, dangling over the edge. He dropped, making a clatter, and crouched, listening, expecting to hear an angry voice or see a familiar face at the kitchen window, but nothing came. He unhooked the ladder and let it slide down. He climbed down to the next landing, releasing each ladder in turn until he finally dropped into Uncle Max's weed-filled garden.

Baxter fluttered down, landing on his shoulder. Newton danced through the air ahead of Darkus, zipping about excitedly. Darkus felt like he could do anything when he was with the beetles.

Beetles and boy threw themselves up onto the shed roof at the bottom of the garden and shimmied over the neighboring wall, tumbling blind into the mass of junk that Darkus had named Furniture Forest when he'd first discovered it. A place that now, even in the dead of night, held no secrets for Darkus. He knew every corner and every cushion. He scrambled on all fours to the black door with a silver 73 that was the entrance to Base Camp.

Pushing it open, he was greeted with a warm yellow light and smiles from his two favorite people.

"What took you so long?" Virginia smiled.

Hanging from one of her braids, Marvin waved a red claw at Darkus.

"What are you doing here?" Darkus laughed. "I thought you were banned from seeing me."

"From tomorrow." Virginia grinned. "We're banned from tomorrow, so we thought we'd better see you tonight or we'd be disobeying our parents, and we wouldn't want to do that, now, would we?"

"And you?" Darkus looked at Bertolt.

"I stuffed cushions under my duvet and crept out. Mum doesn't really make rules." Bertolt pushed his glasses up his nose. "She said she'd like me to stay out of trouble and not make your dad angry, but ultimately I had to make the decision about what was the right thing to do."

"I had to practically drag him here," Virginia said flatly.

"You didn't," Bertolt protested. "I just don't want to disappoint Mum."

"You won't." Virginia flopped down onto the olive-green sofa. "Once we've found out what Lucretia Cutter's done with Spencer Crips, saved him, and stopped her from doing whatever evil thing she's planning, you'll be a hero. Your mother will be proud."

Bertolt didn't look happy. "The Morse code is a cool trick," Darkus said, changing the subject.

"Isn't it?" Bertolt flushed with pride. "Newton picked it up really quickly. He can spell out complicated sentences now. I wasn't sure if you'd be able to decipher it."

"I learned at Cub Scouts," Darkus said. "And it's a great idea to use a code. I wonder if the other beetles can learn it, too?"

"Not all of them have lamps in their abdomens," Virginia pointed out.

"Morse code can be done with sound," Darkus said. "Baxter could tap out a message with his horn, or use stridulation."

"That *is* a good idea." Virginia sat forward. "Marvin can tap-dance a message using his back legs."

Bertolt sat down beside Virginia, pulling out a pen and notebook. "I'll write that down, shall I?"

"Write what down?" Darkus asked.

"We don't know when we'll next see each other," Virginia said, pulling a giant atlas out of her backpack and slamming it down on the coffee table. "So we're making a case file to keep here in Base Camp. We can all make entries and read each other's."

"It's an atlas."

"No, it isn't. It just *looks* like an atlas." She flipped open the cover of the book. Inside, where there should have been maps, was a folder instead. "I found it in one of the wet boxes, rotting over by the wall. The maps were ruined, so I ripped out the pages and stuck this folder into the inside of the back cover. Now no one will know."

She pulled out several sheets of paper. One was the article about Spencer Crips, and another was titled *Fabre Project* and had several names on it.

"These should go in there, too, then." Darkus reached into the back pocket of his pajamas and pulled out the rolled-up photographs. "I found them in Dad's research folders."

"It's the picture!" Bertolt exclaimed, taking the large photograph from Darkus's hands. "The one from Lucretia Cutter's desk."

"Look on the back," Darkus said.

Bertolt turned it over and saw the names. "Look, Virginia!"

"Brilliant!" She pulled a pen from her jeans. "Read them out."

"Dr. Danny Laroche, Dr. Yuki Ishikawa, Dr. Henrik Lenka, Dr. Lucy Johnstone, then Darkus's dad and mum, Dr. Bartholomew Cuttle and Esme Martín-Piera," Bertolt read, "and Professor Andrew Appleyard."

Virginia looked at Darkus, her eyes shining. "That's three new names! They could be possible leads."

"I brought this for the case file." Bertolt pulled a newspaper out of his bag. "Look who's on the front page."

The front page featured a picture of Lucretia Cutter in her trademark white lab coat and sunglasses, two black sticks dangling from straps around her wrists like ski poles. Beside her, giving the camera her best movie-star smile, was Novak.

"The story inside says that Lucretia Cutter is dressing all the actresses in the Best Actress category at the Film Awards, including Novak. Did you know she's been nominated for an award? She's in a movie called *Taming of a Dragon*, about a blind girl with a pet dragon."

Darkus thought back to when he'd first met Novak, at the library in Towering Heights. "She did say something about being in a film."

"We should go to the cinema and see it," Bertolt said excitedly. "I bet she's wonderful."

"How would you know?" Virginia snorted. "You've never met her."

"No." Bertolt sighed. "But I feel like I have, what with her being Darkus's friend and helping rescue his dad . . . and she has a beetle. It's like she's one of us."

"She *is* one of us," Darkus said. "I wish there was a way I could talk to her."

"We don't know what trouble she might have gotten in for helping rescue your dad," Virginia said softly. "You don't want to make it worse."

Bertolt pointed at Novak's picture in the newspaper. "At least we know she's alive and well."

"Yes." Darkus smiled. "That's true."

Bertolt put the newspaper into the case file. "If Lucretia Cutter's going to the Film Awards, perhaps she's given up looking for the beetles," he said hopefully.

"Then it's just my dad we've got to worry about," Darkus said glumly. He knew he was going to have to tell them that he was being sent away.

"SSSHHHHHHHHHHHHHH!!!!" Virginia grabbed Bertolt's arm, her face a picture of alarm, her finger to her lips.

They heard a loud clatter beyond the door of Base Camp. All three of them turned and looked as the door was wrenched open. Uncle Max stumbled in.

"Oh, thank goodness you're here, Darkus!" Uncle Max was waving an envelope around and gasping, his leathery skin purple from the effort of scrambling through Furniture Forest.

Darkus jumped to his feet. "What's the matter?"

"I heard a noise. I thought it was Barty coming home from the hospital. I went into his room and found this on his bed. It's addressed to you." He passed over the envelope. "I don't think I was meant to find it until the morning. My suitcase is gone, and all his new clothes."

Darkus took the envelope and ripped it open, dread tugging at his insides. His hand shook as he held the letter and read out loud:

> Dear Darkus,
>
> I have to go away for a while. I know this will be hard for you to understand, but there is something I must do, and I cannot take you with me.
>
> Uncle Max will take good care of you, at Nana and Pop-Pop's house, away from the city. Be good for him, he loves you very much and none of this is his fault.
>
> I need you to be brave, as I may be gone some time. I'm sorry, it's unlikely I'll be home in time for

*Christmas, but I promise to come back as soon as
I can and then I'll make it up to you.*

*I wish I could explain better, but please know that
your mother would have agreed, that I must go.
There is no other way.*

I love you more than anything in the world.

Dad.

He let the letter drop to the floor and looked at Uncle Max, whose mouth was hanging open.

"Well of all the stupid, pig-headed, idiotic things . . ." Uncle Max lifted his safari hat and dragged his fingers through his silver hair in frustration.

"He's going back to Lucretia Cutter," Darkus said, his voice thick with emotion.

"He might not be," Bertolt said.

"He is," Darkus replied flatly. "I've worked out why he's got new clothes and shaved off his beard." He picked up the Fabre Project photograph. "He wants to look exactly like he used to when he was young"—he pointed at his dad in the picture—"when they were friends."

"He says he loves you," Bertolt said. "That bit's nice."

"Hang on. What does he mean, *at Nana and Pop-Pop's house, away from the city?*" Virginia looked at Uncle Max, her hands on her hips.

"Well, I thought the three of us were going to stay in our parents' old house in Wales for Christmas," Uncle Max said. "But Barty obviously had other ideas he didn't see fit to share with me." He shook his head. "That vile woman has put some kind of a spell on him."

"I'm not going." Darkus rubbed his hands over his face. "You can't make me."

"Darkus, I promised your dad I'd take you out of London." Uncle Max put a hand on his shoulder. "However, what I *didn't* promise him was when, or where I'd take you, which gives us some wiggle room."

"Us?" Darkus looked at his uncle.

"Oh yes." Uncle Max put his hat on the table and sat down on the sofa with a grunt. "Whatever you're planning, I'm in."

"Darkus." Virginia looked at him. "What should we do?"

"Dad's in danger." He swallowed. "Only a powerful force is capable of stopping Lucretia Cutter. He can't do it alone. We have to help him."

"We're not a powerful force." Bertolt's white eyebrows rose above his oversize spectacles.

"A tiny thing, like a beetle, or a kid, might seem weak or unimportant," Darkus said. "But tiny things can get into places and see things." He looked at his friends. "And if one tiny thing joins with another tiny thing, and another, together they become a powerful *big* thing, a force to be reckoned with."

"But we don't know what Lucretia Cutter's planning to do!" Bertolt protested.

"We know that she's building up an army of transgenic beetles, we just don't know what for." Darkus sighed. "But I'll bet Dad knows." He turned to his uncle. "You and Dad talk; has he told you anything that would help?"

"There was one thing." Uncle Max nodded. "In the hospital, Barty was reading a journal article about an outbreak of mountain pine beetles in the Rocky Mountain National Park in Colorado. The beetle is only five millimeters long"—he pinched his thumb and forefinger together to show its size—"but the outbreak has destroyed millions of acres of forest. Your father seemed to think it was something to do with Lucretia Cutter."

"She destroyed a whole forest?" Bertolt said, dismayed.

"I also might have had a bit of a rummage around his desk," Uncle Max admitted, his cheeks flushing. "Barty's been collecting reports and information about unexplainable invasive beetle species appearing in unusual habitats from before he was kidnapped. I asked our old friend Emma Lamb, the news reporter, if she'd look into it. I'm still waiting for her to get back to me."

Virginia pushed the Fabre Project photo across the coffee table, indicating the three unknown faces. "Do you know any of these people?"

"Yes." Uncle Max pointed at a tall blond man with an athletic build. "That brute is Henrik Lenka, a chemist. He was a disagreeable sort. He was Lucy's boyfriend for a brief spell. Danny"—he pointed at a diminutive woman with round glasses—"was a good friend of your mother's." He sighed. "Tragic what happened to her."

Bertolt gulped. "Is she dead?"

"No, but"—Uncle Max closed his eyes briefly—"she's not well."

"Does she live in London?" Virginia asked. "Could we ask her some questions?"

Uncle Max shook his head. "She's French, from a little village in the Loire Valley, and I'm not sure she'd want a visit from us."

"What about him?" Virginia pointed to the last stranger in the lineup.

"Dr. Yuki Ishikawa." Uncle Max smiled. "A Japanese microbiologist and all-around lovely chap. He used to wear a tiny bamboo cage of crickets around his neck, letting the insects roam about the lab as he worked. He said their song helped him think."

"Like the ones in Professor Appleyard's meditation room," Bertolt said.

Uncle Max nodded. "He and Andrew are good friends, I believe."

There was a heavy silence as they thought of Professor Appleyard, lying unconscious in a hospital bed.

"So, Dr. Ishikawa, is he alive and well?" Virginia said.

"Last I heard he'd gone to Greenland for research."

"Greenland's a bit far away." Bertolt sighed.

"We need to find out if those invasive beetle outbreaks have anything to do with Lucretia Cutter's transgenic beetles," Darkus said, thinking out loud. "But first, we need to get Dad back. If he's joining Lucretia Cutter, then we know where he's gone."

"Towering Heights," Virginia said with a nod.

"It may be too late," Bertolt pointed out. "It's nearly eleven o'clock. He could have been gone for hours."

"We have to try." Darkus stood up. "I've got a horrible feeling he's walking into a trap."

"We'll never get in there again." Uncle Max scratched his chin.

"We could take the beetles," Virginia suggested. "They can go in and look for him."

"Oh dear." Bertolt fidgeted, his thumbs rolling over one another nervously. "What if we get caught? I don't want to end up in one of Lucretia Cutter's cells. Mum will panic if she wakes up in the morning and I'm not in my bed."

"You can stay here with Newton," Darkus said. "Write down what we know about the Fabre Project team, and the stories about invasive species of beetle."

"Thanks." Bertolt gave him a relieved smile.

Darkus looked at Uncle Max. "Will you drive us to Towering Heights?"

"It'd be my pleasure." Uncle Max put his hat back on.

"We'll pick up volunteers from Beetle Mountain on our way to the car," Darkus said, already at the door.

Virginia jumped up. "You're not leaving me behind."

"I wouldn't dream of it." Darkus gave her a wry smile. "You'd make too much of a fuss."

Virginia punched his shoulder.

"OUCH!" Darkus rubbed his arm. "What was that for?"

Virginia smirked as she marched past him. "Toughen you up."

CHAPTER THIRTEEN

Lady Macbeth

At the Empress Hotel, Novak was whisked upstairs to the Cutter Suite. Mater pointed at a purple tapestry chair at the edge of the dressing area. Novak bowed her head, obediently going and sitting down, only realizing as she did so that standing in front of her was Stella Manning, the most acclaimed actress in the world.

Stella Manning was as famous for performing Shakespeare on the stage as she was for her countless award-winning film roles. Her face was a magnet you couldn't pull your eyes from. She wasn't wearing a scrap of makeup, and her long red hair was pulled up into a high ponytail, but she looked magnificent.

"In this dress," Mater said, pursing her gold lips, "your pedigree as a peerless actress will be indisputable." Reaching down, she took the long green skirt between her thumbs and forefingers and wafted the fabric so that it rippled out across the floor.

Novak felt a wave of revulsion as she saw that the dress was decorated with hundreds of emerald-green jewel beetles. *Those poor dead beetles!* she thought, closing her hand protectively over the bangle on her wrist. The jewel beetles on the dress were a different species to Hepburn—one she'd never seen before—but still, Novak didn't want Hepburn to see or hear about the dress.

"It's called the *Lady Macbeth*. It's inspired by the dress worn by the actress Ellen Terry in 1888, depicted in John Singer Sargent's famous painting."

Stella Manning stared at herself in the mirror, extending her arm as if she were about to command an army. "Lucretia, darling, you have surpassed yourself. It's exquisite." Her familiar voice sounded like sandpaper dripping with honey. Novak could see that Stella Manning enjoyed the way the flared sleeves, which widened at the elbow into bells of velvet, gave her every gesture emphasis.

"The dress has a spandex corset that pulls in the stretched skin from your pregnancy. Do you see that?"

Stella Manning murmured that she did. She looked at her reflection in the mirror, her hands resting on the tiny waist that the corset created. "It's like looking at my younger self."

"It is a powerful dress, made for a queen of the stage. Demure yet sultry," Lucretia Cutter declared.

Stella Manning frowned. "I have played the Scottish king's wife many times," she said. "The name carries bad luck." She stroked the bodice of the forest-green gown. "For the Film Awards, I will need all the luck I can get." She looked at Lucretia Cutter. "I'm not getting any younger."

"An actress of your talents doesn't need luck," Lucretia Cutter purred. "Are you really going to let a silly superstition put you off wearing it?"

Stella Manning frowned.

"I made the dress for you. The color perfectly complements your hair and skin."

"It does," Stella Manning agreed. "I look amazing."

"But if you don't want it, I will find another actress to wear the dress." Novak watched Stella Manning struggle with her superstition. Mater looked away. "Ruby Hisolo Jr., perhaps?"

"No!" Stella Manning spat, her face suddenly spoiled by the ugliness of jealousy. "Not that glorified waitress."

"She's very pretty," Lucretia Cutter murmured. "The next big thing, I hear."

"This dress is simply too beautiful to be unlucky," Stella Manning declared. "I love it." She turned around and looked at Lucretia. "I'll buy it."

Lucretia Cutter shook her head. "It's not for sale, but I would be honored if you'd wear the dress to the Film Awards."

"Really? A loan?"

"The Film Awards is to be my greatest fashion show yet," Lucretia Cutter replied. "This dress was made to be worn by a true artist, and I would be honored if the great Stella Manning would wear my *Lady Macbeth* to the awards."

Stella Manning pivoted slowly, unable to take her eyes off her reflection.

"The world will be stunned and awed by you in this dress." Lucretia Cutter's voice was a whisper.

"Yes." Stella Manning nodded. "You are a master of your art, you really are."

"The dress would have very little impact if *you* weren't wearing it." Lucretia Cutter's gold lips twitched. "The combination will be explosive."

Novak thought that Mater looked like a hungry cat about to devour an unsuspecting mouse, and she wondered why the Film Awards were so important. Mater had always refused to dress celebrities for awards ceremonies in the past, saying it devalued her art. And now here she was almost *begging* an actress to wear her dress to the Film Awards. Novak stared at *Lady Macbeth*. Was it something to do with the dress?

"Can I take it with me now?"

Lucretia Cutter shook her head. "This dress is under embargo. On the morning of the awards, my team will bring it to you, dress you, and chauffeur you to the ceremony." She signaled to Gerard, who stepped forward. "I don't want anyone to see it until you step out of the limousine onto the red carpet."

Stella Manning looked at Gerard, reluctant to take the dress off, then sighed and turned her back so he could unfasten her. Gerard looked the other way as the actress carefully stepped out of the dress and stood in her lingerie, pulling at the skin on her stomach.

"Pity the world doesn't like a baby belly." She sighed and looked at Mater. "Do you hate yours, too?"

"Mine?" Lucretia Cutter frowned.

Stella Manning looked at Novak and then back at Lucretia Cutter, confused.

"Oh, I see. No. I used a surrogate for Novak," Mater replied, her face expressionless. "My work is too important to be interrupted by a pregnancy."

"Oh!" Stella Manning's eyes flickered over Novak.

Novak stared blankly back. She'd always known that she'd been grown in a test tube and delivered by a different mother, although she didn't know the woman's name. Gerard called her "The Stork."

Stella Manning smiled at her. "Novak is a pretty name." She picked up her black cashmere sweater and pulled it over her head.

"I named her after a handbag." Lucretia Cutter's voice was flat. "She makes a great accessory, don't you think?"

Novak didn't move a muscle. She knew she was being scrutinized. Gerard had told her she was named after a famous movie star, from the days when the movies were in black and white. He'd shown her pictures of a beautiful platinum-blond woman called Kim Novak.

"A handbag? Huh!" Stella Manning picked up her jeans, sliding first one leg and then the other into the figure-hugging denim. "Well, Novak. You must be excited about being nominated for a Film Award? It's a rare honor."

Novak nodded.

"You mustn't be disappointed if you don't win. It's an amazing achievement just to get nominated."

Novak nodded again.

Stella Manning gave her a look tinged with pity and turned back to

Lucretia Cutter, who was watching Gerard as he gently placed *Lady Macbeth* in its wardrobe box. "I'm grateful you thought of me for one of your dresses, Lucretia." She slipped on her leather jacket and picked up her sunglasses from the sideboard. "I'm looking forward to the awards this year."

"Me too," Lucretia Cutter said, her face splitting with an alarming smile. "It's going to be the most memorable awards in the history of the academy."

As Stella Manning turned to the mirrors to put on her sunglasses, the door opened and a tall, thin man with sandy hair and very blue eyes entered the room.

"Ah, come in, my dear." Lucretia Cutter stepped forward.

Novak cried out and jumped to her feet before she could stop herself.

Standing in front of her was Darkus's dad. He'd gotten a haircut and the beard was gone, but it was definitely him. She could see the scars on his neck, the same scars she had on her own body, scars from the assassin bugs.

All the adults were staring at her.

"What is it?" Lucretia Cutter's voice cracked like a whip, a penciled eyebrow raised above her sunglasses.

Novak sat back down and fixed her eyes on the floor. "I'm sorry, Mater. I . . . I didn't realize you knew him. I thought he was an intruder."

"Stupid child." Lucretia Cutter laughed. "Bartholomew, allow me to introduce Stella Manning, the greatest actress of our time."

Novak watched, her stomach knotting itself up, as Darkus's dad took Stella Manning's outstretched hand, bent down, and kissed it. "Of course," he said. "It's a great honor to meet you."

Novak studied his face for signs of grief and pain, but saw none. Her body was shaking with anger. Didn't he care about what had happened to Darkus? Darkus had risked everything to save him. Why was he smiling at her mother in that way?

Novak fizzed with fear and outrage: Darkus's own father had betrayed him.

She watched her mother wrap an arm around Darkus's dad's waist and kiss his cheek. "Stella, this is one of my oldest and dearest friends, Bartholomew Cuttle. After more than a decade apart, we're working together again, on something really big."

CHAPTER FOURTEEN
Darkened Heights

*D*arkus poked his head between the front seats of the car, and Virginia grinned at the green tiger beetles sitting on his head. Uncle Max changed into third gear and the car bunny-hopped through the streets of Camden toward Regent's Park and Towering Heights.

"What are you going to say to your dad?" Virginia asked. "He might not be happy to see us."

"I don't know." Darkus frowned, thinking back to the argument they'd had that evening. "I need to make him see that he's in danger." He shrugged. "I don't care if he shouts at me."

"I just wish he'd talked to me before he ran off trying to be a hero," Uncle Max said. "We're all on the same side, for goodness' sake."

"Are we?" Virginia asked. "How can we know that? We don't know what Darkus's dad is planning to do."

Darkus opened his mouth to protest, to say that they were all fighting for the same thing, but he had to admit his dad was behaving strangely. What if he *wanted* to be with Lucretia Cutter? What if her research into beetles was too tempting for him to resist? What if Darkus was in the way, and that was why Dad had wanted Uncle Max to take him to Wales?

The car was thick with an uncomfortable silence.

Darkus reached up and lifted Baxter onto his palm, looking into his friend's shining eyes. He smiled at the rhinoceros beetle, who opened his mouth, smiling in reply. At least with Dad gone, there'd be no more talk of him giving up Baxter. He looked down at the beetles lined up on either side of him on the backseat: a compact battalion of luminous-spotted fire beetles to combat darkness, mottled Hercules beetles for their strength, bombardiers for their talent with firing acid, and titan beetles, which had a vicious bite. They were experienced fighters now; Darkus had been training with them ever since the Battle of Nelson Parade.

He stroked Baxter's elytra. "When we send the beetles into Towering Heights," he said, "we should get them to check the cells for Spencer Crips."

"That's a good idea!" Virginia nodded. "And we need to keep our eyes peeled for yellow ladybugs."

"Yellow ladybugs?" Uncle Max said. "There was a very large one in the front room yesterday."

Virginia's and Darkus's heads snapped around.

"I'm afraid to say"—Uncle Max lowered his voice to an exaggerated whisper—"I accidentally squashed it with the sole of my shoe!"

Virginia burst out laughing as Uncle Max waggled his eyebrows.

"I'll not have Lucretia Cutter's spies in my house."

Despite the late hour, Camden Town was alive with staggering revelers. The closer they got to Towering Heights, the more nervous Darkus felt. He hadn't returned to the big white house since they'd busted his dad out of Lucretia Cutter's cell. He shook his head; he still couldn't believe that Dad would voluntarily walk back into that house. Darkus felt his nails cutting into his palms and realized he was clenching his fists.

He looked out of the window; the familiar parkland of London Zoo was on their left. Uncle Max pulled over. "I don't want to get any closer, in case the car is recognized," he said over his shoulder.

Darkus nodded. The old mint-green Renault 4 was pretty memorable.

They cautiously got out of the car, the beetles following Darkus like a scuttling shadow. As they got close to the house, Darkus became aware his heart was thumping like a bass drum. The familiar brick wall rose up in front of them, behind it the tall copper-beech hedge.

"Can you get up and over?" Darkus whispered to Uncle Max.

"Don't worry about me, lad." Uncle Max reached up and jumped, pulling himself up and over the wall. Darkus heard a thud as he landed safely on the other side.

Virginia bent her knees, clasping her hands together, offering him a step up. Darkus slipped his foot into her hands, and in a second was sitting on top of the wall, reaching down to grab Virginia's hands and pulling her up to sit beside him. The beetles scurried up the wall and over it as the children dropped to the ground in unison. Darkus and Virginia wriggled through the copper-beech hedge, their arms over their faces to avoid getting scratched.

Uncle Max was standing on the edge of the giant paved chessboard patio. "The whole house is dark," he whispered.

"It's the middle of the night," Darkus replied.

"There are no cars in her driveway." Uncle Max pointed. "And there's a large padlock on the garage door. I think the house is empty."

Darkus looked at each of the windows, trying to detect a source of light, but there was nothing. All the ground-floor window shutters were closed. He ran lightly across the patio and pushed his face up against the glass, cupping his hands around his eyes. Peering between the slats of the shutters, he could make out a giant white shape. He pulled away and frowned.

"The furniture is covered in sheets." He looked at Uncle Max.

Virginia ran straight up to the black front door. She fell to her knees and pushed her fingers into the letterbox, lifting the flap and peering through. "It's empty," she hissed.

"The house is closed up," Uncle Max said. "There's no one home."

"It can't be." Darkus's voice faltered. "Where's Dad?"

Uncle Max walked over to Virginia and hammered the brass scarab knocker down onto the door. Darkus and Virginia jumped. "What are you doing?" Virginia stepped back, her eyes wide.

"I'm seeing if there's anyone in," Uncle Max replied.

Darkus held his breath, staring at the door, but no one came. His shoulders dropped as he started breathing again.

"Shall we look around the back?" Virginia suggested, becoming braver now she knew there was no one home. "We might find a clue."

Darkus nodded, and they crept around the side of the building.

"Where did everybody go?" Darkus whispered. "Where's Novak?"

"This isn't the only building Lucretia Cutter owns, Darkus," Uncle Max replied. "She could be anywhere."

"If Dad came here and found the house closed up, he might have gone back home. He could be there right now, wondering where we are," Darkus said hopefully.

"There's the servants' entrance." Virginia strode across the white gravel of the driveway, to the blue door, and pushed her ear against it. As she did, the door swung open and Virginia stumbled into the skirts of a woman, who screamed.

Virginia flew backward, yelling, as Uncle Max and Darkus rushed forward.

The woman in the house saw Darkus and screamed even louder.

Uncle Max held his hands up. "It's okay! It's okay! We mean no harm."

"*It's you!* The . . . the beetle boy," the woman gasped, shock written across her face. "You're dead! She shot you! Novak said!"

"Hello, Millie." Darkus smiled. "She did shoot me, but I'm not dead."

"A thousand apologies, my good lady." Uncle Max gave a courteous bow. "We didn't mean to startle you."

Millie looked crossly at Uncle Max. "Was it you doing that terrible knocking?"

"Ah yes, sorry." Uncle Max cleared his throat. "I thought no one was in. My apologies if I woke you."

"You gave me a terrible fright," Millie said, her hand on her heart as she tried to calm herself. She looked at Darkus. "If you're looking for the little miss, she's gone. They're all gone, to America, for the Film Awards."

"Millie, did a man come here this evening?" Darkus asked. "Clean-shaven, short wavy hair, sandy-colored with gray bits. He has blue eyes . . ."

"There were these two horrible men here, not two hours ago—one giant bald man and one skinny half-crazed creature. They were banging and knocking, insisting they had an appointment to see Madame Cutter, that she owed them money."

Virginia grabbed Darkus's arm. "Humphrey and Pickering!" she hissed.

"They wouldn't believe me when I said she'd gone away. I had to shut the door on them, and they smashed a window! They only went away when I told them I'd called the police." Millie put her hand over her heart again. "When you started knocking, I thought you were them, come back to rob the place."

"I can assure you, we have no such intentions. My name is Maximilian Cuttle. We are looking for my brother."

"Oh no!" Millie's hands flew up to her cheeks. "I forgot!" She thrust a hand into her white apron and pulled out a lavender envelope. "Are you the Maximilian Cuttle who lives on Nelson Parade?"

"Why yes, I am." Uncle Max nodded.

"Then this is for you. I'm so sorry, I was meant to bring it to you earlier this evening, but when those two men came knocking and shouting, I forgot all about it."

"What is it?" Darkus asked as Uncle Max tore open the envelope.

"Thank goodness you came." Millie shook her head. "I'd have felt terrible forgetting a thing like that. I promised little Novak that I'd get the letter to you as soon as I could."

"Darkus." Uncle Max's head snapped up, his voice urgent. "Lucretia Cutter knows where the beetles are. She's going to burn them."

Darkus stumbled backward, his mouth open in horror, tears pricking his eyes. "We have to get back! We have to save them!"

"Bertolt's there!" Virginia exclaimed, fear in her eyes.

And then they were running, footsteps on gravel, back up the driveway to the car and Nelson Parade.

CHAPTER FIFTEEN

Forest Fire

*B*ertolt looked up from the newspaper. Newton was darting around his head, manically flickering and flashing, dive-bombing his face.

"What is it, Newton?"

He folded up the newspaper and put it down on his workbench. He'd been reading about Lucretia Cutter's sudden decision to attend the Film Awards. The newspaper confirmed what he'd thought, that in the past Lucretia Cutter had condemned awards ceremonies, refused to attend them because they were vulgar, and she'd even singled out the Film Awards as particularly vacuous. The article's author didn't know why she'd made such a dramatic U-turn, not only attending the awards but dressing all the actresses nominated for Best Actress.

Bertolt wondered if Lucretia Cutter had changed her mind for Novak, but the way Darkus had described her brutal treatment of her daughter made that seem unlikely. She didn't need publicity, either; she was rarely out of the papers. Bertolt scratched his forehead. He couldn't think of one good reason why Lucretia Cutter would want to be a part of the movie world. Unless, of course, she didn't . . . but then why would she be going to the awards?

Newton zoomed in front of his face and bumped off his glasses.

"I'm sorry." Bertolt sniffed. "What's the matter?" An acrid smell filled his sinuses. "Newton, can you smell burning?"

Newton hovered in front of Bertolt's face, flickering and flashing.

"FIRE?!" Bertolt cried, reading the Morse code.

He ran to the door, yanked it open, and scrambled along the main tunnel to the sycamore tree. He had to get out of Furniture Forest. If it caught light, he'd be roasted alive!

He burst out from underneath the foldaway table and stopped dead. The back door of the Emporium was hanging open, and a fountain of flames shot out of the manhole.

"NO!" he screamed, running to the doorway, a terrible image in his mind of the beetles being burnt alive in their teacups. Tears streamed down his face. The smoke was making him cough, and a wave of heat pushed him back.

Terrified beetles flew and ran from the doorway, fluttering in the air, confused coleoptera bashing into each other and then sinking to the ground as their wings melted in the heat of the fire.

"TO ME! TO ME!" Bertolt's high voice cried. "Beetles, fly to me!" He struggled forward, falling to his knees and scooping up as many as he could, putting them onto his shoulders as more beetles landed in his hair. A line of them clambered up his legs.

He looked back at Furniture Forest. It was a death trap of rotting wood; he didn't want to be anywhere near it if it caught fire. He looked through the Emporium's back door. He needed to get out, to the safety of the street, but to do that he'd have to run through the burning building. He'd have to be quick: The back kitchen was catching fire.

Bertolt darted forward, covering his face with his arms. The heat pushed against his skin. He remembered a fireman coming into the school and telling them that the most dangerous thing about fires was not the flames, but the smoke. The toxic smoke that could make you pass out in minutes.

He looked up. There was a mushroom cloud of dark, menacing smoke growing against the ceiling. He pulled his sweater up to cover his mouth, and dashed forward past the burning bathroom, into the kitchenette, and through the archway into the ruined shop.

He came to an abrupt halt.

Standing in the doorway of the shop was a giant mountain of a man, a scrawny skeletal figure clutching his arm.

"IT'S THE BOY!" Pickering shrieked.

"GET HIM!" Humphrey roared.

Bertolt stumbled backward, spinning around and running back through the burning kitchen. His eyes spewed tears, making him blind, but he knew where the doorway was. He shot out into the backyard, beetles clinging to every part of him.

"Newton!" he called out, and the flickering firefly swooped down. "Get the Base Camp fireflies. Light the way to safety for any survivors."

Using Bertolt as a safety raft, the beetles climbed up, gathering on his back and shoulders. Those that were able to fly took off and joined the fireflies to aid the rescue of their brothers and sisters. Bertolt fell to his knees and crawled as fast as he could under the foldaway table.

"Where is he?" he heard Humphrey shout.

Bertolt's heart was beating faster than the wings of a hummingbird. He flicked a switch, setting the Grandfather Clock booby trap, and scrambled into the labyrinth of Furniture Forest.

"There!" Pickering screamed. "He went under that table."

Bertolt came to the Grand Archway of bicycles and looked right, down Dung Ball Avenue. He didn't want to lead Pickering and Humphrey to Base Camp. There was a crashing noise behind him, and a howl of pain as Pickering became a victim of the grandfather clock's pendulum. Bertolt imagined it swinging down with force and smashing into Pickering's head, and felt a moment of satisfaction.

"Argh! Humphrey! The boy hit me in the face with a sword! I'm bleeding!"

Bertolt looked down; beetles were collecting in puddles around his shins and hands. "Climb on," he whispered. "We have to get out of here." He turned his back on Dung Ball Avenue and headed into Tok-Tokkie Tunnel. Moving as quickly as he could, he scrambled to the

Oyster, a safety pod he and Virginia had built in case of emergency. The pod was made of two bathtubs, one upside-down on top of the other, joined at the back by a giant hinge, and four springs he'd pulled out of an old pinball machine to make lifting the top bathtub easy. Bertolt raised it.

"Right, all of you, get in here," he whispered to the beetles, "until I can come back and get you."

The beetles flew, tumbled, and dropped into the empty bathtub.

"I'll be back as soon as I can." Bertolt closed the Oyster and scrambled back to the Grand Archway.

"Get out of my way," Humphrey was shouting at his wailing cousin. "I'll squash that little gnat!" Bertolt heard a clatter as Humphrey ripped the foldaway table away from the forest, tossing it behind him.

"Newton," Bertolt called up to the firefly, who was dancing up above Furniture Forest, "I need a halo. We need the ogre to see me."

Humphrey was on all fours, trying to squeeze between the two wardrobes that leaned against each other like sleeping tramps.

Newton and a chain of his brothers, who were up above Furniture Forest looking for any surviving beetles, swooped down and formed a ring above Bertolt's head.

"I see you!" Humphrey shouted with menacing glee.

"Oh no! Please don't get me!" Bertolt cried, hoping Humphrey would take the bait. "Help me! Somebody!" And he twisted left, scrambling through a rarely used tunnel, which quickly narrowed. He'd waited for ages to test his booby traps, and he knew the perfect one for Humphrey.

The tunnel was a dead end, a heavy oak dresser barring the way. Bertolt opened one of the cupboard doors in the dresser and wriggled through a small round hole that he'd cut out of its back. On the other side of the dresser, framing the hole, a toilet seat was screwed into the wood. Bertolt smiled to himself; Humphrey would never be able to fit through that hole.

"I'm coming to get you!" Humphrey called out, grunting and straining as he crawled toward the dresser. "I'll teach you to set fire to my house."

"Please don't!" Bertolt cried as he doubled back through chair legs to a spy hole. He watched as the angry Humphrey huffed and puffed his way past on all fours, then silently slid a sheet of chipboard across the tunnel, slotting it between two bookcases on the opposite side, and pushing a heavy marble fireplace to lean against the chipboard. Humphrey was trapped.

Feeling braver, Bertolt scurried back to the toilet seat, poking his head through it. "You're trapped, you nasty great bully!" he said to Humphrey.

"You're not the boy!" Humphrey snorted, like an angry bull, and tried to back out of the tunnel. His feet kicked against the chipboard, but it was no use. He couldn't get out the way he'd come in.

"What have you done, you little rat?"

"You're caught in my Bog Seat booby trap," Bertolt called out proudly. "And it serves you right for setting fire to the beetles."

"I didn't set fire to any beetles!" Humphrey shouted. "Why would I set fire to what's left of my home?"

Bertolt blinked. A cold tide of fear washed over him. If it hadn't been Humphrey and Pickering who started the fire, then it must have been . . . "Lucretia Cutter," he said aloud.

"Let me out!" Humphrey shouted.

"Actually, I can't. Sorry," Bertolt called back. "I'm not strong enough on my own."

"What?" Humphrey thrashed about, kicking and butting his shoulders against his furniture cage until he realized he was well and truly trapped.

Bertolt poked his head back through the hole in the back of the dresser. "Sorry!" he said, grinning.

Humphrey's nostrils flared. "Why, you little pipsqueak!" he roared, thrusting his head into the dresser, gnashing his teeth like a rabid dog, trying to bite Bertolt. "I didn't get out of prison just to be trapped by a ridiculous-looking chipmunk wearing a bow tie!" His face poked out of the back of the dresser, framed by the toilet seat.

Bertolt darted forward and grabbed the rim of the toilet seat, turning it ninety degrees.

Humphrey tried to pull his head back out of the hole, but couldn't. He was utterly stuck.

"Right, back in a bit," Bertolt said, with a little wave, and as fast as he could, he headed back toward the Grand Archway.

He heard Pickering before he saw him.

"My antiques! No! Oh no!"

Where Furniture Forest brushed up against the Emporium, Bertolt saw that flames had caught the rotting tables and chairs. Pickering, almost encircled by flames, was leaping around beating them out with an old rug.

"Hey!" Bertolt called. "Pickering!"

Pickering turned around, a crazy look in his eyes. Bertolt ducked back into Furniture Forest, running as fast as he could to the tunnel off Dung Ball Avenue containing the Tangle Tunnel trap. He wriggled into it on his belly, leaving his feet sticking out.

"Newton," he hissed, "show him my feet."

A moment later he heard a shriek of delight from Pickering. "I see you! You little punk!"

Bertolt pulled his legs into a squatting position. Reaching up above his head in the darkness, he found the ladder and pulled himself up silently. He held his breath as he watched Pickering below, writhing on his belly like an angry snake, moving into the pitch-black Tangle Tunnel.

"I'm going to catch you, you little thief, and when I do, I'm going to . . . urgh! What's this? It's sticky. Ugh. What? Get it off! Ouch! Arghh! Oh, help! Humphrey!"

Bertolt pressed his eyes closed and imagined all the strips of flypaper that were stapled to the floor and dangling down into the darkness distracting Pickering from the wire snares on the floor of the tunnel.

"Let go of my leg! Humphrey? Is that you? Ouch!" There was a series of curses and mutterings as Pickering wriggled around, getting more tangled in a web of black string, wire snares, and the sticky paper that butchers used to trap flies.

"Can you hear me, boy?" he called out. "You must think you're ever so clever, but you'd better hope I never get out of here, because if I do, I'm going to find you and let my cousin bake you into a pie and EAT

YOU!" He laughed, a horrible, chilling gurgle. "WITH CRANBERRY SAUCE!"

Bertolt silently clambered up the ladder and out onto the bed frame that reared up in the middle of the yard. The sycamore tree was on fire, and the fringes of the forest were burning. He felt a bolt of panic as he saw how fast the furniture was catching fire. The flames were creeping along the wall, blocking any escape.

CHAPTER SIXTEEN
Rescue and Ruin

*N*elson Parade loomed out of the darkness, the silhouette of the Emporium backlit by a strange orange glow.

"Good lord!" Uncle Max slammed his foot on the brake, and the Renault 4 threw them all forward as it screeched to a stop. He leapt out of the car.

Darkus lifted Baxter down from his shoulder and put him on the backseat with the other beetles. "Stay in the car," he said.

Baxter refused to be put down, gripping onto Darkus's hand with his strong claws.

"Baxter, it's too dangerous." As he spoke, Darkus realized that he was saying the same words to Baxter that his father had said to him, and he stopped struggling with the beetle. Baxter had every right to want to save his family.

The rhinoceros beetle marched determinedly up Darkus's arm to his shoulder and stood alert, looking forward as Darkus got out of the car to stand beside his uncle and Virginia, staring at the burning building.

"Bertolt!" Virginia screamed. Before Darkus or Uncle Max could stop her, she darted into the ruin of the Emporium.

"NO!" Uncle Max was after her in a flash. "Virginia, get back here!"

Darkus's feet felt like concrete. He was rooted to the spot. Where had the fire come from? Where were the beetles?

"Darkus!" he heard Virginia shout. "Furniture Forest is catching fire! Bertolt's in there!"

And then he was running, too, leaping over the rubble and wreckage in the Emporium. The heat radiating out of the manhole cover was overpowering, the hairs of his wool sweater melting and singeing from the power of it, and he knew in every fiber of his being that any beetle down in the sewer was dead.

He grabbed Baxter off his shoulder and held him in his cupped hands, close to his chest. Tears spilled out of his eyes as he coughed and choked on the smoke. A tsunami of emotion crashed against his rib cage, and he stumbled. Before he hit the ground a strong hand grabbed the back of his sweater, lifted him to his feet, and yanked him out of the back of the building.

"You okay? Darkus?" Uncle Max hugged him to his chest.

Darkus nodded, pushing the image of Beetle Mountain as a towering inferno out of his head.

Uncle Max was looking about him in a panic. "Foolish girl, she's disappeared into that mess!" He pointed past the sycamore tree to a gaping hole in the furniture where the foldaway table had once stood. "It's a death trap."

Darkus saw that the sycamore tree was on fire and flames had embraced the fringes of the forest. He put Baxter back on his shoulder and grabbed Uncle Max's sleeve.

"Call the fire brigade. I'll get Virginia over the wall and into our yard." Not waiting for a response, he dived into the forest and found the tunnels thick with smoke. He scurried down Dung Ball Avenue, pulling his sweater up over his mouth.

"Virginia!" he called out.

"Darkus. Over here."

Darkus followed Virginia's voice. She was standing in Base Camp. It was empty, but she was pointing at the wall. Two of the booby trap alarms were jangling, the Bog Seat and the Tangle Tunnel. Virginia looked at him and he nodded.

"I'll take the Bog Seat. You check the Tangle Tunnel."

"Wait!" Virginia grabbed two tea towels that were folded neatly on Bertolt's workbench. She thrust them into the bucket of water they used for washing up. "Tie this over your mouth."

Darkus gratefully received the damp cloth, and the two of them ran out of Base Camp, securing the towels over their mouths.

He ducked and scrambled to the edge of the Bog Seat trap and peeped around the corner. To his astonishment he saw Humphrey's head poking through a toilet seat, looking like a mounted and stuffed pig's head. Darkus doubled back and met Virginia beside the Tangle Tunnel.

"Pickering's caught in there!" Virginia mumbled through her cloth.

Darkus pointed over his shoulder. "Humphrey's in that one."

"But where's Bertolt?" Her dark eyes darted about in panic.

The heat of the fire was increasing and the smoke was getting thicker. They needed to get to safety.

"Safety!" Darkus shouted. "The Oyster!"

Virginia's eyes widened and she nodded, already running and sliding down the passageway that led to the safety pod. Darkus was hot on her heels. They burst out of the opening in front of the two bathtubs, and Virginia grabbed a corner and tried to push it up.

"It won't budge."

Darkus was by her side in a second and pulling, but the upturned bath wouldn't open. They struggled for a minute, and then Darkus let go.

"He's locked it from the inside," he said, banging on the bathtub bottom, lifting his tea towel and shouting, "BERTOLT! IT'S US!"

There was a clunking sound and the top bathtub sprang open to reveal Bertolt, sitting in the bottom bathtub surrounded by a hundred beetles.

"You knucklehead!" Virginia threw her arms around Bertolt's face, knocking off his glasses. "I thought you were dead!" She squeezed his head hard as tears ran down her cheeks.

Darkus wondered if she would have thrown her arms around him like that if it had been him in the bathtub.

"LET GO!" Bertolt gave a muffled cry. "You're suffocating me."

Virginia smiled and stepped backward. "You're alive!"

"The beetles . . ." Darkus found he was unable to speak.

"I tried, Darkus, I really tried." Bertolt pressed his lips together, trying not to cry. "But Humphrey and Pickering chased me, and the fire was so hot, and these were all the beetles I managed to save." He looked down at the insects around him in the tub. "Some of them are hurt."

Darkus closed his eyes. He felt like a part of him was burning, too; all those wonderful, clever beetles gone. He slumped forward, gripping the edge of the bathtub.

"This is not the time or the place to talk about this," Virginia said, putting her hand on his shoulder. "The smoke is getting thicker. We need to get out of here."

Darkus leaned in and gently sank his hands into the bathtub. "Climb up, little friends," he whispered. Virginia walked around to the other side of Bertolt and did the same.

Bertolt carefully clambered out of the tub, still with beetles on his shoulders and head.

"We need to get to the ladder and over the wall into your uncle Max's," Virginia said.

"The flames are all along the wall," Bertolt said. "The ladder will be on fire."

"Grab the washing-up bucket—we'll put out the flames," Virginia said to Darkus.

Darkus didn't wait—he sprinted into Base Camp, picked up the bucket, and ran back. He stepped onto a chair, climbing up onto the melting tarpaulin skin of the forest. "We'll go up and over," he said. "That way we can see where the fires are and avoid the smoke."

"What about Humphrey and Pickering?" Bertolt said, following Virginia up onto the chair. "We can't let them die."

"Uncle Max has called the fire brigade. They'll be here any minute," Darkus replied.

"But the smoke?" Bertolt said.

"Their heads are close to the ground," Darkus replied. "Smoke rises. They'll live."

"*They* wouldn't care if *we* got roasted," Virginia said, unconcerned, offering Bertolt a hand up.

As they clambered across the roof of Furniture Forest, the welcome yowl of approaching fire engines gave them strength. Darkus hurled the bucket of water over the singed ladder, and one by one they made it safely over the wall.

The three children watched from Uncle Max's kitchen window as the firemen trained their hoses on Furniture Forest. They used sticks with metal hooks to pull apart the burning-hot furniture, putting out the many small fires they encountered as they searched for the trapped men. Darkus saw the relief on Bertolt's face as Humphrey and Pickering were freed from their traps, thoroughly soaked and a bit singed but fully alive and as angry as pestered hornets. Humphrey was charging around shouting at firemen, while Pickering was frantically trying to save items from the charred mountain of burnt junk that had once been their Furniture Forest. A strip of flypaper was stuck to the side of his head, his straggly hair matted around it. A sheet of newspaper had gotten stuck to it, too, and was flapping in the wind. He looked ridiculous, but no one felt like laughing.

Several escaping beetles—stragglers, hurt and confused—made it to the window ledge. Baxter, Marvin, and Newton welcomed them in, but there were only a few, and then no more came.

Darkus made the injured beetles a makeshift hospital in a roasting tin with oakwood mulch on the bottom, a pile of fruit, and a couple of teacups at one end. The other beetles made their way into dark corners of the room to rest.

The fire was washed out of Furniture Forest, and what was left looked like the burnt and shattered hull of a shipwreck.

The firemen packed away their hoses as an ambulance arrived to take Humphrey and Pickering away. Uncle Max pulled the children away from the window and ordered Virginia and Bertolt down to the car to take them home. Darkus said good-bye and trudged up the stairs to bed with Baxter.

As he climbed into his hammock, Darkus noticed the blue light of early morning creeping through the skylight. He curled the edges of the hammock over, cocooning himself in darkness. Cupping his hands protectively around Baxter, who was unusually still, he hugged him to his chest.

There couldn't be more than a hundred and sixty or seventy beetles who had escaped the sewer inferno—tens of thousands had died.

The beetles were gone, and so was Dad.

Lucretia Cutter had won.

CHAPTER SEVENTEEN
Daily News

Humphrey and Pickering lay opposite each other on stretchers in the back of the ambulance.

"What's this?" Humphrey grabbed at the flypaper stuck to the side of Pickering's head.

"Arghhhhh!" screamed Pickering as Humphrey tore the strip away, bringing with it a layer of skin and a clump of hair. "What did you do that for?" He thumped Humphrey, but his cousin didn't even grunt. He was studying the newspaper article that had been stuck to the side of Pickering's head.

"What are you looking at?" asked Pickering.

"Lucretia Cutter," Humphrey replied.

"What?! Let me see." Pickering tumbled out of his stretcher and shuffled over to his cousin on his knees.

Humphrey showed him the picture of Lucretia Cutter and Novak next to the story about her dressing the three nominated actresses at the Film Awards. "The boy who trapped me—the little blond rat—accused us of starting the fire. When I said it wasn't us, he said her name."

"How would that little rat know her name?" Pickering wondered.

Humphrey shrugged. "Don't know, but if Lucretia Cutter burnt down our house, then she owes us big-time."

"She owes us anyway," Pickering said. "We signed a contract."

Humphrey waggled the newspaper. "Well, now we know where she is." He smiled. "I think we should take a trip to Los Angeles. Pay her a visit. Maybe even go to these Film Awards."

"Oh yes!" Pickering clapped his hands with delight. "I've always wanted to go to America."

Humphrey nodded and rubbed his tummy. "They have giant burgers over there."

"Lucretia Cutter might take us to the awards as her guests," Pickering said, clutching his hands over his heart and sighing.

The ambulance came to a halt.

"Quick, get back in your stretcher and pretend to feel ill." Humphrey shoved Pickering backward. "We've no bed to sleep in tonight, and if we stay in the hospital we'll get a free breakfast in the morning."

Pickering jumped back on his stretcher and pulled the red blanket over his body. "Los Angeles!" he whispered to himself. "To see Lucretia Cutter! How wonderful!"

"Once we've eaten our fill of hospital food," Humphrey said, "we'll go to the airport."

"Hang on, how will we afford the tickets?" Pickering sat up. "We haven't got any money."

"We've got your life savings." Humphrey smiled.

"I'm saving that for a rainy day!" Pickering exclaimed.

"It's raining, Pickers." Humphrey sniffed. "If ever a day could be called rainy, it's the one when your house burns down—after it's already exploded."

CHAPTER EIGHTEEN

Bombardier Jet

Novak stepped out of her mother's car onto the runway. She walked toward the black Bombardier Learjet emblazoned with the gold scarab of Cutter Couture. She concentrated on keeping her hand flat across the top of her shoulder bag, ensuring Hepburn was the right way up inside her secret compartment. She'd worried that keeping Hepburn hidden from Mater, with her heightened senses, would be difficult, but now that Bartholomew Cuttle was by her side, Lucretia Cutter barely looked at Novak, and she did her best not to draw attention to herself.

She was concerned that Darkus's dad might recognize her from the rescue, but if he did, she saw no trace of it in his face. When he looked at her, she thought she saw concern or pity in his eyes, but that must have been fake. He had betrayed his dead son—he wouldn't be concerned for Novak.

Gerard stood at the bottom of the steps that led up to the cabin door of the plane. He offered his hand, and Novak took it as she climbed onto the portable staircase. He gave her hand a gentle squeeze and they exchanged a glance.

The cabin of Lucretia Cutter's private Learjet was upholstered in white leather. Eight reclining chairs faced each other in two sets of four. There were two lone seats at the rear of the plane, facing the backs of the chairs in front; Novak made a beeline for one of the isolated seats and sat down.

Ling Ling was the captain and Craven her copilot. Dankish and Mawling sat at the front, with Gerard. In the central quad, facing one another, were Mater and Bartholomew Cuttle.

The flight was eleven hours long. Novak had planned out the whole thing. She was going to sleep and read her way across the Atlantic. She'd brought a book, a slim volume she'd taken from Mater's library, called *The Beetle Collector's Handbook*, which Darkus had mentioned. Mater had every book ever written about beetles, so it hadn't been hard to find it. Not wanting anyone to see she was learning about beetles, Novak had taken the dust jacket from one of her other books, a story about a girl who wanted to be a ballerina, and wrapped Darkus's beetle book inside it. When she read, she felt close to him, as if he was looking over her shoulder and approved.

She had the plastic container of watermelon from Millie in her handbag. At two-hour intervals she'd go to the bathroom and let Hepburn out of the bracelet to stretch her legs and eat.

Novak fastened her seat belt and, gazing out of the window, wondered if this was the last time she would be in England.

If I was going to grow up like a normal person, she thought, *I'd want to have a home here. I love England, especially when it rains.*

Novak's head was heavy. She leaned against her headrest and closed her eyes.

She wasn't aware of time passing, or takeoff, but when she awoke the black Bombardier jet was high above the clouds. She became aware that Hepburn was out of her secret compartment and pinching the skin between her thumb and forefinger.

Novak was about to silently chide the beetle when she noticed Hepburn was waggling her forelegs and flicking her antennae in alarm. The beetle was trying to tell her to listen to the conversation in the seats in front.

"Wait until you see just how far the seeds of our work together has taken me," Lucretia Cutter said.

"I hardly think I can take credit for what you've achieved."

"On the contrary, Bartholomew, I wouldn't be in this position if you hadn't opened my eyes to the astonishing skills and adaptability of beetles. It was your passion and knowledge that started me on this journey. You're my inspiration. Finally to be back in a laboratory together . . ."

"I thought Lenka was working with you?" Bartholomew Cuttle sounded uncomfortable.

"Yes, he did, for a while." She snorted. "He's no use to me now."

Novak remembered Henrik Lenka, a stony-faced blond man with cruelty chiseled into his bone structure. It had been nearly two years since he'd wrenched her out of the pupation chamber in the Biome. She'd be happy never to see him again.

"Do you know, I have a lab assistant that reminds me of you?" Lucretia Cutter said. "He's not as bright, but he has an amazing way with beetles." She sighed. "Such a shame you gave it all up. It could've been you in my Biome, instead of the Crips boy."

"Crips?" Bartholomew Cuttle sat bolt upright.

"Not jealous, are we?" Mater smiled.

"No." He relaxed back into his seat. "So, what's the Biome?"

"My secret laboratory."

"And where is this secret laboratory?"

"If I told you, it wouldn't be a secret, would it?" Lucretia Cutter gave a low, guttural cackle. "You'll find out soon enough. You're going to do your life's greatest work there."

"You're too kind. I fear I may have already done my best work."

"Kindness is a waste of time and energy," Mater sneered. Novak rolled her head toward the window, her eyes half-closed. The window reflected a reverse image of Mater.

"Come on," Bartholomew Cuttle said, "you don't believe that. Look at the effort you've gone to, taking your daughter to the Film Awards. You must be proud . . ."

This time Mater's laugh was a shocking staccato sound. "Oh, my dear Bartholomew. You don't get it, do you?"

"Get what?"

"The girl is a genetic reproduction of me, nothing more."

"Your daughter?"

"You can call her that. I don't."

"I don't understand."

Novak watched Lucretia Cutter lean forward. She held her breath; Mater was going to tell him her secret.

"In my Biome, I have built a pupation chamber." She looked for a reaction on Bartholomew Cuttle's face. "Once the chamber is sealed, it cannot be opened and the process cannot be stopped. The subject is pulled apart molecule by molecule, turned into soup, retaining memory and notions of previous form. It is at this point that I introduce a new gene to the subject and it begins the transformation into a new form, replicating the change from larva to beetle."

"Lucy!" Novak heard the shock in Darkus's dad's voice. "You can't mean . . ."

"Oh yes, I do. I've experienced the process myself." She slowly removed her enormous sunglasses, revealing two glistening black orb eyes. "It's exquisitely painful."

Bartholomew Cuttle gasped. "You could've killed yourself!"

"Aww." Lucretia Cutter mocked him with a pout of her gold lips. "I didn't know you cared!" She sat back, leaning her head against the leather headrest, and replaced her glasses. "You needn't worry. I test everything on a guinea pig before I apply it to myself. It's something I picked up from the cosmetic industry." She smiled. "The girl is my current guinea pig."

"Novak?"

"There have been others, but unfortunately"—she paused—"they all died."

Novak couldn't see Bartholomew Cuttle's face, but she could see Mater's smile, and it made her shiver.

"But, but, the girl . . . she isn't as changed as you?"

"No," Lucretia Cutter snapped. "I'm not sure why. I think it may be her youth. When she goes through the changes of human puberty she will most likely develop more beetle features. Not that it matters. She will pupate again."

"Again?"

"I'm happy with this stage in my metamorphosis, but it's not enough."

"Not enough?" Bartholomew Cuttle's voice sounded hollow. "You've already gone beyond the boundaries of modern science. You're—you're no longer human! What do you hope to achieve?"

"Why spoil the fun by giving the game away?" Lucretia Cutter laughed.

"Lucy, surely you're not thinking of performing a full metamorphosis?" Bartholomew Cuttle rasped. "It will kill you. Even if the transformation worked, there's not enough oxygen in the atmosphere to support a beetle of your size! And how would you communicate? You'd have no lungs, no voice box."

"Do you think I haven't thought of all of these things?" Lucretia Cutter sneered. "They are minor irritations. We'll test them on the girl first."

"This is what you *really* need me for, isn't it? To help you once you've changed."

"I don't *need* you," Lucretia Cutter hissed. "I have the Crips boy—his affinity with beetles is almost as strong as yours—but you and I, we have a shared vision, an intellectual history. Our ability to understand one another is superior. Once I've completed the holometaboly, I'll need humans around me who can communicate with invertebrates. You and I are tied together by so much history. I know you, above all people, will be able to interpret my will. We'll be together forever."

"You're crazy," Bartholomew Cuttle whispered.

"That's what people say about you right before you're recognized to be a genius."

Novak was rigid with fear. She vividly remembered the horror of the pupation chamber, the agonizing pain as she was pulled apart, changed forever. She'd rather die than go through that again. She squeezed her eyes tightly shut and mouthed a silent prayer to Darkus for help, knowing she was utterly alone and no help was coming.

CHAPTER NINETEEN

The Darkest Hour

Darkus didn't think he could face going to school, but Uncle Max insisted he go. He sat through the morning lessons in a daze. At lunchtime he, Bertolt, and Virginia sat at their usual table and took out their packed lunches.

"Mum was up when your uncle dropped me home. He told her he'd caught us having a secret sleepover," Virginia said as she bit into her tuna sandwich. "She didn't believe him. I got the full interrogation after he left."

Bertolt sighed. "I don't know why you can't wait until you've finished speaking before you eat."

Virginia ignored him and swallowed. "I kept to the story. In the end, Mum had to admit that I was in one piece and had no bruises, so I got away with being grounded for one month."

"I didn't get punished," Bertolt said quietly. "My mum just cried."

"Oh! That's awful." Darkus had left his lunch box closed. He wasn't hungry.

"Not as awful as what happened to the beetles," Bertolt whispered.

"I'm going to go down there after school." Darkus looked at his hands. "I need to see."

"Are you sure that's a good idea?" Virginia said.

"I have to." Darkus swallowed. "I want to give them a proper funeral . . ."

"Yes." Bertolt blinked. "I'd like to do that, too."

"Yeah, okay." Virginia nodded. "They deserve a good send-off."

"But you're grounded." Darkus looked at Virginia.

She shrugged. "I'm supposed to do gymnastics club after school. No one expects me home till six. This is more important."

There was silence as they imagined the sight that would greet them when they got down into the sewer.

"What about Base Camp?" Bertolt said.

"I went out on Uncle Max's fire escape this morning. It's ruined," Darkus said blankly. "She's won."

"No, Darkus . . ." Virginia shook her head.

"Virginia, she's *won*," he said again. "Base Camp is destroyed, we haven't found Spencer Crips, Professor Appleyard is in a coma, the beetles are dead, and Dad . . . we don't even know where he is."

He dropped his head into his hands. "Lucretia Cutter is in America and there's nothing you or I, or anyone, can do about whatever it is she's planning. It's hopeless."

"Well, *you* might not be able to do anything, but together *we* certainly can," Bertolt said, "and with a bit of grit and determination . . ."

"You two aren't even allowed to see me outside school!" Darkus snapped.

Virginia and Bertolt looked at each other. "We might have fixed that," Virginia said.

"How?" Darkus frowned. "Dad told your parents you're not allowed to see me."

"Yes, well," Bertolt coughed, "um . . ."

"You mustn't get cross," Virginia said.

"Cross about what?" Darkus looked at Bertolt.

"Well, we may have told our parents that, um, that, well . . ." Bertolt spluttered.

"We said that your dad's having a nervous breakdown and is doing mad things . . . like disappearing," Virginia said, her shoulders up by her ears and an apologetic smile on her face.

Darkus couldn't believe what he was hearing.

"Mum's only met your dad once, but she knew the story about him disappearing before, and you being a lonely orphan and being looked after by your uncle, so when he turned up on the doorstep raving about how it wasn't good for us to see each other, Mum took it to mean that your dad thought *I* was a bad influence on *you*. She was pretty mad about that. But this morning when your uncle Max dropped me home, he was all charming and apologetic, saying I was kind to care about you so much, and that he was grateful to me, as my friendship meant a lot to you, and how I was a lovely, polite girl to have around. Mum lapped it up. Your uncle said your father had gone away for a short spell, and Mum smelled a rat. As soon as he'd left, she asked me heaps of questions. I couldn't tell her the truth, so I sort of made up the nervous breakdown stuff. I said that your dad had had a funny turn the day before—when she'd met him—and the doctors had decided he should be sent away to get better, in a special hospital, and that you were really upset, and that Bertolt and I had snuck out in the middle of the night to comfort you, because we are such brilliant friends." Virginia sat back proudly. "So, you see, we *are* allowed to see you. Only I'm still grounded for sneaking out."

"Virginia's mum rang my mum and told her the whole story," Bertolt said.

Darkus blinked. "You're telling people that my dad's been locked up in a mental hospital?"

"Um, that's not the right way to say it." Bertolt gave a distressed shake of his head. "We said your dad was in a special hospital, because he's having a nervous breakdown due to the tragic death of your mother."

"What?" Darkus pushed his chair away from the table as he got to his feet. "You don't know anything about my mother!" He spun on his heel and stormed out of the cafeteria into the playground.

"Oh dear." Bertolt looked at Virginia. "I don't think we handled that at all well."

"Is that you, Darkus?" Uncle Max's voice greeted him as he opened the door of the flat.

"Who else would it be?" Darkus replied.

"Wonderful!" Uncle Max appeared at the top of the stairs, dusting off his hands. He smiled broadly at his nephew.

Darkus looked at him suspiciously. "Why are you looking so cheerful?"

"Why don't you come up into the front room?" Uncle Max said, beckoning to him.

Darkus slid off his backpack and coat and dropped them on the floor by the door.

"Oh, Darkus, how many times do I have to tell you to hang your coat on the hook? You've got a memory like a fruit bat." Uncle Max chuckled and went back into the living room.

Darkus picked up his coat, hanging it on the wall, and followed his uncle upstairs. He pushed the living-room door open. Uncle Max was standing in the middle of the room, his arms spread wide.

"Ta-da!" he sang.

Darkus stared.

All the furniture had been moved. The sofa and armchairs were in a line under the window, and the coffee table was pushed up against the fireplace. Above the carriage clock and below the row of African masks hung a corkboard, pinned with soiled and crumpled scraps of paper. Darkus stepped closer. It was all the clues from the back of the wardrobe in Base Camp: Novak's card, and Virginia's list of facts about beetles. Behind him, at the far end of the room, was a sky-blue paddling pool, its bottom lined with oakwood mulch. On one side of the paddling pool, part buried and piled up in a mound, was a miniature mountain of mugs, and on the other side were chopped-up bits of melon, cucumber, and banana. The surviving beetles from the mountain were busily burrowing, munching, and generally making themselves at home. Against the left wall of the room, where the sofa had previously lived, was Bertolt's workbench, and lined up on top of the ironing board were his tools from Base Camp. Draped about the workbench, attached to four hooks screwed into the ceiling, was the square of tarpaulin that Bertolt had stitched all the chandelier crystals to, and nestled at base of each crystal was a sleeping clump of fireflies.

"So? What do you think?" Uncle Max asked.

"What? I—it's—it's amazing!" Darkus whispered, stunned.

Uncle Max nodded as he surveyed the room proudly.

"Not a bad bit of redecorating, if I do say so myself! Cleaning the chandelier crystals took an age, and of course it's not a patch on your Base Camp, but . . ."

Darkus threw himself at his uncle, hurling his arms around him and burying the side of his face in his safari shirt.

"OEUFFF! Steady on, lad!"

"It's great." Darkus's voice was hoarse. "It's really great." And then suddenly he was crying. Silent, body-racking sobs, brought on by his uncle's kindness. Tears of grief for the beetles, tears of anger at his father, tears at the injustice and hopelessness of everything.

"There, there. Let it all out." Uncle Max patted his head. "A good cry helps you think clearly, and it's good for the soul."

Uncle Max carefully shuffled backward to the sofa and sat the two of them down. He stroked Darkus's hair as he gulped air and sobbed into his uncle's belly. Eventually he was all cried out, and his breathing calmed. He lay for a bit, slumped over Uncle Max, listening to his belly gurgle.

"How are we doing?" Uncle Max asked gently.

Darkus sat up. He wiped his sleeve across his face. His eyes felt sore. "Better."

"Good—then, if it would be all right by you, I'd like to put on a new shirt." Uncle Max looked down at his stomach and made a face.

Darkus laughed. Uncle Max's shirt was wet through, and Darkus had left a couple of unpleasant snot trails across his chest. "Sorry."

"Not a bit. We'll have a nice cup of tea with heaps of sugar—that makes everyone feel better." Uncle Max climbed to his feet. "To be honest, I would've been worried if you *hadn't* had a good cry. It's not healthy to hold it all inside. I'll be back in a minute."

Darkus looked around the room. Uncle Max must have worked all day to bring this upstairs. He walked over to Bertolt's workbench and ran his hand along the soldering iron, thinking how happy Bertolt would be to see it again. He lifted his fingers to his face; they smelled of bonfires.

He thought about Bertolt and Virginia, and felt bad for ignoring them all afternoon. His head ached. The past twenty-four hours seemed to have gone on forever, yet at the same time they seemed to have sped past. Everything had utterly changed.

A familiar weight pressing on his shoulder told him Baxter was landing. He sighed and turned his head.

"Hello, Baxter." He stroked the rhinoceros beetle's elytra. Baxter's face was downcast. "It's time we mourned for our lost friends. We're going to give them a proper funeral."

Baxter nuzzled the side of his head against Darkus's neck.

"I know, Baxter. I feel it, too."

Uncle Max came into the room backward, carrying a tray of sugary tea and a plate of custard creams. After gulping down a cup of tea, Darkus felt stronger, and it seemed that Uncle Max had been right about the crying. It had made things clearer. Right now the only thing that was important was saying a proper good-bye to his beetles.

He went upstairs and changed into black jeans, sneakers, and a black sweater. When he came down, Uncle Max was wearing his funeral suit.

"You can't go into the Emporium anymore," Uncle Max said. "The fire has made the building unsafe. But I paid a visit to Claire, the woman who runs the shop downstairs. She has a manhole in her stockroom. It leads down to a chamber next door to Beetle Mountain. I went down there this afternoon." He took a deep breath. "I have to warn you, Darkus, it's not a pretty sight."

"You've been in there?"

"I had to," Uncle Max replied. "I knew you'd want to go down there, and I needed to make sure it was safe."

"If you can look at it, then I can look at it." Darkus gritted his teeth. He felt his nostrils flare as emotion welled up inside him again, but he managed to control it this time. "I have to look at it. They were my friends."

"Very well, then." Uncle Max nodded.

Darkus leaned his head back and mimicked the sound that Baxter made when he rubbed his back leg against his elytra by sucking his teeth. All the beetles in the room responded to his call. Those that flew formed a flotilla, and those that crawled formed an orderly procession, marching soberly below their flying brothers. The fireflies kept their lamps dark.

Uncle Max, Darkus, with Baxter on his shoulder, and the beetles soberly made their way out of the flat and down into the street. When Uncle Max opened the door, Darkus saw Virginia and Bertolt standing there, dressed in black. Virginia was biting her lip and looked like she was about to cry.

Darkus had never seen her look upset before. He smiled at her as she and Bertolt fell in step behind Uncle Max, who led them all into the Mother Earth store and down into the sewers.

They gathered together in the main tunnel outside the chamber that held Beetle Mountain, making sure they had all the beetles with them.

"I thought, if you want, we could begin with a bit of music?" Uncle Max raised his eyebrows, looking at Darkus questioningly.

Darkus felt lost. He wanted to give the beetles a proper send-off, but he hadn't thought about the way to do it.

"And then, I thought, we could make a ceremony, a beetle ceremony," Virginia said, taking a piece of paper from her pocket. "Marvin and I came up with something, if you're happy for us to do it?"

"Obviously, you and Baxter should give the eulogy," Bertolt said, "so Newton and I thought we would take care of closing the ceremony."

"That sounds good." Darkus nodded.

Uncle Max pulled a miniature set of panpipes out of the breast pocket of his jacket. He blew a long haunting note, which wavered as his breath ran out, then led into a melancholy tune as he walked solemnly into the chamber that held the ashes of their coleopteran friends.

Darkus felt Bertolt take his hand, and together they walked into the chamber. Virginia followed them, the beetles swarming around and over their feet.

The smell shocked Darkus. The room stank of gasoline; the fumes were so strong it made his head spin. Beetle Mountain was barely a third of its original size. Some cups had shattered in the intense heat of the fire, but plenty of the thicker mugs were still in one piece. The black skeleton of the buddleia tree reached out from what was left of the mountain like a desperate hand grasping for help. The upturned bodies of larger species of beetle were clearly visible—the Goliath, the Atlas, the Hercules—but Darkus knew that there were thousands of tiny beetles deep in the black pile, invisible in the darkness. He reached up and stroked Baxter. This couldn't be an easy thing for the beetle to see. He needed to be strong for him.

Uncle Max's haunting tune came to an end and he stepped respect-fully to one side. Virginia walked forward, standing at the foot of the monstrous mountain of ash and death. She licked her lips and swallowed. Reaching into her coat pocket, she took out a small box and lifted the lid. She held it out, offering it to the mountain, and then bowed her head. Kneeling down, she placed the box in front of her. "What happened here was"—her voice wavered—"a cruel thing, a murder, a stopping of the cycle of life. And it happened to our dear friends, our special beetles." She bit her lip. "But"—she reached into her box and pulled out a tiny blue sparrow's egg—"the cycle of life is more powerful than cruel humans."

Virginia held the egg up above her head. "This egg represents the beetle's egg." With her other hand she reached into her coat pocket and pulled out a palm-shaped, rubbery green leaf, taken from her mother's potted plant. "This leaf is for the habitat." She placed the leaf down like a blanket on the ashes and carefully laid the egg on the leaf. "From the egg hatches the larva." From her box she lifted a lump of stone and held it high. Darkus could see it had a spiral of marks on it. "This fossil, that lay in the earth for hundreds of years, represents the larva." She placed the larva beside the egg on the leaf and reached into the box again, lifting out a purple crystal. "The larva becomes a pupa; this crystal is the pupa." She placed it beside the larva. "And from the pupa comes the beetle." Her voice was thick with emotion as Marvin dropped down from her hair onto the green leaf, standing beside the crystal.

Virginia spread her arms wide, as if she wanted to embrace the whole mountain. "These beetles will lay no more eggs," she said. Her shoulders were shaking, but she held her voice steady. "Dearest beetles," she continued, "your ashes will go into the ground and become food for larvae, where you will rejoin the cycle of life. Nothing ever really dies," she said, bowing her head.

Darkus gritted his teeth together, holding back the grief that was threatening to overwhelm him.

After a moment of silence Virginia gathered Marvin in her hands, got up, and moved back to stand beside Bertolt. Darkus nodded at her, reassuring her she'd performed a good ceremony, and then stepped forward. "My friends." He coughed to clear his throat and took a deep breath, fixing his eyes on the charred rims of teacups and the black exoskeletons scattered across the funeral pyre. "We are sorry. Sorry that we could not do more to protect you. Sorry that we couldn't save you. Sorry that it was humans who did this to you." His head dropped, and he felt Baxter nuzzle his horn against his neck.

He pulled himself up straight. "But we will *never* forget you, and we will *never* forget what was done to you." He raised his hand. "I swear, whenever I feel I haven't got the strength to fight, I will think of you, and I will be stronger. I swear that I will dedicate my life to understanding the natural world and protecting it. I do this in your name, for the beetles of Beetle Mountain: my saviors, my teachers, my friends." And then in a voice like stone, he added. "But first, I swear, I will find Lucretia Cutter and I will stop her."

Virginia stepped up beside him, tears flowing freely down her face, and raised her hand. "I swear, I will stop her."

Bertolt silently joined them, his hand raised. "I will stop her, too."

Uncle Max stepped up beside Virginia and raised his hand. "And me," he whispered in a voice thick with emotion.

Newton rose up into the air, flying to the mountain, followed by his family of fireflies. And the mourning fireflies danced in the air, a slow, graceful, flickering waltz of tiny lanterns, dipping and rising as they encircled what was left of their friends. The surviving beetles, half-hidden by the shadows in the chamber, made a strange high-pitched chirping sound as they rubbed their back legs against their elytra, an otherworldly accompaniment to the dance of the fireflies.

Bertolt wiped tears away from beneath his glasses, and Darkus noticed that even Uncle Max's eyes were glistening—but he himself had cried his eyes dry and what remained was a steely resolve, a driving purpose that he understood for the first time in his life.

He was the Beetle Boy. He was going to protect his beetles and destroy Lucretia Cutter.

CHAPTER TWENTY
Beetle Wake

"Now then, who wants a piece of chocolate cake?" Uncle Max asked as they trooped back through the door of the flat. "I've got ice cream, brightly colored fizzy drinks, and a whole heap of sweets." He hung his safari hat on a hook beside the door. "Not having had a beetle funeral before, I wasn't quite sure what would be required."

"This isn't a party!" Bertolt exclaimed, aghast.

"Have you ever been to a funeral, Bertolt?"

"No." Bertolt looked down. "This was my first."

"Well, after the funeral ceremony there's always a wake. The wake is a celebration of the life of the person—or, in this case, the beetles—who have passed away. It's important that we remember just how wonderful and brave and clever the beetles were. To do that, we need treats and high spirits. Can't celebrate life by being somber."

"I would like some chocolate cake and ice cream in the same bowl with sweets on top," Virginia said, embracing the idea. "I'm starving."

"Me too," Darkus nodded.

"Okay," Bertolt agreed reluctantly. "I'll have the same."

"Ha! That's more like it. You go into the front room. I'll bring it up." And Uncle Max disappeared into the kitchen.

Darkus smiled sheepishly at Bertolt and Virginia. "Sorry for shouting at you at school. I mean, I . . ."

"It's all right." Bertolt pushed his glasses up his nose. "I would have shouted at us, too. We were horrible. We're sorry, aren't we, Virginia?"

Virginia nodded, but looked the opposite of apologetic.

"I'm glad you came for the funeral. It wouldn't have been proper without you," Darkus said. "Virginia, your ceremony was really good."

"Did you think so?" Virginia's eyes widened with relief.

Darkus nodded.

"Oh, I *am* glad. I wanted it to be about the beetles, you know? Relevant to their lives. All the usual stuff about heaven and angels didn't seem right."

"It was brilliant." Bertolt nodded.

Darkus pushed open the living-room door and walked over to the paddling pool, carefully placing one foot into the mulch, so that all the beetles who had hitched a ride out of the sewer could crawl off into their new home.

"My workbench!" Bertolt exclaimed. "Oh, and my chandelier crystals! I don't believe it!"

"No way!" Virginia shouted, rushing over to the fireplace and gripping the mantel as she studied all the clues and fragments of information that Uncle Max had salvaged from Base Camp and pinned to the board. "It's all here! Look! It's the Fabre Project picture. I thought we'd lost that in the fire." She wrinkled her nose. "It smells of barbecues." She spun around. "When did you do all this?"

Darkus shook his head. "Not me. Uncle Max."

"Really?" Bertolt looked up at the tarpaulin. "That was kind of him."

"We can't go back into Furniture Forest. It's too dangerous," Darkus said.

"Base Camp is gone for good?" Bertolt asked, crestfallen.

Darkus nodded. "Uncle Max rescued what he could and carried it up here. The rest is ruined."

"And the paddling pool?" Virginia asked.

"I was improvising," Uncle Max replied, coming through the door with a large tray of goodies. "The beetles were searching out dark corners and soft wood. I thought I'd better find them a more appealing habitat before they reduced my furniture to sawdust. This beauty"—he pointed to the paddling pool—"is the biggest container I could find in Mr. Patel's newsstand. I'm rather pleased with it."

"It's perfect," Darkus said.

"Thank you, Professor," Bertolt said, pointing at the tarpaulin, hanging low with the weight of the chandelier crystals and fireflies. "Especially for bringing our roof. It took me ages to stitch on all those crystals, and the fireflies love it."

"My pleasure." Uncle Max bowed to Bertolt. "I know this is no Base Camp, but I was hoping perhaps it might make do as our head-quarters."

"Headquarters?" Darkus asked.

"Sit down, all of you," Uncle Max said, shooing them to the sofa and handing each of them a large bowl heaped with chocolate cake and vanilla ice cream. "This is the way I see things. Barty's dis-appeared, we're not sure exactly where to. Lucretia Cutter's set fire to the house next door, killing thousands of poor, innocent creatures. Your wonderful den has been destroyed, and I don't want to think about poor Andrew in the hospital. I'm not one for conflict, but that woman has gone too far. How she can have the audacity to flit off to America to have a party at these Film Awards I don't know!"

"Oh!" Bertolt's hands flew up to his cheeks. "I've remembered something I was thinking about before the fire!"

"What?" Virginia asked.

"I was looking at that newspaper article, and thinking it's odd that Lucretia Cutter is going to the Film Awards. She's never cared about awards before—in fact, she hates them. She's refused even to let actresses wear her dresses to the ceremonies in the past."

"Maybe it's for Novak." Virginia shrugged, looking at Darkus. "You said Lucretia Cutter paid for the film that Novak's in?"

Darkus shook his head. "She doesn't care about her daughter one bit."

Virginia frowned. "Then why . . . ?"

"What if she's not interested in the Film Awards *at all*?" Bertolt said, jumping and tipping his cake and ice cream into his lap. "Oh! Whoops!"

"Steady on there, Bertolt." Uncle Max leaned over and scooped the cake and ice cream back into the bowl.

"But that doesn't make sense," Virginia said. "Why would she be there if she doesn't care about the awards?"

"Because," Darkus said, feeling his body grow cold, "she wants to stand onstage at an event that's being broadcast live around the world. She wants all the cameras on her, because that's when she's going to do it."

"Flipping fleabags!" Virginia's mouth dropped open. "That's it!"

"Yes!" Bertolt nodded as he wiped a napkin over his leg. "The twenty-second of December—that's when it's going to happen."

"But we don't know what *it* is!" Darkus threw his hands up in frustration, and Virginia caught his arm in midair.

"But we've got a spy." Her eyes were wide. "We've got Novak. She tried to save the beetles with her letter, didn't she? She's on our side. She'll help us."

"That poor girl." Uncle Max shook his head.

"She's going to be at the awards, Darkus," Virginia said. "And with her help, we might be able to stop Lucretia Cutter somehow."

"We need to reach her." Darkus nodded. "And we need to tell her I'm alive."

"Well then, what we need is a cover story that will enable us to go to America without arousing suspicion." Uncle Max sat down and scratched his chin. "How about a Christmas trip to Disneyland?"

Virginia clapped. "I've always wanted to go to Disneyland!"

"But we won't really be going to the theme park?" Darkus said.

"No, we'll tell everyone that we're going to Disneyland, when really we'll go to LA, to the Film Awards, to try and find Novak."

"Isn't that lying?" Bertolt asked.

"A little bit," Uncle Max admitted.

"Would I be back in time for Christmas Day?" Bertolt wrung his hands. "I can't leave Mum on her own for Christmas Day."

"We'll be back before Christmas Eve," Uncle Max assured him.

"We're going to need an army," Darkus whispered.

"The beetles are gone," Virginia said mournfully.

"Not all of them." Darkus looked at the paddling pool. "But three children, a bunch of beetles, and an archaeologist aren't going to be enough to stop Lucretia Cutter."

"Four children," Bertolt said, "if you count Novak."

"I've got it!" Uncle Max sat up, his hands on his knees. "What if we enlisted the help of a scientist and entomologist every bit as clever as Lucretia Cutter? We'd have to take a detour through Greenland, but it might just give us the advantage we need."

"It'd certainly help." Virginia nodded.

"But who?" Bertolt asked.

Darkus looked at his uncle and smiled. "Dr. Yuki Ishikawa."

CHAPTER TWENTY-ONE
A Meddle of Mothers

*D*arkus and Virginia carefully slid the suitcase full of beetles into the trunk of Uncle Max's car just as a motorbike roared up the road, slowing to stop beside them. The motorcyclist lifted off her helmet to reveal the blond bob and well-known face of Emma Lamb, the TV reporter. She winked at Darkus. "Any kidnappings happen around here recently?"

"What are you doing here?" Virginia asked, gazing admiringly at the motorbike. She reached out and stroked the shiny red fuel tank. "Nice bike."

"Ah, Emma! Good to see you," Uncle Max said, carrying two duffel bags to the car, followed by Bertolt, wheeling a mini suitcase.

"Thought I'd check in before you check out," Emma Lamb replied. "Poking your nose into Lucretia Cutter's affairs is a dangerous thing to do."

"Are you helping us?" Bertolt asked.

"I have my own score to settle with that woman." Emma Lamb nodded. "Did you hear? I lost my job."

"They fired you?" Virginia was outraged.

Emma Lamb leaned toward her. "*And* all my memory cards—the ones with the camera footage of Lucretia Cutter's weird black eyes—they've all been wiped."

"Wiped?" Bertolt gasped.

"That's awful!" Darkus said.

"Yeah, well, Lucretia Cutter made a mistake when she decided to mess with me," Emma Lamb said, grimacing, "because I fight back."

"Have you found something?" Uncle Max asked.

"Not sure," Emma Lamb replied. "From what I can tell, Lucretia Cutter is a one-woman mafia. She has a chain of businesses under the umbrella of Cutter Couture. Some of them are legit, some of them are grim, and some of them are invisible. I've heard rumors about factories farming insects."

"Insects that could destroy a forest in Colorado?" Darkus asked.

"Perhaps." She shrugged. "I'm interested in the acres and acres of Amazon rain forest that Lucretia Cutter has bought. It's impossible to get any information about what's happening there. There are no satellite images of it. Nothing. It's invisible." She raised a finger. "And where there is an absence of information, there's a story."

"The Amazon rain forest is a perfect habitat for beetle breeding," Darkus said. "The best and biggest species can be found there."

"You could hide anything in there." Bertolt nodded.

"Well, that's where I'm headed." She lifted her helmet. "I came by to tell you"—she looked at Uncle Max—"you know, in case I disappear."

"You're going to the Amazon?" Virginia's eyes grew wide.

"Hidden in that jungle is a juicy story with my name written all over it." She pulled her helmet on. "I'm going to bring down that power-hungry witch and scoop up the Pulitzer Prize at the same time."

"Be careful," Uncle Max warned.

"Look who's talking!" Emma Lamb laughed. "Unless I'm wrong, you're planning to grab the tiger by the tail." She put on her gloves. "Good luck!" She flipped down the helmet visor, turned the key in the ignition, and backed the bike into the road, waiting for a break in the traffic.

"Hey, wait!" Darkus shouted. He leapt forward, grabbing at the air, but Emma Lamb didn't hear him over the roar of the engine. The bike jumped forward and she was gone.

"What is it?" Virginia asked, coming to his side.

Darkus held out his fist, lifting one finger for a second, showing Virginia a flash of a yellow ladybug. "It was on her back. Quick, grab the pill pot from my pocket."

Virginia pulled a plastic pot from Darkus's coat pocket, and he forced the struggling beetle inside.

"I'll put it in the jar with the others," Virginia said.

"We need to get a move on or we'll be late for the plane." Uncle Max ushered the children into the car.

"I still can't believe you got my mum to say yes to this," Virginia said gleefully as they drove out of the city.

"I can't see why any parent would say no to their child getting an all-expenses-paid trip to Disneyland the weekend before Christmas, can you?" Uncle Max laughed.

"I feel bad about lying." Bertolt shook his head. "I've never lied to my mum like this before."

"Of course you haven't," Virginia scoffed. "There's never been anything like this before. This is an adventure times a thousand." She bounced up and down on the backseat, causing Bertolt to bob unhappily beside her. "They'll make a movie about *us* one day."

"As long as we're not the collateral damage," Bertolt muttered.

Darkus looked at his worried friend. "If you don't want to come, we'd understand."

"I *do* want to come," Bertolt replied. "I just don't like lying to my mum."

"We *can't* tell our parents the truth." Virginia threw her hands up in the air. "I mean, c'mon, how do you even convince a grown-up that this is real? Have you tried to talk to anyone about your intelligent beetle?"

"Ahem." Uncle Max pointedly cleared his throat. "*I'm* a grown-up!" He paused. "Although I do see your point."

"And we don't want Lucretia Cutter to know we're coming," Darkus added. "She has spies everywhere."

Bertolt sighed unhappily and looked out of the window. "I know."

The airfield was not much to look at: an expanse of scrubland with patches of old tarmac that rose like islands out of the grasses and weeds. A dirt track led to two dilapidated buildings that looked more like cowsheds than aircraft hangers.

"Are you sure this is the right place?" Darkus asked.

"Absolutely. This old airfield hasn't been used for over twenty years, which means it's unlikely it's being watched."

As they parked, a woman strode out to meet them. She was tiny, with gray hair scraped into a tight bun. Her face was like a bulldog's, her features bunched together in the middle while her cheeks and chin rolled into folds. Gold-rimmed circular glasses perched on her tiny upturned nose, framing two bright hazel eyes that darted about constantly, taking in every detail.

"Motty, so marvelous to see you." Uncle Max took her tiny hand in both of his. "Thank you for doing this."

"I must be getting soft in my old age," the woman said, smiling, "but I needed to get back to my place in LA anyway, and you're a hard man to resist, Maximilian."

"Ha!" Uncle Max laughed. "Meet the children: Bertolt Roberts, Virginia Wallace, and this is my nephew, Darkus."

"Good afternoon, young man." She held out her hand. "I'm Motticilla Braithwaite." She shook Darkus's hand hard enough to make him lose his balance. "Call me Motty," she said, letting go and grabbing Bertolt's hand. "Everyone else does."

Uncle Max lifted the suitcases and bags out of the car, and they followed Motty into one of the dilapidated buildings.

"It's nothing but a giant shed!" Virginia said as they trooped through the door.

"What more do you need?" Motty replied.

"It's a bit old," Virginia said, wrinkling her nose.

"*I'm* a bit old, young lady," Motty said, peering over her glasses, "but I could pick your pocket before you could remember my full name."

Virginia stopped walking, surprised by Motty's retort, and Darkus couldn't help grinning.

"We really are grateful to you for helping us like this," Uncle Max said.

"If everything you've told me about Lucretia Cutter is true," Motty said, "I'm happy to be flying you to America."

"You're the pilot?" Virginia gawped at her.

"Well, I'm not going to let anyone else fly *my* plane, am I?" Motty's eyes twinkled with mischief. She looked at Darkus. "It took several phone calls from your uncle to get me to take him on as copilot."

Darkus looked at Uncle Max. "You can fly?"

"I'm a bit out of practice," he admitted, "but I have a license, and I haven't died in a plane crash yet."

Motty snorted. "Flying short trips across the desert is a bit different from flying to the West Coast of America."

"Well, this will give me a chance to learn what all the knobs and buttons do," Uncle Max replied.

Motty looked at the children. "Don't worry. He's not actually going to be flying. A single pilot can fly a plane—we only need a second pilot in case anything happens to me."

"We'll take great care of you," Bertolt replied earnestly.

"We refuel in Narsarsuaq," Uncle Max said.

"In Greenland," Darkus added, "where we're going to find Dr. Yuki Ishikawa."

"I'm hoping he'll be at the Arboretum Groenlandicum," Uncle Max said. "Last anyone heard, he was there studying the whirligig beetle."

"He'll help us." Darkus felt a thrill of excitement. "I know he will, and I'll bet if anyone knows how to stop Lucretia Cutter, it'll be him."

"So"—Motty cleared her throat—"we have three children, one adult copilot . . . and we'll be picking up one more passenger in Narsarsuaq?"

"Don't forget the beetles," Darkus said, pointing at the suitcase he was dragging behind him.

"Beetles?" Motty frowned.

Darkus carefully laid the suitcase flat on the ground, flipped up the catches, and lifted the lid. Inside was a honeycomb construction of plastic cups, wedged and wadded with moss and newspaper. Poking their heads and antennae out from nooks and crannies were beetles of varying sizes. "There are one hundred and eighty-seven of them."

"Eighty-eight," Virginia said, holding up the plastic pill pot containing the yellow ladybug. She knelt down beside Darkus, lifting a jam jar with a perforated lid from a pocket on the front of the case. It contained nine yellow ladybugs; all but three were dead. The three surviving yellow beetles had eleven spots on their elytra.

Darkus unscrewed the lid, holding it in place until Virginia had her fingers over the edges of the pill pot lid. In one fluid movement he lifted it as Virginia tossed the yellow ladybug into the jar, and then he slammed the lid back on, screwing it tight.

Motty looked at Uncle Max. "Is this the 'controversial cargo' you mentioned?"

Uncle Max nodded. "We can't let anyone discover the particular talents of these beetles, or they'll be confiscated and killed. We need to get them in and out of America without anyone knowing."

"Right, then we'd better not get caught." Motty smiled. "If we're asked, you are the family and friends of the eccentric British millionaire Maximilian Cuttle"—Uncle Max bowed—"and he's taking you on his private plane to Disneyland. Got it?"

"Got it!" they cried.

"Right, let's get flying." Motty strode off in the direction of a giant pair of double doors.

There was a loud bang behind them, and everyone jumped and spun around.

"Oh no!" Bertolt looked like he was about to faint.

Two women stood in the doorway to the hangar.

"MUM! What are you doing here?" Virginia yelped.

"I might ask you the same question, Virginia," Mrs. Wallace replied, her hands on her hips, her lips clamped together in an angry pout.

"Ah, Mrs. Wallace . . ." Uncle Max began apologetically.

"Don't you be trying to smooth-talk me with your lies." Mrs. Wallace held up her hand. "I don't want to hear them. I came here to get my daughter and take her home."

"Mum, *no!*" Virginia shouted.

"Bertie"—Calista Bloom's eyes were like a hurt puppy's—"you lied to me."

"I'm sorry." Bertolt had gone purple.

"Don't be too hard on Bertolt. If he hadn't told Iris Crips what was going on, we'd never have known," Mrs. Wallace reminded Calista Bloom.

Darkus looked at Bertolt. "You told Mrs. Crips?"

Bertolt's head dropped and he nodded. "She's so lonely. I've been visiting her," he admitted. "I didn't mean to tell her, but I was so worried about lying. I thought she could explain to Mum if, you know, if anything happened to me."

"Mrs. Crips is a mother who knows what it is to lose a child," Barbara Wallace said to Uncle Max. "Of course she told us. What were you thinking?"

Uncle Max's face flushed. "You are quite right, of course. I got carried away with the situation. I'm sorry. Utterly unforgivable of me. Sorry. Terribly sorry."

"You're as bad as the children," Barbara Wallace chastised him. "You're meant to be the responsible one, the grown-up."

"Bertie, my little chickpea." His mother held out her arms, and Bertolt scurried into her embrace. She looked over his head at Darkus. "Has this boy been leading you astray?"

"No, Mum." Bertolt shook his head, and Darkus was surprised to see him step back, out of his mother's arms. "I'm sorry for lying. I really am. But I have to do this. You must let me go. There are dark things happening, things that will affect all of us." He blinked.

"Mrs. Crips's son is missing, our friend Novak is in danger, and Darkus's dad has gone—to stop Lucretia Cutter from doing something terrible at the Film Awards, we think."

"The Film Awards?" Bertolt's mother looked startled. "Oh, I love the Film Awards!" She smiled brightly and clasped her hands together. "Everyone looks so handsome—oh, and the dresses are so twinkly . . ."

"Mum." Bertolt took his mother's hand to get her attention. "I want to go, Mum. I have to."

Virginia nodded, stepping toward her mother. "I'm sorry I lied, Mum." The words tumbled out. "I only did it because I didn't think you'd let me go, and this is the most important thing I've ever done in my life. They need me. I *have* to go. Please!"

Mrs. Wallace looked at Darkus. "You told me his father was in the hospital."

"I lied," Virginia admitted.

"There's been a lot of lying." Barbara Wallace sucked her teeth as she stared at Darkus. "Your father told me that my daughter should stay away from you."

"He was protecting her," Darkus replied, holding Mrs. Wallace's gaze. "He knew we'd try and fight Lucretia Cutter. He thought by keeping us apart, he'd stop us."

"Sounds like he was right." Barbara Wallace shook her head. "You should not be fighting anybody. You should be doing your schoolwork. You are only children."

"We're not *only* children," Darkus replied. "We're children with one hundred and eighty-eight special beetles, and an uncle who understands that any young person can fight as hard as an adult."

Mrs. Wallace scowled at Uncle Max, who rocked back on his heels, silently apologizing.

"Virginia, you believe this is something you must do?" Barbara Wallace asked her daughter.

With clenched fists and a determined pout, Virginia nodded an emphatic yes.

Barbara Wallace let out a sigh and shook her head. "If I could come with you, then maybe . . . but it's Christmas, and someone's got to look after Keisha and Darnell."

"I could go," Bertolt's mum blurted out.

"What?" Bertolt squeaked.

"I could go to Hollywood." Calista Bloom looked surprised at her own words. She giggled. "I mean, I'm hopeless at fighting, and I'm frightened of creepy-crawlies, but I could make sure the children eat properly, and tuck them in at night with a nice mug of cocoa."

"But what about the Christmas play?" Bertolt said, blinking furiously. "You can't just walk out—you're the good fairy."

Calista Bloom rolled her eyes. "Oh, I play that part every Christmas. Let the understudy have a go. This is much more exciting!" She twirled around. "I've always dreamt of going to the Film Awards. I'll have to buy a dress and shoes and a handbag."

"Would you really go, Calista?" Barbara Wallace said. "That *would* be a weight off my mind."

"Wait!" Virginia looked confused. "Are you letting me go?"

"You've always been a fine fighter." Barbara Wallace gave Virginia a proud smile. "If you are set on fighting this bad lady, then who am I to stop you? I just want you to be safe, daughter, and Calista will make sure of that; she's a mother, just like me." She looked at Uncle Max and pointed threateningly. "But no one is going to hurt my daughter without them hurting you first, you get me?"

"Of course!" Uncle Max spluttered. "No question."

Darkus found himself looking at Barbara Wallace and feeling envious. He wished his dad believed in him the way Virginia's mum believed in her.

"You keep an eye on him," Barbara Wallace said to Calista Bloom, pointing at Uncle Max.

"But—but . . ." Bertolt stammered. "Mum, you don't have your passport."

Calista Bloom's eyes brightened. "Actually, I do." She fished around in her turquoise handbag and pulled out a passport, spilling a tube of lipstick and her keys onto the floor. "Whoops!" She bent down and picked everything up. "I keep it with me, just in case Hollywood calls." She giggled.

"Well, that settles it!" Uncle Max clapped his hands together. "We'll add Mrs. Bloom to the passenger list."

"Miss," Calista Bloom corrected him.

"I beg your pardon, *Miss* Bloom." Uncle Max bowed.

Bertolt's mum turned to him and flapped her hands. "Isn't this exciting, Bertie?"

Bertolt nodded, a forced smile on his face.

"We need to get airborne," Motty interjected, "or we'll not make it to Narsarsuaq before the end of the day." She pulled open a huge door.

Two hundred feet in front of them, on the tarmac in the dazzling winter sunshine, was a small white plane with red markings. Its twin propellers reached forward from the wings in line with a cockpit that sat high in the pointed nose.

"This is Bernadette—she's a Beechcraft 90," Motty said, striding out of the hangar. Darkus saw that *Bernadette* was written in swirly red writing on the tail of the plane.

"Are there in-flight refreshments?" Calista Bloom asked. "I didn't have breakfast."

"We have packed a picnic," Uncle Max reassured her.

Darkus felt Bertolt take his hand. His pale face was a picture of anxiety. "Are you frightened of flying?" he asked.

"No." Bertolt shook his head. "If you understand the mechanics of a plane, it's impossible to be scared. Flying is the safest mode of transport there is." He paused. "It's just, well, this is a big thing we are about to do."

"Yes." Darkus nodded. "It is."

"And, I'm afraid, if anyone's going to muck it up or get hurt . . ." Bertolt frowned. "It'll be my mum."

CHAPTER TWENTY-TWO
Narsarsuaq

*T*his is going to be our greatest adventure yet," Virginia said as the two propellers spluttered into life. She leaned forward, wedging her face between Bertolt's and Darkus's seats, grinning at them. "I thought my mum'd make me go home for sure. Can you believe *your* mum's coming, Bertolt?"

Darkus looked at Calista Bloom, who was at the front of the plane, talking nervously to Uncle Max. Her hands were scrunching up her brightly patterned skirt as she talked.

"I feel sick," Bertolt said, following Darkus's eyeline. "I'd prefer not to have an adventure right now."

"You don't mean that!" Virginia said.

"I do. I'd like Lucretia Cutter not to exist, and for everything to be normal."

"Yeah, well, normal isn't much fun for some people." Virginia turned to look out of the window. "Normal means being invisible." She waved to her mother, who was standing on the tarmac.

"No one could call *you* invisible!" Darkus protested.

"What, because I'm a *Big Bird*?" Virginia snapped.

"Hey, Virginia," Bertolt chided, "that's not fair! He didn't mean that."

"I mean, you've got guts"—Darkus caught her eye—"and a big mouth, which makes you pretty hard to ignore."

A wry smile twisted Virginia's pout. Darkus hadn't realized her school nickname bothered her so much. She never seemed to care what people called her.

"I don't want to live an ordinary life. I'm not good at it," Virginia huffed. "Adventures are tough, but that's the point of them, isn't it?"

"What we're about to try and do is a bit harder than tough," Bertolt pointed out.

"We fought Lucretia Cutter before and we won," Virginia reminded him.

"She got the beetles in the end, though, didn't she?" Darkus said, looking out of the airplane window at Barbara Wallace, who had her arms crossed and a grim look on her face.

"Not all of them," Virginia said.

"I'm not going to let her hurt one more," Darkus said, "or Novak, or Dad, or anyone."

"She has all the power, the money, and the science." Bertolt blinked at Darkus through his big glasses. "How do you plan on stopping her?"

"I don't know," Darkus said. "But I *am* going to stop her, and this time, for good."

"That's the spirit." Virginia thumped Darkus's arm with approval.

Calista Bloom tottered down the aisle of the plane. "Darkus," she said sweetly, "would you mind if I sat next to my little Bertie-kins?"

Darkus tried not to smile as he shuffled past a blushing Bertolt to let Calista Bloom sit next to her son. He fell into the seat next to Virginia, and they grinned at each other as the plane's engines roared to life.

"Put your seat belts on, children," Calista Bloom said in her bell-like voice, fastening her own.

The Beechcraft 90 picked up speed, and Darkus felt his stomach lean against his spine and his head push into the headrest as Bernadette climbed steeply into the sky.

As soon as the seat belt light went off, Virginia sprang up. "I'm going to the cockpit. You coming?" She clambered over Darkus, not waiting for a reply.

Darkus leaned forward and tapped Bertolt. "Want to come?"

"I'm going to stay with Mum." He shook his head and mouthed: "She's not great with flying."

Darkus looked at Calista Bloom, who had her eyes clamped shut and was gripping the armrests tightly. He nodded and followed Virginia.

Pulling aside the curtain that hid the cockpit from the cabin, Darkus saw Virginia sitting in the copilot's chair, ogling the dashboard as Motty described what the switches and knobs did. Two handlebar joysticks stuck out of the control panel, and when Motty nodded, Virginia reverently took hold of one.

"She's done me out of a job," Uncle Max said, hovering behind the copilot's seat.

Darkus looked out through the windshield. They were above the clouds now; the horizon was pure blue. He pictured the trillions of beetles who crawled the surface of the planet below him. When this was over, he was going to dedicate his life to learning about those invertebrates. The more he thought about it, the more certain he was that the idea behind the Fabre Project was a good one. Beetles *could* be employed in environmental healing. He imagined beetles working in landfill sites, breaking down waste. He imagined insect farms cultivated to help with pest control and pollination. He thought about Professor Appleyard's book, and a world where humans farmed insects instead of cattle. It sounded like a good world to live in, something worth fighting for.

He wondered, again, about Lucretia Cutter's transgenic beetles, and something his father had said sounded in his head: *A force that is made to do good can also be used for evil. Whoever controls that force has the power to choose.*

Who knew what kinds of insects Lucretia Cutter was creating in her laboratories, or what she planned to do with them? But Darkus knew she'd also made the creatures that had become his friends and had built Beetle Mountain, which meant that beetles created to do bad could also be good.

His hand went up to Baxter sitting on his shoulder. The rhinoceros beetle was living proof that good could come out of whatever it was Lucretia Cutter was doing. He wished his father could see that. At the thought of his dad, Darkus's heart ached. Where was he? Was he with Lucretia Cutter? Was he fighting her or working for her?

Baxter nuzzled Darkus's finger.

"Are you hungry, Baxter?" Darkus backed out of the cockpit, walking down the aisle to the end of the cabin, where he'd strapped the suitcase of beetles into a seat. He released the seat belt, unzipped the case, and lifted the lid. Some of the beetles clambered away from the sudden light, burrowing into the oak mulch stuffed in between the teacups; others reared up and waggled their legs at Darkus.

"Hello." Darkus reached into the front pocket of the case, pulling out two bags, one containing pieces of banana and melon, and the other containing tiny jars of jelly. "Baxter says it's dinnertime." He placed jelly jars and fruit pieces around the case, so the beetles could easily find something to eat, and then put a lump of banana on his shoulder. Baxter immediately climbed onto it with his front two legs and began to nibble it.

"I'm going to have to shut you back in now," he said to the beetles. "I can't have you roaming around the plane. I'm going to need every last one of you when we confront Lucretia Cutter."

He sat down in the chair next to the case, while Baxter ate his banana. Bertolt's mum peered at Baxter from across the aisle.

"He's very big, isn't he?" She wrinkled her nose as she studied the rhinoceros beetle from a safe distance. "I don't really understand why you children are so obsessed with bugs." She shook her head, and her long, dyed-blond ringlets bounced around. "Bertie used to let me brush his hair, but since that fire-bug thingy decided to live in it, he won't let me near his head. It's dirty."

"Without beetles, Mum, you'd be up to your knees in animal dung," Bertolt replied.

"Oh, Bertie-kins, how revolting!" She turned and frowned at her son. "Poop is hardly a suitable subject for conversation, is it?"

"Mum!" Bertolt's face scrunched up. "I've told you a thousand times. Stop calling me that."

"Beetles do more than get rid of . . . dung." Darkus smiled. "They're an important part of the food chain for birds and other small mammals, and they pollinate all sorts of plants."

"I thought bees did that." Calista Bloom pouted. "I like bees. They make honey."

"Bees *do* pollinate plants," Darkus replied, "but so do beetles." He stroked Baxter's elytra and turned to stare out of the window while the rhinoceros beetle ate his dinner.

Darkus was awoken by the thud of feet as Uncle Max marched Virginia down the aisle toward them, and Motty's voice came over the intercom. "Lock up your beetles and take your seats, folks. We're coming up on Narsarsuaq."

"I need to get back to the cockpit and help with the landing," Uncle Max said apologetically as he hurried away.

"I wanted to do that," Virginia grumbled, "but they wouldn't let me. It's not my fault I turned off the autopilot."

"Maybe take some flying lessons before you try landing a plane,"

Darkus suggested as Virginia helped him lift and strap the beetle suitcase into the seat before they scurried back to their own.

As the plane descended over the charcoal sea, Darkus saw white icebergs thrusting up from the water, like the tops of drowning mountains. The sea ended abruptly, and a strip of tarmac painted with white lines climbed out of the water, marking the path inland to the Narsarsuaq Air Base.

The plane lowered its wheels, grazing the runway as it landed steadily and slowed to a stop.

"Nice landing, Motty!" Virginia shouted, cupping her hands around her mouth so the sound would carry.

"This is your captain speaking." Motty's voice came over the intercom. "You are now free to undo your seat belts and hop off the plane."

CHAPTER TWENTY-THREE
Dr. Yuki Ishikawa

A man in a US military uniform was waiting for them on the runway.

Uncle Max handed out padded coats with fur-lined hoods to the children, giving Calista Bloom his own.

Uncle Max opened the door and jumped down. He spoke a few words with the uniformed man, who walked around to the back of his truck and pulled out a standard army-issue jacket with hood. Uncle Max pulled it on gratefully, while the children passed down their overnight bags and the suitcase containing the beetles.

Darkus's breath was a heavy white fog that made the top of his lip sting. It was bitterly cold, even with the coat.

The military man pointed to a minibus with its engine running. Bertolt and Virginia piled their bags onto the backseat and sat down. Darkus lifted up the suitcase of beetles to sit beside him. Motty stayed with the plane, to refuel for the second leg of the journey.

It was only four in the afternoon Greenland time, but it was as dark as midnight. Uncle Max explained that this far north, there were only a few hours of daylight in winter.

The bus drove down a cleared road, passing a series of single-story square wooden houses painted red, tucked into three or four feet of snow. The bus driver informed them that there were only 160 inhabitants in Narsarsuaq, which doubled when the adventure tourists arrived or the scientists descended on the town. He said that in the winter the temperature fell below freezing, but that the long dark nights made it a perfect place to experience the aurora borealis—the northern lights.

"This place we're going to," Virginia whispered to Darkus, "the ar-bor-e-tum. What is it?"

"It's a collection of trees," Bertolt replied, his whole body juddering with the cold.

"The University of Copenhagen tends the Greenlandic Arboretum," Uncle Max explained. "It is almost five hundred acres of trees. The area is also a climate station, collecting data on temperature, soil properties, and things that tell us about climate change."

"And that's where we're hoping Dr. Yuki Ishikawa is," Darkus added, with a shiver.

The bus pulled to a halt. "Bus wait here," the driver said. "Don't want to get stuck in snow."

"I feel the same as the bus," Calista Bloom said through chattering teeth.

Darkus, Bertolt, and Virginia set out, keenly striding up a gravel road softened by shallow snow. The headlights of the bus lit their path. To the left was a fjord, the water appearing black in the darkness, pierced by ghostlike icebergs. To the right of the road the rocky foundations of a mountain were visible, but reached up into a white mist.

"Oh dear." Calista Bloom's plaintive cry came from behind them. "I'm really not wearing the right shoes for this weather."

Darkus turned to look, and suppressed a snort as he watched Bertolt's mum's red stilettos, decorated with pink hearts, sinking into the snow. Her knees were knocking, poorly protected from the cold by a thin pair of nylon tights.

Bertolt sighed and walked back to his mother. He held her hand as she struggled through the snow.

"Look!" Darkus cried, spying a light ahead. "The arboretum."

"Hopefully Dr. Ishikawa will be there to meet us," Uncle Max said.

"Hopefully?" Calista Bloom wailed. "Please don't tell me we've come all the way to Greenland, in freezing snow, to pay a surprise visit to someone who might not be home?"

"You told him we were coming, right?" Darkus asked Uncle Max.

"I tried." Uncle Max smiled apologetically. "I sent a message on ahead, addressed to the forest technician. I mentioned we'd be passing through, and if Dr. Ishikawa would agree to see us, we'd like to talk to him."

"Couldn't you just call him?" Virginia looked unimpressed.

"He doesn't have a phone," Uncle Max replied. "I'm reliably informed he is only found when he wants to be."

"Why all the mystery?" Darkus asked.

"Dr. Ishikawa prefers the company of insects over people," Uncle Max said. "He's a recluse and lives alone somewhere in the arboretum. His only contact with the outside world is through the university."

"What does a microbiologist do, exactly?" Bertolt asked.

"They are masters of the microscope," Uncle Max replied. "They identify diseases, test medicines, and investigate microorganisms—Dr. Ishikawa's specialist area is the use of microorganisms to break down toxic substances. He has discovered several natural ways to combat pollution."

"Why was he part of the Fabre Project?" Darkus asked.

"Back then, Dr. Ishikawa's work was focused on food. He tested food for bacteria, viruses, and toxins. Dr. Ishikawa was interested in proving the safety of entomophagy. That means—"

"Eating bugs," Virginia butted in. "Yeah. We know."

Uncle Max raised his eyebrows. "Dr. Ishikawa worked closely with your mother, Darkus."

"Really?" Darkus felt his stomach twist. "Then I hope he's here."

A long rectangular building with a row of square windows appeared out of the darkness. It was painted the same red as the town buildings.

"Here we are. The Department of Geosciences and Natural Resource Management." Uncle Max raised his fist and knocked. The door was opened by a tall, bearded man in a thick blue sweater.

"Welcome, Professor Cuttle." He shook Uncle Max's hand vigorously. "I'm Viggo. I've been expecting you."

Uncle Max stepped in, introducing each member of their party as they surged over the threshold, eager to get out of the freezing night and into the warmth.

Viggo led them down a corridor into a central room with a wood-burning stove and a kitchenette, explaining that he was a forest technician. "We don't normally get visits in the winter months," he said.

"We are hoping to speak with Dr. Yuki Ishikawa," Uncle Max said.

Viggo raised his eyebrows. "You may have a long wait. Can I make you a cup of coffee?"

"T-t-t-t-tea. Tea? Do you have tea?" Calista Bloom's whole body was shuddering. "I need a cup of tea. I think I've got hypothermia. Is my skin blue?"

Viggo looked at her shoes. "Would you like a pair of slippers?"

"I don't want to be any trouble." Calista Bloom fluttered her eyelashes at the forest technician and made a whimpering noise.

Bertolt stepped in front of his mother. "The slippers would be great, thank you, and a pair of tracksuit bottoms if you have any to spare, and perhaps a blanket?" He led his mother to the wood-burning stove and sat her down, lifting off her high heels and rubbing her feet between his hands until Viggo came back with an armful of clothes.

Uncle Max put the kettle on, opening and closing cupboards until he found cups.

Virginia looked at Darkus. "Do you think Yuki's gonna show up?"

"I don't know." He shrugged. "But I'm more worried about Baxter. Look"—Darkus lifted his hand to show Virginia the rhinoceros beetle—"it's like he's sleeping, except he's not." He rubbed his finger under the beetle's head, a gesture that would normally rouse the insect. "Is Marvin okay?"

Virginia lifted down her hood and tipped her head so the braid that Marvin clung to hung away from her face. She ran her thumb and forefinger down the plait, holding her free hand below it. Marvin dropped onto her palm. He seemed a bit stunned, but he was more alert than Baxter.

"Bertolt." Darkus called him over. "Is Newton okay? Baxter's really sleepy, and Marvin's a bit slow."

"Newton?" Bertolt whispered up to his spring of white curls. "Wake up."

There was a jerky hum as the firefly lifted up, dropping midair and clumsily lifting again. Bertolt held out his hands to catch the beetle.

Darkus looked down at the immobile rhinoceros beetle he loved so dearly. "I don't understand what's wrong with him."

"They are cold," a strange voice whispered from the darkness of the corridor.

Darkus looked up. He could make out the silhouette of a man.

"Cold?" he repeated.

"Yes. Think. Where are your invertebrates from? Not lands of snow and ice."

The man was wearing a thick coat and wasn't much taller than Darkus.

"Your beetles are from lands of great heat, where moisture is carried in the air."

Darkus looked down at Baxter. "He's cold?"

"And thirsty."

"What should I do?"

The man gestured and Darkus moved into the corridor, Virginia and Bertolt following behind, unsure of the stranger. The man unbuttoned the toggles on his coat and unzipped a second insulating jacket. Hanging around his neck on a fine chain was a filigree latticework cage the size of a pencil case. On the floor of the cage was the stem of a leafy plant, and built into the base was a thimble of water. Inside the cage was the prettiest praying mantis Darkus had ever seen.

"This is *Idolomantis diabolica*, the giant devil's flower mantis. I call him Akio. He is from Ethiopia and does not like the cold, so I must make him warm here, inside my coat, beside my heart."

Darkus looked into the man's eyes. They were dark and calm. The skin of his face was leathered by the weather and his eyebrows were gray. Lines of kindness appeared around his eyes as he smiled. "Do you have a cage for your *Chalcosoma*?"

Darkus shook his head. "Baxter likes to be free."

"Better to be in a cage of warmth and comfort than free and frozen. Don't you agree?"

Darkus nodded.

"I'm sure we can find something for your friend." He reached into his pocket and pulled out a little basket made of woven rushes. He lifted the lid and Darkus saw that it was a glasses case. The man pulled a safety pin from his other pocket. Taking the lid, he instructed

Darkus to open his coat, deftly pinning the rush basket to the lining of the coat, at the height of his heart. He pointed at Baxter. "Put your friend in the basket, and keep your coat closed when you are outside."

"You're Dr. Yuki Ishikawa, aren't you?" Darkus said, putting Baxter in his new bed and doing up his coat.

The man brought his hands together and bowed his head. "And you are the progeny of the eminent Dr. Cuttle and most wondrous Dr. Martín-Piera?"

Darkus bowed, trying to mimic Dr. Yuki Ishikawa. "My name is Darkus."

Virginia and Bertolt shuffled forward.

"Have you come to help us?" Bertolt asked.

"Do you have cold beetles, too?" Dr. Yuki Ishikawa's eyebrows lifted.

"Yes, but," Virginia said, "we need your help to stop Lucretia Cutter as well."

"Stop Lucretia Cutter?" Dr. Yuki Ishikawa cocked his head. "What does that mean?"

"Lucy Johnstone is Lucretia Cutter. She's kidnapped people—a boy called Spencer, and my dad—and she's breeding transgenic beetles," Darkus said.

"She's going to do something bad—on TV, in front of the world, at the Film Awards," Bertolt added.

"Children, I am a scientist." Dr. Yuki Ishikawa's brow furrowed. "My research is important." He shook his head. "I cannot take time away from my work for kidnappings and television. The climate is changing, and fast." He bowed his head and took a step backward. "It was a pleasure to meet you, Darkus Cuttle. I have a deep fondness and respect for your mother. Take care of your beetles."

"Wait!" Darkus cried. "My dad's trying to stop Lucretia Cutter from doing something terrible. He can't fight her alone. You *have* to help him."

"Your father is with Lucy Johnstone?" Dr. Yuki Ishikawa's eyebrows rose.

Darkus nodded.

He shook his head. "I do not fight, I have no talent for it." He patted his stomach and chuckled. "My stature alone should tell you that. No, my interest is in observing nature in its tiniest forms. If I find a man-made imbalance, I seek a natural counterbalance."

"But you *must* help." Darkus felt bereft. "Uncle Max says Lucretia Cutter is afraid of you."

"Ha! This is compliment I have not earned." He smiled.

"But you're all we have." Darkus's heart sank. "Professor Appleyard is in a coma, bitten by one of her beetles, and Dad's gone." His voice trembled. "People I care about are getting hurt. You can't just sit back and do nothing."

"What would you have me do, Master Cuttle?"

"I don't know," Darkus admitted. "It's just . . . she's not human."

"We are all flesh and bone."

"No!" Darkus shook his head. "Lucretia Cutter is part beetle."

Dr. Yuki Ishikawa's head jerked back. "Part beetle?"

"She has compound eyes." Virginia nodded vigorously.

"And spiked chitinous legs, with claws for feet," Bertolt added.

Dr. Yuki Ishikawa's eyes grew wide. "You have seen these things?"

The three children nodded.

"To transform oneself into an insect . . ." His eyebrows rose. "A metamorphosis from the human form . . ." He shook his head. "That would take the most complex science."

"We're not lying," Darkus insisted.

Dr. Yuki Ishikawa smiled. "To invent a lie of this size would be foolish. A lie must at least be plausible. How many people believe you when you tell them what you have seen?"

"None," Darkus admitted.

"Which is precisely why I believe it to be true . . . but still, I cannot help you." He placed his hand on Darkus's shoulder. "The greatest weapon you have is knowledge. Think, Darkus. You know what she is. Every creature has a predator. That is how balance is maintained."

"We're staying at the Narsarsuaq Air Base tonight." Uncle Max's voice came from behind him. Darkus turned to see him standing a respectful distance away. "In the air base. If you change your mind, we fly to Los Angeles tomorrow morning," he added.

"I'm sorry." Dr. Yuki Ishikawa looked at the three children. "I am not the warrior you are looking for." He pointed at Darkus's heart. "Your beetles do not like the climate in Greenland, keep them warm."

He bowed and was gone.

CHAPTER TWENTY-FOUR

Hark the Herald Angels

*L*A was a contradiction—it was covered in fake snow and dripping with glitter, but the weather was warm and the sky blue and cloudless. Jaw-dropping Christmas installations and sparkling decorations covered restaurant forecourts and the roofs of houses. A medley of Christmas songs played loudly from shops and cafés, wafting in through the open car windows as Uncle Max drove them from the airport. Bertolt's mum happily hummed each song, switching from one to the next as they traveled. "Don't you just love Christmas carols? Bertolt and I go to the carol service every Christmas Eve." She sighed. "It's magical."

They were driving inland, to the Hollywood Theatre to see where the Film Awards would take place. Motty was sitting up front with Uncle Max, and Calista Bloom was squeezed in the back between Darkus and Bertolt. Bertolt and Virginia hung their heads out of the car window, like dogs, as they drove along the palm-tree-lined avenue beside the sea.

"We're not in gray old rainy England any more!" Virginia hooted, her eyes shining and her smile wide. "LA is brilliant. It's like you're looking through a yellow filter."

Darkus smiled weakly, but he couldn't share Virginia's excitement. He'd been worrying about the Film Awards ever since Dr. Yuki Ishikawa had refused to help them. He'd been so sure that the scientist would have all the answers, be their secret weapon. Now, Darkus realized, it was going to be up to them and the beetles.

Mrs. Wallace's words—*You're only children*—kept coming back to him, and his father's: *You and your friends think this is some sort of childish detective game.* Darkus was uncomfortably aware that he still didn't know where his dad was or how to help him. He didn't know what Lucretia Cutter was planning to do, and his strong words about making her pay for burning the beetles felt hollow and meaningless.

Scaffolding was going up outside the Hollywood Theatre; a giant gold facade was being erected to receive the celebrity guests on the red carpet. An army of men in black suits with walkie-talkies and earpieces stood and sauntered around the perimeter of the site, while gaggles of tourists took pictures.

"How are we going to get in there without an invitation?" Darkus wondered out loud.

"We're going to need Novak's help," Bertolt replied.

"And an absurd amount of luck." Virginia nodded.

"I could dazzle them with my talent!" Calista Bloom said, pushing her blond curls up on top of her head and pouting.

"Um, I don't think that will work," Bertolt muttered.

"Perhaps I'll get spotted by a Hollywood agent, and he'll invite me to go to the awards as his guest!" Calista gasped, imagining the moment and making a series of faces as she played out the scenario in her head.

"I thought we were here to find Darkus's dad and help him fight Lucretia Cutter," Motty said bluntly.

"Oh yes, of course," Calista replied. "What I meant was, if an agent happened to notice me . . . I mean, of course we'd do the rescuing and fighting bit first . . . but maybe afterward, if there was time, I could do a couple of castings . . ." Her voice petered out as she saw the look of disapproval on Motty's face.

"I've seen it on television so many times," Bertolt said, looking out of the window at the theatre. "It seems smaller in real life."

They stared at the Hollywood Theatre, realizing the challenge they'd set themselves. They noted down the details of the building and then Motty declared it was time to go. They'd had a long day.

Motty's house was across town, in Lincoln Heights, an old suburb of Los Angeles north of a large park. Mozart Street was characterized by a smattering of Victorian mansions dotted among sprawling single-story houses. "That's it." Motty pointed at a sky-blue clapboarded house with steps up to the front door. The paint was peeling in places, and a tile or two was loose on the roof, but it looked welcoming.

Uncle Max pulled up and parked, and they piled out of the car, stiff and weary from their traveling. Darkus helped his uncle unload the bags and took charge of the beetles' suitcase.

"Do you live here?" Bertolt asked as Motty took a set of keys from her pocket and opened the front door.

"No," Motty replied. "I live in Cairo. I bought this place when I worked for the Natural History Museum of Los Angeles. I usually rent it out, but I haven't been back in a while. My neighbor, Valentina, keeps an eye on it for me when it's empty." She strolled into the open-plan living space and flung open the curtains, stirring the dormant dust.

Bertolt coughed. "How long is *a while*?"

"Three years."

"Well, isn't this lovely?" Uncle Max said, putting the bags down.

"It's brilliant," Virginia agreed, looking around at the bare house.

"It's dirty," Calista Bloom said, rolling up her sleeves and marching over to the kitchen sink to find a cloth.

Motty rolled her eyes and pushed her circular spectacles up her nose. "The children and the beetles can have the big bedroom. Max, you're on the sofa, and Calista can bunk up with me."

"Bunk up?" Calista turned around.

"You can share my bed."

"Oh, I see," Calista said, looking unhappy. "Thank you."

"Wonderful." Uncle Max clapped his hands together. "Now, shall we get some coffee on the go? I'm fit to fall out of my boots, I'm that tired."

Darkus sat down cross-legged in the middle of the floor and opened the suitcase, systematically checking that all the beetles were okay after their long journey. Virginia and Bertolt sat down beside him as Bertolt's mum wiped surfaces around the room, tutting at the dust she found there.

"Are they all okay?" Bertolt asked, leaning over the suitcase.

Darkus nodded. "All present and correct."

"What's up?" Virginia cocked her head. "You've barely said a word since we left Greenland."

"I'm worried about Dad," Darkus admitted. "What if we've come all this way, and we can't get into the theatre—or . . ." He paused. "What if he's angry to see us?"

"Darkus." Virginia dipped her head so she could look into his eyes. "Your dad can't fight Lucretia Cutter's beetles. No human can. We need to match like against like. Beetles versus beetles." She pointed at the suitcase. "You are the only person, other than Lucretia Cutter, with an army of beetles. He will need your help."

"And Novak will help us to get into the theatre. I know it." Bertolt nodded. "We just need to find her."

"But the ceremony is in two days, and we don't even know where Lucretia Cutter's house is," Darkus said. "How are we going to find Novak?"

"I know where Lucretia Cutter lives," Bertolt's mum said brightly.

"You do?" Bertolt frowned, and they all looked up at her with surprised expressions.

"Of course. Lucretia Cutter owns 227 Hillcrest. She bought it seven years ago from Dom Shanks, who had to sell it because of his divorce from Faith Peeters. It was in *Sizzle* magazine."

"Mum, you're amazing." Bertolt smiled at his mother, who flushed with pleasure and returned to her dusting, happily humming "Hark! The Herald Angels Sing" as she cleaned.

"That's it! I've just had an idea." Virginia slapped her hands down on the floor in front of her. She looked at Darkus and Bertolt, a mischievous glint in her eye. "I know how we're going to get to Novak, but we'll need disguises."

"Oh! Oh! Me! Me!" Bertolt's mum jumped up and down. "Sorry, I really wasn't listening in—well, maybe I was a bit, but I can help with that." She twirled around on the spot. "I'm great with costumes. Theatres are full of them."

"Disguises," Virginia corrected her.

"Yes, of course, disguises." Calista Bloom giggled.

CHAPTER TWENTY-FIVE

Hosanna in ex-Darkus

"Now's our chance. *QUICK!*" Darkus hissed as a delivery van pulled up to the gates and a young man leaned out of the window, pressing the intercom.

The three of them were hiding in a thicket of trees across the road from 227 Hillcrest, and had been waiting, dressed up in their disguises, for over an hour. Darkus was wearing a cap, Bertolt's oversize glasses, and a camo jacket with the collar popped up, to hide as much of his face as possible, as he was the most likely to be recognized. Virginia had chosen to dress as a boy, wearing a large short-sleeved skater T-shirt over a long-sleeved one, a beanie hat, and jeans. Bertolt's mum had slicked his hair back at the sides and dressed him in surfing shorts and a Hawaiian shirt that was way too big.

Darting out of the trees, Darkus, Virginia, and Bertolt ran to the back of the delivery van and slipped through the closing gate. They walked cautiously up a long curving driveway that circled around the palatial house, taking in the overgroomed garden of stunted box hedges in swirling patterns surrounding ostentatious fountains.

"Check out the swimming pool." Virginia whistled, pointing at the turquoise infinity pool on the far side of the house.

"I'm scared," Bertolt muttered.

"Nothing wrong with being scared," Virginia said, tucking a loose braid back into the beanie hat. "Makes you run faster."

The man delivering groceries had disappeared around the back of the house, and there seemed to be no one about. "What are we going to do now?" Bertolt whispered.

"I say we go right up to the front door and ring the bell," Darkus said.

"Good idea." Virginia nodded.

"What if she has attack dogs," Bertolt said, nervously pulling at the Hawaiian shirt, "or attack *beetles*?"

"Then the sooner we get to the front door, the better," Darkus replied, drawing Bertolt's glasses down to the end of his nose and pulling his cap down over his eyes. "It's time to bring a bit of festive spirit to Cutter Mansion." He grinned, jamming his hands in the pockets of his jeans and hunching his shoulders up by his ears.

Novak felt a bead of sweat trickle down her hairline; the heat of the afternoon seemed intensified by the threat in the room. She was perched on the corner of a giant black leather sofa, a blank expression on her face.

America made Novak feel small. Everything was so big: The roads were wider, the rooms were bigger, even the furniture was huge. She desperately wanted to get to the safety of the bland room in the east wing that was her bedroom, but Mater had insisted they have drinks before dinner.

"You must be excited about the Film Awards?" Darkus's dad said. "It's pretty special to get nominated for Best Actress."

Novak felt her cheeks glow hot, and nodded.

"The film is a turgid piece of sentimental claptrap," Mater said, topping up his glass from a crystal decanter. "The nomination came about because I bribed the right people."

"Oh!" Novak said, crestfallen. "I thought it was because I'm good at acting."

Lucretia Cutter laughed. "Child, you are lucky that you will never have to earn a living from it."

Darkus's dad looked into his glass as if he found the ice at the bottom intensely interesting. "I don't understand what you're doing at these awards, Lucy," he admitted. "You hate ceremonies of any kind, always have. Couldn't we skip them and go straight to your Biome?" He looked up and smiled winningly at her. "You never did say where it was?"

"No." Lucretia Cutter ran her fingertip around the rim of her glass. "And you'll never know exactly where it is, because you're going there blindfolded, after the awards."

"I see." Bartholomew Cuttle laughed uncomfortably. "Don't you think we're a bit old for party games?"

"I don't want the world knowing where I keep my secrets, now, do I?"

"I guess not." He raised an eyebrow. "At least explain the Film Awards to me."

"You never were much of a showman, Bartholomew," Lucretia Cutter replied, "but I understand the power of pageantry. Great kings and queens use it to assert their authority. The Film Awards is the moment I have chosen to burst onto the world stage"—she flung her hand, heavy with diamonds, in the air—"as a new kind of leader."

There was silence, and Novak stared at the floor, feeling horribly uncomfortable.

"I don't wish to pour cold water on the idea," Bartholomew Cuttle said, "but what makes you think anyone will take the slightest bit of notice?"

"Oh, they'll notice." Lucretia Cutter drew herself up tall. "The world will fall to its knees and tremble before me."

"Right. I see." He gave a little shrug. "I have one other question."

"Yes?" Mater barked, irritated that he hadn't been more impressed.

"When are we actually going to get into a laboratory?" Darkus's dad put his glass down. "All of this swanning about in Learjets, meeting famous actresses in hotel rooms, and planning to take over the world is great, but it's not really me. You promised me that I would get to work at the cutting edge of transgenic coleopteran research. That's why I'm here. I'm itching to get started, and I have to admit"—he looked about the room as if searching for a chessboard or something that might occupy him—"I'm getting a little bored."

It was all Novak could do to suppress a laugh at the expression on Mater's face.

"Bored?" she spat.

"Well, yes." Darkus's dad nodded. "But only a little bit."

Lucretia Cutter was suddenly on her feet. "Well, we can't have that," she snapped. "Let me introduce you to my flying *Sitophilus granarius.*"

"What?" Bartholomew stood up. "Wheat weevils don't fly!"

"Oh, but mine do," Lucretia Cutter said, stalking out of the room, "and they like their wheat fresh."

Darkus's dad followed her and Novak suddenly found herself alone. She sat perfectly still for a minute, to make sure no one was coming back, and then hunched over her wrist.

"Hepburn," she whispered, lifting the lid of the secret compartment in her bracelet. "Are you okay?"

A pair of delicate antennae waggled at her and Novak felt a flood of warm relief.

"C'mon, let's go and get you some dinner."

Darkus pulled on the bell cord and they heard a distant ringing sound. He wondered if his dad was somewhere in this house. He closed his eyes and made a fierce wish for Novak to open the door.

The door swung open. It was Gerard. Darkus kept his head down, so the butler wouldn't see his face.

"Yes?" The butler stared at the three children. "How may I help you?"

"WE WISH YOU A MERRY CHRISTMAS . . ." Darkus half sang, half yelled.

Virginia and Bertolt joined in, singing raucously. "WE WISH YOU A MERRY CHRISTMAS, WE WISH YOU A MERRY CHRISTMAS AND A *DARKUS* NEW YEAR!"

"Good day, sir," Virginia said, grabbing the butler's hand and shaking it. "We are collecting for the, er, the . . ."

"The Orphans of Los Angeles charity," Bertolt said with a perfect American drawl. "We hope that in exchange for a festive melody, you will make a generous donation to help the poor orphans at Christmastime."

"SILENT NIGHT," Darkus wailed, "*DARKUS* NIGHT, ALL IS CALM, ALL IS BRIGHT . . ."

"Yeah, yeah, yeah, DARKUS!" Virginia shouted, jumping about and trying to impersonate a rapper.

"Children, please!" Gerard interrupted. "This is a terrible noise. Christmas it may be, but I'm afraid I cannot help you. We do not donate to charity."

"But look at your crib!" Virginia exclaimed, following Bertolt's lead and getting into character. "It's wall-to-wall dollars, man." She whistled through her teeth as she hopped forward and then backward over the doorstep.

Gerard shooed her out of the house, and Darkus started singing again, as loudly as he could. They needed Novak to hear them. "GOD REST YE MERRY GENTLEMEN, LET NOTHING YOU DISMAY, 'CAUSE *DARKUS* HAS A MESSAGE FOR YOU THIS CHRISTMAS DAY."

Bertolt took a big breath and wailed: "GLOOOO-OOOOOOOO-OOOOOOOOOOOOO-OOOOOOOOOOOOO-OOOORIA, HOSANNA IN EX-*DARKUS*!"

"Enough!" Gerard cried. "I shall call the police if you do not leave."

"Dude!" Bertolt exclaimed. "Call the police? What will you tell them, sir? That three children are singing for you, to help the needy? It's not murder or robbery, is it, sir? We're armed with nothing but our voices and a good cause. I'm certain the police will tell you to donate to the poor orphans of Los Angeles at this festive time of year."

Darkus stared at Bertolt, surprised by how good his acting was. Out of the corner of his eye, he saw Novak appear in a doorway. He waved at her, pulling off his glasses and lifting his hat.

She let out a scream.

Darkus pulled his hat and glasses back on and jigged on the spot, rapping: "ONCE IN ROYAL *DARKUS* CITY STOOD A LOWLY BEETLE SHED. UH! HUH! UH! HUH! THAT'S RIGHT, *I'M NOT DEAD*!"

"*ARRÊTEZ!*" Gerard held up his hands. "STOP! ENOUGH! FINISH! You are scaring the lady of the house."

"They're not scaring me, Gerard." Novak rushed forward. "I was surprised, that's all."

"We're collecting money for the orphans of Los Angeles," Bertolt said. "So they can have presents at Christmastime."

"Oh, well, that sounds like a wonderful charity." Novak smiled. "I'd love to make a donation."

"Mademoiselle," Gerard said in a low voice, "your mother will not be happy if she sees these children here."

"Yes, I know," Novak nodded. "I'll see them to the gate and give them a donation there."

"No, I will do this."

"Oh, Gerard." Novak looked up at him, her eyelashes fluttering. "I'd like to. I don't see children my own age very often."

"As you wish, Mademoiselle—but," Gerard said, dipping his head, "don't let Madame see you."

"Thank you," Novak gushed and turned back to Darkus, her eyes shining. "Follow me," she said, walking past him.

Darkus followed her, looking over his shoulder once. Gerard was watching them.

"I thought you were dead!" Novak hissed. "Mater said she shot you, but you're alive! *You're alive!* How could you let me think you were dead? Do you know how awful it's been? I cried and cried. I know you can't exactly visit, but it's been nearly two months. *Two months!* You could have at least sent a message."

The butler could no longer hear them, but he was still watching.

"She did shoot me," Darkus said, "in my shoulder. The bullet went right through."

"Oh." Novak's stride faltered, but she kept walking. "I'm sorry."

"No, I'm sorry. You're right. I should have sent a message when I got out of the hospital. I was worried about getting you into trouble," Darkus said, risking glancing at her and smiling. "Novak, have you seen my dad? I need to find him."

"Why, yes, he's here, but . . ." Novak paused. "He's working with Mater."

"Oh! Right!" Darkus said, noticing Virginia giving Bertolt a look. "So he's okay, then?"

"Yes, Mater adores him." Novak nodded. "She even lets him disagree with her!"

Darkus didn't know what to say. He felt sick.

As the driveway curved around the lawn of box hedges, they were finally hidden from view. Bertolt scurried forward, pulling his glasses from Darkus's face so that he could see, and grabbed Novak's hand, shaking it up and down.

"I'm so pleased to meet you," he said, not letting go. "I think you're wonderful. I'm Bertolt. I'm Darkus's friend. I don't normally look like this. I'm normally much better dressed. Is that Chanel you're wearing? You look fabulous."

"Hi, Bertolt." Novak giggled, retrieving her hand. "Darkus told me all about you, but he didn't tell me you could do such a marvelous American accent."

"I didn't know," Darkus said.

"Thanks." Bertolt blushed with pleasure. "I help my mum practice for her auditions, but I'm not a natural talent, not like you."

"Oh, I have no talent," Novak replied, her head dropping. "Not really."

"You mustn't say that," Bertolt gasped. "Look at how you helped Darkus. Why, you must have to act your socks off every single day just to stay out of trouble."

"He's right." Virginia stepped forward and nodded. "You must be pretty good. Hi, I'm Virginia."

Novak beamed. "I'm so happy to meet you, both of you." She looked at Darkus. "But what are you doing here, in America? Did your uncle get my letter? Are the beetles okay?"

"We got your letter," Darkus said.

"Oh, thank goodness!" Novak clapped her hands together. "Did you save Beetle Mountain?"

Darkus shook his head, and there was a horrible silence.

Novak's hands dropped. "Oh no."

"They didn't all die," Bertolt said. "We managed to save some of them."

"I'm sorry." Novak's bottom lip wobbled. "I—I tried . . ."

"It's not your fault," Darkus said. "If we hadn't gotten your letter, it would've been a lot worse."

"You saved my life." Bertolt nodded. "I might have been burnt to a crisp."

"Novak," Darkus said, "we know Lucretia Cutter's planning to do something terrible at the Film Awards. Do you know what it is?"

"Oh dear." Novak bit her bottom lip. "Well, I heard her tell your dad something about pageantry and being a leader, but I didn't really understand what she was talking about."

"What did Dad do?" Darkus asked, leaning forward.

"It was funny." Novak giggled. "He looked bored by Mater's plans, and asked when they were going to get down to doing the scientific work she'd promised him."

"He wasn't trying to stop her?" Darkus was shocked.

"Um, no." Novak shook her head. "He seemed most put out that she'd made a weevil that could fly."

Darkus frowned. What was Dad doing? Could he actually be working *with* Lucretia Cutter?

"Do you know how Lucretia Cutter is planning to take over the awards ceremony?" Virginia asked.

"No, but what I do know is that she's made these dresses for the actresses in my award category. I haven't seen mine yet, but Stella Manning's dress is covered in green jewel beetles. They're a kind I've never seen before, like a cross with tiger beetles."

"You met Stella Manning?" Bertolt squealed.

Novak nodded. "Her dress is to die for."

"I can't wait to see it." Bertolt clapped. "Oh, I have something for you." He checked his pockets and pulled out a piece of paper. "This is Morse code. We've taught it to our beetles. If you teach Hepburn, she can bring us messages."

Novak flipped open the top of her bracelet and Hepburn flew out, looping the loop and settling on her hand.

"You have a beetle, too?" she asked Bertolt.

"Yes." Bertolt looked up. "Newton, come out and say hello."

Newton bobbed up out of the top of Bertolt's hair and flashed his belly at Novak.

"Oh, how beautiful!" she gasped.

"He looks better at night, when it's dark."

"Novak, I know the Film Awards are tomorrow, but do you think you'd be able to get us into the theatre?" Darkus asked. "Whatever Lucretia Cutter's planning to do, we want to be there to help Dad when he tries to stop her."

"He's going to stop her?" Novak said, surprised.

"I'm certain of it." Darkus nodded.

A bald, muscle-bound silhouette walked out onto the lawn in front of Lucretia Cutter's house.

"It's Mawling!" Novak looked frightened. "Leave it with me. I'll get you into the awards somehow," she promised, shuffling backward. "Get as close to the theatre as you can, and I'll send Hepburn to you with a message." She looked across the lawn at Mawling.

"There's six of us," Darkus said. "Us and three adults."

"I'm sorry. I have to go." She turned and walked away, looking back over her shoulder. "Thank you for coming," she said. "I thought I was alone."

CHAPTER TWENTY-SIX
Baggage

*H*umphrey Gamble ignored people's stares as he stomped through the Los Angeles airport looking for signs to the baggage collection area. He was dressed in an assortment of ill-fitting clothes that he and Pickering had found in a recycling bin beside the airport parking lot. All of the items he was wearing were too small. A brightly colored paisley tie was threaded through the belt loops of his trousers, not to hold them up but to hold them together, as the fly wouldn't fasten. The green flares extended only as far as his shins, and his garish pink-and-yellow-striped shirt strangled him despite the top two buttons being undone. He wore a supersize puce tank top to hide the fact the shirt didn't cover his belly.

Spotting the circular conveyor belts, he headed toward the one underneath the flight number of the plane that had brought him from London to America. He was looking for a large navy-blue suitcase and was dismayed to see that many of the suitcases on the conveyor belt were blue. His was a battered, blackened case, pulled from the charred wreckage behind the Emporium. He stared at the square hole covered with hanging strips of plastic, hypnotized as case after case dropped onto the belt.

"Did you hear that?" a woman said to her husband. "That case made a noise!"

Humphrey saw that it was his case the woman was pointing at. He shoved people aside to get to the belt. Grabbing at the handle, he heaved the suitcase onto the floor.

"Ouch!" the case squawked. "Careful!"

"There!" The woman grabbed her husband's arm. "It did it again."

"Will you shut up!" Humphrey hissed at the case. "People can hear you." He hurriedly dragged the case across the floor, away from the staring crowd.

"Try not to bump me around so much!" Pickering's voice hissed back. "It hurts."

Humphrey ignored the case as he dragged it toward the sign that said NOTHING TO DECLARE. He kept his eyes fixed on the exit sign as he stomped through the white corridor, charging forward.

"Excuse me, sir." An American customs official in a smart uniform stepped in front of him with his hand up. "We'd like to check your bag and ask you a few questions about your visit to the United States."

"Um, of course, yes. I'm here for a holiday." Humphrey looked around. Two more officers were standing on either side of a doorway to a room off the corridor. "And my bag is full of clothes."

"This way, please." The officer guided him toward the room.

"Oh right." Beads of sweat rolled down Humphrey's forehead, getting in his eyes. He blinked, trying to smile charmingly. "Is there a problem, officers?"

"No problem at all, sir, just routine procedure," the officer assured him.

Humphrey stepped away from the suitcase.

"Please, sir, bring your bag."

Humphrey nodded and dragged it behind him into the room, which was furnished with a single table and chair.

"Would you mind putting your case up onto the table, and opening it for us," the officer directed.

Humphrey looked at the other two officers, one male and one female. They weren't very big. He heaved the case up, slamming it onto the table while coughing loudly to cover any noise Pickering might make.

"Would you mind unzipping your case, and then stepping over to face the wall?"

Humphrey noticed that all three of the officers had guns in holsters on their belts. He bent down and slowly unzipped the lid, stepped away from the table, and faced the wall.

One of the officers put a hand on his shoulder. "Spread your legs."

There was a terrific ripping sound as Humphrey did as he was told and his trousers split. He looked over his shoulder just as the female officer flipped the lid of the suitcase open.

"Hello, officers!" shrieked Pickering, leaping up with a can of pepper spray in each fist and firing it in their faces.

The customs officials howled, stumbling backward. The officer guarding Humphrey spun around, reaching for his gun. Humphrey hammered his fist down on the officer's head, knocking him unconscious.

"RUN! RUN! RUN!" screamed Pickering as he fell face-first off the table onto the floor.

Humphrey grabbed his cousin under the arms and heaved him over his shoulder, bolting for the door. He charged through the customs hallway and out into the airport, with Pickering aiming his canisters of pepper spray at anyone who looked at them. "They're coming," he shrieked to Humphrey as a commotion arose behind them.

The rip in Humphrey's trousers had freed him up to run, and he pounded through the arrivals lounge, bursting out into the line at the taxi stand. An elderly couple were passing their suitcases to a cabdriver, who was lifting them into the trunk. Humphrey shoved past the elderly gentleman, knocking him over, and ran around to the driver's door. It was open. The keys were in the ignition and the engine running. He threw Pickering into the passenger seat. Pickering yelped as his head hit the glove compartment.

Humphrey jumped into the driver's seat and wrenched the door shut.

The taxi driver ran toward him, shouting at Humphrey to get out of his car.

Humphrey's fist shot out of the open window and punched the taxi driver's lights out. He put the car in gear, slammed his foot on the accelerator, and shot forward into the traffic leaving the airport. He looked in the rearview mirror; the trunk was still open. He accelerated over a speed bump, and the trunk slammed shut. Through his rearview mirror he could see police and airport officials all swarming around the old couple and the unconscious taxi driver.

Pickering righted himself, looked out of the window, and waved. "Bye-eeeeeeee!"

"We're going to have to ditch this car and get new clothes as soon as possible," Humphrey said. "We need to get somewhere where there's lots of people, so we can hide."

"Wheeeeeeee!" Pickering clapped his hands. "We did it! We're in America!"

"Shut up and get the map out." Humphrey could hear the distant wail of sirens. "I haven't come this far just to end up back in prison."

They had brought a map of Los Angeles with them. Marked with a large red X was the venue for the Film Awards, the Hollywood Theatre. The awards were tomorrow, so they needed to find somewhere to stay for the night, and then in the morning they'd go and wait for Lucretia Cutter.

"We need to get as close to the Hollywood Theatre as possible before we give up the car."

"Then you'd better step on it, Humpty!" Pickering cackled. "Because they're coming to get us!"

CHAPTER TWENTY-SEVEN
Einstein's Workshop

Spurred on by Novak's promise to get them into the Hollywood Theatre, Darkus, Virginia, and Bertolt spent the evening before the Film Awards with Uncle Max and Motty, rummaging through Motty's garage in search of anything that might help them fight Lucretia Cutter. The floor was covered with boxes and bags stuffed with assorted things that had been cleared out of the house when Motty had first rented it.

"What's this?" Bertolt pulled a clear plastic cylinder from one of the boxes. It had two tubes sticking out of it.

"That's a pooter," Uncle Max replied. He looked at Darkus. "Your dad's got a trunk full of those in varying sizes."

"What's it for?"

"Collecting bugs." Uncle Max pointed to one of the tubes. "You suck on this tube, and it creates a vacuum here." He moved his finger to the cylinder. "Then you point the other tube at the bug you want to pick up, and it draws the bug up the tube and captures it in the cylinder. This bit of mesh here stops you from swallowing the bug." He smiled. "You unscrew the top to take your specimens out."

"Cool." Bertolt blinked rapidly as he stared at the pooter.

"Why have you got one?" Darkus asked Motty.

"I got it from a man called Smithers, an entomologist who came to a conference at the museum," Motty said as she pulled things out of a big box. "I admitted to him that I wasn't a fan of spiders."

"You're scared of spiders?" Virginia said, incredulous.

Motty nodded. "He gave it to me so I could collect them and take them outside, but it's an awful pain. It's easier to use a glass and a bit of cardboard."

"Can I have it?" Bertolt asked.

"Yes." She nodded. "I'll never use it."

"Thank you." Bertolt hugged the pooter to his chest.

"What are you going to do with it?" Darkus asked.

"Take it apart," he replied.

"We need to weapon up," Virginia said, picking up a lamp stand and brandishing it like an axe. "We can't go in there unarmed against Lucretia Cutter."

"But they'll never let us in if we're carrying a bunch of weapons," Darkus pointed out.

"So, tomorrow, the plan is that we go to the Hollywood Theatre and wait for Hepburn, who'll have a message telling us how to get inside—but once we are in there, what do you want *us* to do?" Uncle Max gestured to himself and Motty.

Darkus thought for a moment. "Our best weapons are the Base Camp beetles. We'll use them to target Lucretia Cutter and any beetles she has brought with her." He looked from Uncle Max to Motty. "But she has bodyguards, at least four. Craven, Dankish, Mawling, and Ling Ling."

"Leave them to us," Motty said. "We'll take care of the humans."

"We'll need to smuggle the beetles into the theatre somehow," Darkus said.

"I've been thinking about that," Bertolt replied. "We need something that won't draw attention to us, and what do we all have that we carry around with us wherever we go?"

"Bubble gum?" Virginia suggested, putting the lamp stand down.

"Backpacks," Bertolt said, pointing at his.

"You want us to put the beetles into our backpacks?" Darkus asked.

"No, I'm going to turn our backpacks into machines." He smiled.

"What kind of machines?" Virginia asked, suddenly interested.

"Bug-catching machines," Bertolt said, holding up his pooter. "I want to make giant pooters."

"Uh-oh." Virginia poked Darkus. "Einstein's got that look in his eye."

"I'm going to need three empty plastic water bottles, three battery-powered air pumps, and three whirly sound hoses," he said, looking at Uncle Max.

"Whirly sound hoses?" Virginia raised an eyebrow.

"Yes." Bertolt nodded emphatically. "Or a vacuum hose, or extraction piping. Anything like that will do. And gaffer tape. Lots and lots of gaffer tape."

"Right," Uncle Max said, twirling the car keys around his finger. "I'll be back in a jiffy."

"I'll come." Virginia followed him out of the garage. "I love American shops."

"And get three utility belts," Bertolt shouted after them.

"Roger that." Virginia saluted.

"Where's Mum?" Bertolt said, looking at Darkus.

"Hem!" Motty's head pulled back, exhibiting her three chins and a disapproving look. "She's upstairs trying on her new dress." She raised an eyebrow. "Apparently it sparkles like stardust."

"Oh!" Bertolt flushed.

"I'm going to get to work on dinner," Motty said, going through the door that led back into the house. "Help yourself to anything useful in here, and shout if you need me."

"Mum only really came with us to go to the Film Awards, didn't she?" Bertolt said, his mouth twisting.

Darkus sat down beside him. "If she hadn't come, then you and Virginia would still be in London and I'd be on my own."

"I suppose." Bertolt nodded.

"At least we know why your mum is here." Darkus rested his chin on his knees. "I haven't got a clue what Dad's up to. I think he wants to stop Lucretia Cutter, but what if I'm wrong?"

"What do you mean?"

"You heard what Novak said. What if Dad is actually working for her? What if he's on her side?"

"Darkus, your dad would never be on the side of someone who set fire to hundreds of thousands of innocent beetles. You told me yourself he doesn't believe in killing any creature, no matter how small."

"That's true," Darkus said.

"I think you have to trust him." Bertolt blinked.

"I wish I could talk to him before tomorrow." Darkus sighed.

Bertolt patted his back. "All we can do is fight for what we believe in."

Darkus nodded and smiled at his friend. "C'mon then, how are we going to make a giant pooter?"

CHAPTER TWENTY-EIGHT

Cleopatra's Daughter

There was a knock. It was Gerard.

"Wake up, Mademoiselle."

Novak's eyes flickered open.

"It is morning." He came and stood beside her bed. "It's time to get dressed. I have brought your breakfast."

"Dressed?"

"Yes. You cannot have forgotten, today is the Film Awards ceremony." Gerard opened the curtains, letting the Los Angeles sun flood into the room. "It is early, but there is a lot to be done. You have a facial after breakfast, then your feet will be unbound—the podiatrist is already here. The hairdresser and makeup artist come at eleven. Your foundation will be applied before a light lunch, the rest will come after, but first your mother wants you to come and try your dress on."

"Mm-hmm."

"Are you listening?"

"I'm awake," Novak groaned. "Give me five minutes."

Gerard bowed and slipped silently out of the room.

Novak blinked, waiting to be sure he wasn't coming back. Reaching up into the vase of flowers by her bedside, she lifted Hepburn out of the deep bell of a white calla lily.

"This is it, Hepburn." Her heart was dancing as she sat up in bed. They'd spent most of the night learning Morse code and going over the plan. Knowing Darkus was alive had made Novak brave. She'd had an idea of how to get Darkus and his friends into the Hollywood Theatre—and this time, when she saw him, she'd ask him to take her with him, back to England and away from Mater.

"Today's the big day." She hugged Hepburn to her chest.

Gerard knocked insistently.

"Coming!" Novak yelled, putting Hepburn back on the lily and jamming her feet into her slippers. She skipped after Gerard as he led her into the section of the house that was usually out of bounds. He punched a code into a lock and carried on down the hall, putting a white-gloved finger up in the air as he stopped and rapped the knuckle of his index finger against a door.

"Yes," Lucretia Cutter's voice called out.

Gerard opened the door and ushered Novak in.

"I've brought Mademoiselle Novak for her dress fitting."

Novak stepped through the doorway. Even if she'd been teleported into this room, she would have known it was Mater's bedroom. It was dark and the furnishings were black, edged with gold. The floor was black marble, and a thick black bearskin rug was laid out at the end of the bed. An ornate black-and-gold Japanese screen stood on the far side of the room.

Mater's voice came from behind the screen. "Her dress is on the rail."

The wardrobe rail was empty except for one black dress hanging from a gold hanger, a waiflike, floor-length dress made from millions of tiny serrated feathers. It was beautiful.

"I thought I might wear my favorite pink dress to the awards," Novak said bravely. "I brought it with me specially."

Lucretia Cutter's head lurched up above the screen. She was wearing her glasses even in this dark room.

"No," the gold lips snarled, "you will wear the dress I have made for you. A hundred children in India hand-stitched each of those settings, and they're expecting to see their handiwork on the red carpet. You wouldn't want to deprive them of that moment, would you?"

"No. It's just . . ."

"All three nominated actresses *will* be wearing the dresses I have made for them."

"Yes, Mater."

"Do you want to see what I'm wearing?" Mater's voice was dripping with amusement.

"Um, yes," Novak mumbled. "That would be nice."

Lucretia Cutter stalked out from behind the screen.

Novak frowned. Mater's dress was odd-looking. It was a high-necked, floor-length evening gown, with a cinched-in waist and exaggerated hips, seemingly made of bubble wrap, except that where the bubbles should bulge out with air, they curved inwards, making penny-size indentations. Gerard carried a full-length mirror forward so she could see herself.

"Yes." Lucretia Cutter nodded at the mirror. "It's perfect."

"Oh! It's lovely," Novak said, confused. "It really is."

"This is an undergarment, you silly child," Lucretia Cutter snapped.

Novak looked back. There were no other dresses on the rail but hers.

The door opened. Mawling rolled in a tall cabinet on wheels.

"Put it there." Mater pointed at the floor in front of her. "And then get out of here."

Mawling did as instructed, and left. Gerard stepped forward and opened the door of the cabinet. It had a series of entomological specimen drawers in it. Gerard pulled out the first one. It was full of globular golden scarabs.

Lucretia Cutter made an unsettling clicking noise at the back of her throat.

Novak felt goose bumps rise on her arms as the golden scarabs stirred in their drawer. None of the beetles had pins in them. As they rose up, each beetle, called by the alien noise, opened its elytra and took to the air, flying to one of the indentations in Lucretia Cutter's undergarment. Gerard pulled out drawer after drawer, and hundreds of living golden scarabs flew to Lucretia Cutter, filling the dress from floor to neck with the staggeringly rich gold of their wing cases.

Within seconds, Mater stood in front of her in a beautiful gold gown, looking shinier than a Film Award statue.

Lucretia Cutter turned slowly, so that Novak could see her back. High up, where her shoulder blades should have been, were two gold wing cases. Novak watched them with horror as they cracked open and lifted. She gasped as a pair of black wings unfolded from under the giant gold elytra.

"Gerard, I think we should try the diadem."

The butler went to the dressing table, took out a key, and unlocked the deep drawer, lifting out a circlet of heavy gold. At its center was a gold scarab, its exoskeleton marked with hieroglyphics.

"This diadem belonged to Cleopatra," Lucretia Cutter said, taking the circlet from Gerard. "I've improved it. Cleopatra liked asps. There was a snake here." She pointed. "I have replaced the asp with the gold scarab that guarded the sarcophagus of Queen Nefertiti."

"It's beautiful," Novak whispered.

"Do you know the Egyptians worshipped beetles? They believed the sun god was a dung beetle that rolled the sun across the sky." She lifted the circlet above her head. "And now the world will worship me." She settled it on her brow.

"Worship you?" Novak's throat was dry.

Lucretia Cutter turned to face her and Novak could barely breathe.

Unimaginably tall, dressed in gold, the scarab crown on her brow, her black wings spread wide like an abominable angel, Lucretia Cutter removed her sunglasses, and her black, unblinking eyes stared down. "Yes. Worship me."

Novak looked at the floor. Her whole body was trembling with fear. Was Mater planning to proclaim herself a god in front of the world at the Film Awards?

"Now, put your dress on," Lucretia Cutter ordered.

Novak went over to the rail and found Gerard beside her, helping her to step out of her nightie and into the black dress. *"Sois courageuse,"* he whispered.

"We'll paint your eyelids black, and your lips gold," Lucretia Cutter said as Gerard took out a second, smaller circlet with a small gold heart scarab at the center. "You'll be the perfect accessory."

Gerard placed the gold crown on her head and Novak looked at the mirror, horrified by what she saw. The black tassels that she'd thought were feathers were the dangling legs, mandibles, and antennae of giant bombardier beetles.

Lucretia Cutter came to stand beside her.

Novak thought she was going to cry. The closeness of Mater and the black depths of her compound eyes terrified her.

"Watch this," Lucretia Cutter said into the mirror. She moved her head in a strange snakelike side-to-side movement, making a clicking sound at the back of her throat, and Novak felt her dress shiver. The black beetle legs were attached to living insects, and they were stirring. They cycled their legs in a strange dance and the dress came alive, moving as if Novak were underwater or in gravity-less space. The effect was hypnotic.

"Beautiful," Lucretia Cutter muttered to herself. She looked down at her daughter. "It's time to let the world see who you really are, Novak."

CHAPTER TWENTY-NINE
Dumpster Motel

*H*umphrey lifted up the dumpster lid with his head. He looked up and down the alleyway; there was no one about. "Coast's clear," he growled to his cousin, whose ratlike face appeared at his elbow, looking about furtively.

They'd ditched the stolen cab a few blocks away, running from the car only minutes before the police caught up with it. There was a row of dumpsters down an alleyway next to a Chinese food restaurant, and they had thrown themselves into one, deciding to stay hidden until the police had gone away.

Humphrey was amazed and then delighted by the amount of food he found in the dumpster. Rooting around, he uncovered spring rolls, a tray of half-eaten spicy noodles, and half a crispy duck. Chinese food was his favorite. He ate it all hungrily.

It was Pickering who had pointed out that the black bags of rubbish made a reasonably soft bed. Seeing as they had no money until they found Lucretia Cutter, the pair of them had arranged the bags as comfortably as possible, salvaging anything edible and feasting on leftovers before falling asleep.

They checked the map. They were only a block away from the Hollywood Theatre.

Humphrey clambered out of the bin and dusted himself down.

"Pickers, hand me the case."

Thinking on his feet, Humphrey had grabbed a suitcase from the trunk of the cab before they ran away. He knew they couldn't show up at the awards ceremony dressed in ripped recycled clothes and stinking of rubbish. Lucretia Cutter would never speak to them. He was hoping there'd be clean clothes inside the case that they could change into.

Pickering pushed the case out of the dumpster. It dropped to the floor, bursting open. Humphrey bent over and rummaged around. There were slim pickings for a man of his size, but there was a black dinner suit. He lifted out the trousers and hung them over the bottom rung of a fire-escape ladder. He pulled on the white shirt. He could only do up one button, and the cuffs flapped around his chubby wrists. No cuff link was going to be long enough to fasten them. The jacket was tight and pulled his arms backward, but he managed to get it on without ripping it. The man who owned the suit was short in stature but generous in girth, and when it came to the trousers, after taking a deep breath, Humphrey could just about manage to do them up, although they didn't extend past his calves. With midriff, ankles, and wrists bare, he nodded at the improvement.

"How do I look?"

"Like the Incredible Hulk's sickly cousin," Pickering spat, struggling to lift the lid and clamber out of the bin at the same time.

Humphrey snorted and held the dumpster lid open. Pickering fell to the ground. "You're going to have to wear *this*!" Humphrey said, pointing.

"What!" Pickering leapt to his feet. "I'm not wearing that, I'll look ridiculous."

"But this is all that's left." Humphrey grinned.

"There must be something else." Pickering pulled out knickers, a bathing suit, towels, and toiletries. "Why can't I wear the suit?"

"Because it's the only thing I can fit into," Humphrey guffawed.

"Fine." Pickering snatched the garment out of his hand. "Turn around while I put it on."

Despite getting up with the sun and having only a block to walk, Pickering and Humphrey found that there were plenty of other people who'd stayed up all night, or slept on the pavement, to get a good spot outside the Hollywood Theatre for the Film Awards. Crowds of people were gathered behind the cordon next to the red carpet, waiting to see—or perhaps even meet—their movie idols and to soak up the glamorous dresses and dapper suits. The entrance to the theatre was framed by film cameras and photographers with long lenses, on foot, on stools, and on ladders.

Humphrey pushed and shoved, trying to force his way into the crowd, but discovered Americans were not like the British; they didn't take kindly to being pushed around, and they shoved him right back. People were staring at Pickering, who'd pulled up the skirt of the pink flowery dress he was wearing because it kept getting tangled around his ankles. He had one hand on his head, holding on a floppy straw hat, and his skirts yanked so high they exposed his hairy knees.

"What category are you nominated for?" someone shouted. "Ugliest dude in a dress?"

The crowd erupted in roars of laughter.

By the time the first cars started arriving, Humphrey and Pickering were stuck in the middle of the crowd with no way of moving forward and no interest in going back. Each time a long black car pulled up at the end of the red carpet, Humphrey craned his neck to see if Lucretia Cutter stepped out of the vehicle. Pickering, intoxicated by the atmosphere, was gibbering excitedly, and Humphrey had turned sideways, hoping to disassociate himself from his scrawny cousin. Pickering resorted to talking to himself, occasionally giggling and waving his muckminder like a lady's hankie at the people who were arriving early.

The cousins were stupefied by the chiseled, overgroomed, stallion-like men who strutted past them in deftly cut suits, swaggering and blowing kisses to the ladies. They had never seen such an array of Adonises. "Their teeth," Pickering gasped, pawing at Humphrey's arm. "They're so straight! So white!"

Humphrey felt bashful looking at the women, they were so pretty. They fluttered and floated by, sparkling and smiling like ethereal creatures, elegant and lovely.

Suddenly the crowd gasped and surged forward. Humphrey and Pickering both strained to see what everyone was staring at.

"It's *Snow White!*" an excited woman squealed, and the crowd echoed her.

"Snow White! Snow White! Snow White!"

A dainty woman, with platinum-blond hair pinned up in kiss curls around her sultry face, lips a Cupid's kiss of cherry red, accepted the hand of a besuited gentleman and stepped out of the black limousine.

"Ruby! Ruby! Over here!" the photographers shouted.

"Give us a smile, Ruby!"

Cameras flashed and the crowd gasped as light ricocheted off Ruby Hisolo Jr.'s dress. She was so dazzling that Humphrey could barely look at her, and yet he couldn't look away. All he could focus on was the deep red of her perfect lips. She was a walking prism of pure light.

The crowd was awed, as if an angel had fallen out of heaven.

And then she was gone, inside the Hollywood Theatre, and the world was gray once more. Humphrey longed for her to come back.

Other actresses turned up, but people paid them little attention. The dazzling image of Ruby Hisolo Jr. was seared upon their eyeballs and it was all they could talk about.

Humphrey began to get impatient. He didn't like being trapped in the crowd, and he was hungry.

"Where is she? Are you sure she's coming?" he grumbled.

"Yes, yes. It's been in all the papers. She never goes to awards ceremonies. This will be the first." Pickering nodded frantically. "She's coming. I know it. I can *feel* it."

Humphrey rolled his eyes.

Another limousine arrived.

"It's her!" someone cried, and there was a surge forward.

"Who?" Humphrey asked several people around him. "Who's arrived?"

"It's Stella Manning," replied a woman, who was so excited that she didn't even turn around to see who she was talking to. "She's the greatest actress who has ever lived." She screeched excitedly, clasping her hands to her chest. "She's a chameleon, a miracle worker. I love her."

Humphrey puffed out a gasp of frustration. It wasn't Lucretia Cutter, but he may as well see the greatest actress who has ever lived.

A forest-green skirt flooded out of the car door, then a majestic woman stood up, thick red curls of waist-length hair falling over her shoulders, a circlet of burnished gold on her brow.

"It's *Lady Macbeth*!" a young man gasped, his hands on his cheeks. "O-M-G! It's stunning!" He pretended to swoon.

"I thought you said it was Stella Manning," Humphrey said to the woman, who was now desperately holding out an autograph book and pen.

"It is. The dress is the *Lady Macbeth*, designed by Lucretia Cutter."

"Lucretia Cutter? Where?"

"The dress, it's designed by her."

Humphrey frowned. Why would anyone give a dress a name? He looked at Stella Manning, who was parading regally along the red carpet toward him. The dress was mesmerizing, constructed from a highly tailored sheer nude underlayer, showing off every curve and contour of Stella Manning's body while giving her the posture of a female chieftain of a highland clan. The forest-green lace overlay was floor-length and adorned with pretty green shells, which were iridescent and gave the gown a royal purple tinge. Humphrey had to admit Lucretia Cutter was pretty good at making dresses.

There were flashing lights, and Stella Manning lingered to talk to a woman with a microphone.

"Where is she?" Pickering was bouncing up and down like a child who'd eaten too many sweets. And then it arrived, the car that Humphrey had first seen outside their flat in Nelson Parade, more stylish than any limousine, a timeless classic shape hiding a powerful engine. The last time he'd seen Lucretia Cutter, she'd been bundled into that car and driven away by her chauffeur. He wondered how she'd got it to America—perhaps she had a fleet of them.

The chauffeur walked around the iridescent car to the rear door and opened it. Humphrey leaned forward, licking his lips with anticipation. A dainty black claw with hooklike nails appeared, stepping down onto the red carpet; cameras flashed as a tiny girl got out of the car. The clawed feet belonged to her. She was dressed in black, her hair sculpted into a white bob. Her eyes were painted in a strip of black, and her lips shone gold, but it was those weird shoes that made Humphrey stare; they looked so much like black claws that he couldn't see how a foot could fit in them. But then a larger, more vicious pair of claws stepped down onto the red carpet. Lucretia Cutter was getting out of the car, helped by a handsome man in a blue suit.

The crowd drew breath and then erupted into spontaneous applause.

Lucretia Cutter was dressed head to toe in gold. She drew herself up, standing impossibly tall, towering above the man whose arm her hand was resting upon. Her sticks and lab coat were gone, but her trademark sunglasses and the black bob were still there, and a heavy gold crown sat on her head. She looked neither left nor right, and a reverent hush fell over the crowd as she glided along the red carpet, her daughter at her side.

"Woo-hoo!" Pickering shrieked at the top of his voice in the heart of the silence. "Lucretia, darling, it's me. Pickering!"

"And me!" Humphrey bellowed. "Over here!"

"Lucretia!" Pickering shouted. "My sweet, I love you!"

For a millisecond Humphrey thought he saw Lucretia Cutter bristle, but she continued moving forward and didn't look in their direction.

"Oi!" he roared. "We want our money!" But now all the photographers were shouting, too. "GIVE US OUR MONEY! YOU BURNED OUR HOUSE DOWN!" Humphrey shouted, but he couldn't make himself heard.

Lucretia Cutter didn't stop to sign one autograph or do one interview.

"Didn't she hear us?" Pickering asked forlornly. "She could at least have blown me a kiss."

"Sod this." Humphrey turned his back on the red carpet. "I'm done with waiting around. Let's get in there and get our money."

"But how?" Pickering whined, traipsing after Humphrey.

"This place is a theatre," Humphrey said as they walked to the corner. "It's got to have other doors." They looked down the alley that led to the stage door. It was lined with security men in black suits. A man wheeling a cart stacked with golden cages full of colorful, squawking birds was going in through the stage door.

"We'll never get in that way," Pickering said.

"Then we'll have to find a different way in," Humphrey replied, looking upward.

CHAPTER THIRTY

Stage Door

ovak gasped with delight as they entered the auditorium. The inside of the Hollywood Theatre was an opulent palace of red velvet, crystal chandeliers, and glittering gold trim. She was standing in the most famous theatre in the world. She felt a surge of determination, taking strength from the building. It was time for her to do the best acting of her life.

She crossed her legs and started dancing around on the spot.

"I need the bathroom."

Mater ignored her, so she looked at Bartholomew Cuttle with pleading eyes. "Please. I really need to go." She screwed her face up.

"It's probably the excitement," Darkus's dad said to Mater. "You should let her go now, quickly, before it all begins."

"You'd better be in your seat when the awards start. Nominated actresses are all seated in the front row," Mater snapped, stepping forward to receive the air-kisses and gushing gratitude of Stella Manning for her dress.

Novak bowed her head and ran back into the foyer, desperately searching for someone who might help her.

"Excuse me, sir."

The elderly usher looked down and smiled kindly.

"How can I help you, Miss Cutter?"

"You know my name!" Novak fluttered her eyelashes and feigned bashful delight.

"Why, everyone knows your name, missy. You're nominated."

"I know!" She clasped her hands together. "I can't believe it. It's my dream come true." She smiled up at him. "Only, well, I was wondering if you might help me with something?"

"I'll do my best." He bent down so his head was at her height. "What can I get you? Some ice cream, perhaps?"

"No, sir. You see, the thing is, I do charity work, for the orphans of Los Angeles, and well, these orphans, see, they're really poor. They never get to go to awards ceremonies or even watch them on TV, they are so very poor."

"Well, that is mighty good of you."

"Yes, except I promised some of these orphans, the really poorest ones, that they could watch the awards from the side of the stage. I know I shouldn't have, but they were so excited when I told them about being nominated, and"—she bit her lip and looked at the floor for a long moment, then fixed the old man with a wide-eyed, sad look—"I can't bear to let them down. They've been let down by every person they've ever known, their mummies and their daddies. They don't even get to eat much chocolate."

"Oh dear." The usher scratched his head. "I'm afraid the security here is tighter than the White House on Election Day."

"I know." Novak blinked tears into her eyes. "I'm so stupid. I didn't realize how impossible it would be until I arrived and saw all the security." She sniffed. "They're coming here because I told them to, and now I don't know what to do." Her lip trembled and one solitary tear ran down her face.

"Oh now, don't cry. We can't have you ruining your makeup."

"I don't care about my makeup," Novak sobbed. "I don't even care about these awards. I just wanted to give the poor children something incredible to remember for the rest of their lives, and now all they'll remember is being turned away by scary men in suits, and how horrible I am!"

"Now, now." The elderly usher pulled a handkerchief from his waistcoat pocket. "Dry your eyes. Why don't you follow me, and we'll see if we can't speak to my nephew."

Novak hiccupped. "Your nephew?"

"He's on security duty at the stage door." The usher winked.

Novak followed him to a door hidden behind a curtain and watched as he punched in a code. They walked through an empty locker room, through another door and down a corridor, and came out in a lobby. There was a reception desk, and behind it sat a woman playing solitaire with a deck of cards.

"Hello, Nancy, this here is Novak Cutter."

Novak smiled sweetly and waved. "Hi."

"Is Daniel about?"

Nancy didn't look up from her card game. "He's outside."

"Miss Cutter is going to give you some names of orphans from the Los Angeles orphanage." He winked at her. "It's part of some charity thing going on today. They're to be allowed in to watch the ceremony from side stage. Daniel will take care of it."

Nancy tossed a pen down onto an open book and returned her attention to the cards. "Write their names here."

Novak looked up at the usher with wide eyes. "Really?"

"I'll just inform my nephew that he needs to escort them in through the door to the side of the stage," the kindly usher replied, eyes twinkling.

"Thank you," Novak gushed. "There are three children—one girl and two boys—and three carers."

"Right, I'll let Daniel know. Write down their names in the book. Nancy will take care of them."

Novak nodded and picked up the pen, felling a thrill of excitement as she wrote Darkus's, Bertolt's, and Virginia's names, but then she paused. She only knew Maximilian Cuttle's name, not the two others, so she wrote *Max, Baxter, and Hepburn.*

The kindly usher was back five minutes later with Daniel. He looked the same as all the security men: black suit, white shirt, black tie, and sunglasses.

"Daniel will wait on the corner for the orphans."

"Okay, but how will they know who to go to?" Novak opened her handbag and rummaged around, pulling out a fine pink hair ribbon. "Daniel, would you be so kind to kneel down?" she asked politely, fluttering her eyelashes at the security guard.

Daniel laughed and bent down on one knee, lifting his sunglasses. Novak saw that he had the same kindly eyes as his uncle. She looped the thin pink ribbon around the top button of his jacket and tied it in a bow.

"You are doing a wonderful thing, Daniel," Novak said, "and I thank you from the bottom of my heart."

"It's my pleasure, Miss Cutter." Daniel nodded and stood up.

"Darkus will know you by your pink ribbon," she said, feeling a surge of relief and pride.

"You mustn't worry now," Daniel said. "I'll take care of the children."

"Thank you." Novak turned to the kindly usher. "And thank you, sir." She threw her arms around him. "Thank you, thank you, thank you."

"Now, now, Miss Cutter, there's no need for that." He untangled himself, smiling. "We must get you back to your seat before the ceremony begins.

"Could you show me where the bathroom is first, please?" Novak did her best to look embarrassed. "I really need to go."

"Of course. Follow me."

Novak waved to Daniel, with her pink ribbon tied around his top button, and the kindly usher took her back into the theatre and pointed out the bathroom. Novak thanked him and rushed inside, locking the door. She opened her bag and took out a little purse. Unzipping it, she lifted out Hepburn.

"Are you okay?" she whispered.

Hepburn nodded her little bobble of a head.

"Okay. Here's the message: *Go stage door. Look 4 pink ribbon. 3 kids. 3 adults named Max, Baxter, Hepburn.*"

Hepburn's elytra sprang up like flashing rainbows, and moving them in a succession of long and quick flicks repeated the message back to Novak in Morse code.

"Oh, you clever, clever girl." Novak kissed her little finger and touched it to Hepburn's thorax. "Now find Darkus and Baxter. Give them the message, and stay safe."

A bell sounded in the theatre five times, indicating there were five minutes till the awards ceremony started.

She lifted her hand up to the slotted vent above the sealed window.

"Tell him to hurry, Hepburn."

The pretty jewel beetle skipped up into the air and flew away from the theatre, leaving Novak alone.

CHAPTER THIRTY-ONE

Beetle Insurrection

*N*ovak settled into her seat in the front row, between Stella Manning and Mater, just as the lights dimmed. Her heart leapt as a magical swirl of harp strings played and spotlights swept in loops around the ceiling. The curtain lifted, and the lights moved to point at the center of the stage, where the awards would be given out. There were two sets of stairs leading up from the audience onto the platform, one on the left and one on the right, and the proscenium arch above the stage was decorated with strings of twinkling lights that reminded Novak of fireflies. She thought of Newton, Bertolt, and Darkus, and silently wished for Hepburn to find them safely.

A voice boomed over the speakers, "Good evening, ladies and gentleman. Welcome to the Ninety-Second Film Awards. It's going to be an exciting night, so let's get started by welcoming to the stage your host, Leonora Lavish!"

There was an orchestral burst of music and the twinkling lights rippled as the audience applauded the entrance of a beautiful six-foot-tall man with a beard, in an exquisite dress of glittering crystals. He launched into a monologue that had all the adults laughing, but Novak was too nervous to really listen, and then he started singing. He performed a medley about all the movies nominated, and his voice was sweet and powerful. Novak blushed and giggled at the bit where Leonora pretended to be her, befriending a giant dragon, which then ate her. A camera moved along tracks at the side of the stage, and Novak realized she was being filmed, that everyone in the world could see her, and her gut clenched with fear. *This is what Mater wants!* she realized.

She stole a look to her right, where Mater sat perfectly still, staring at the stage with the intensity of a coiled snake about to pounce. Darkus's dad sat beside her, pretending to laugh at Leonora Lavish, but looking anxious, his body tense. Novak wondered if she should try and tell him that Darkus was coming, but it was impossible. Mater kept him by her side, always.

As each award was given out, Novak became more and more nervous. The music and the jokes seemed increasingly garish and unfunny. The Best Actor and Best Actress awards were the big ones, and came toward the end of the ceremony. The waiting was unbearable. Novak kept leaning forward trying to see into the wings, hoping to spot Darkus. She stole glances at Bartholomew Cuttle, but his face was a blank. What kind of game was he playing?

There was a fanfare. "Please welcome to the stage Billy Vanity."

People got to their feet, applauding the man who had won Best Actor last year. He held a solid gold Film Award and an envelope in his hands. Novak sucked in her breath. This was it. Whatever was going to happen was going to happen now. She closed her eyes and thought of Darkus.

Billy Vanity stopped at the microphone.

"Let's get straight down to business," he said, smiling at the camera. "Nominated in the category of Best Actress are: Ruby Hisolo Jr. for Sarah Lane in *A Bridge Over Your Heart*, a tragic story of unrequited love set in the world of eighteenth-century bridge construction." He paused for the applause. "Stella Manning for Hedda Tesman in *Hedda Gabler*, a screen adaptation of Ibsen's classic play about a passionate woman throwing off the shackles of married life." He paused again while there was riotous applause. "And Novak Cutter for Lyla in *Taming of a Dragon*, an epic fantasy about a blind girl and her pet dragon." He paused. There was a polite spattering of clapping. "And the winner is . . ." He tore open the envelope. "Novak Cutter for Lyla in *Taming of a Dragon*."

There was an audible moment of surprised silence before the ripple of applause came.

Novak stood up like a robot. Lucretia Cutter stood up beside her, taking her hand and ushering her onto the stage.

Billy Vanity couldn't hide the look of surprise on his face as he handed the Film Award to Novak Cutter.

"I'm sorry," Novak whispered as she took it. He bowed to her and stepped to one side.

Standing center stage, Lucretia Cutter leaned into the microphone and smiled.

"I'm sure many of you are wondering why we are standing up here. After all, *Taming of a Dragon* was a vacuous fantasy and this child is a terrible actor." She laughed.

Novak's insides turned to ice. She was frightened.

"I paid handsomely to have the opportunity to stand here tonight, when every screen in the world is trained on this stage. So I for one would like to dedicate this award to the greedy and pliable fools who voted for *Taming of a Dragon*."

There was an uncomfortable murmur from the audience, and loud music suddenly played out over the sound system.

"You CANNOT silence me!" Lucretia Cutter shook her head and tutted. "Dankish! Deal with the sound man, would you?"

There was a cry, and the music abruptly stopped playing. A concerned murmur rippled through the audience.

"That's better. Now, where were we?"

A pair of security guards ran onto the stage. Mawling stepped through the heavy red curtains and swung his fist, knocking them both to the ground with one punch. Neither man got up. He pulled out a gun and pointed it at the audience of startled film stars. Billy Vanity started to shuffle backward off the stage, looking terrified.

"Ling Ling, have you dealt with security?"

The chauffeur was there at Lucretia Cutter's feet, her hat gone, her palms together and her head bowed.

"Good. Now there will be no more interruptions." She pointed at the audience. "You are not why I'm here, but if any of you move, Mawling will shoot you." She looked down the barrel of the camera with the red light. "Hello, world. *Bonjour, hola, hej, nín hǎo, merhaba, konnichiwa.* Sorry to interrupt your vapid enjoyment of the annual Film Awards, but I'm here with a live documentary of history in the making." She threw her arms in the air and the red curtains behind her opened, revealing a giant screen. "This movie is going to change your miserable lives."

An image of a rolling landscape of wheat fields appeared on the screen.

"Isn't that beautiful?" She pointed. "It's the wheat harvest for next year. That's what will make the bread that you eat, your pasta, your burger buns, your bagels." She lifted a phone out of an unseen pocket. "You may not be aware of this, but there is a power greater than money." She bent her head to the phone. "Craven, can you hear me? Wave to the people of the world." Craven's face leered into view as he waved at the camera. "Craven is in Texas, in the Wheat Belt of America. Did you know that the US is the third-biggest wheat producer in the world? The industry is valued at around nine billion dollars." She lifted the phone. "Craven? Release the beetles."

The camera panned back to show Craven standing up on the back of a cylindrical tank atop a truck. He wrenched a lever and the tank flew open. There was a loud buzzing sound as the air became thick with millions of small black beetles, obscuring the camera and the view of the fields.

There were gasps and suppressed cries of distress in the auditorium.

"Live TV, everyone!" Lucretia Cutter gestured to the screen and gave it a little round of applause. "Oh dear, it looks like my beetles are hungry." The camera zoomed in to a close-up of an ear of wheat being decimated by a horde of beetles. "I guess some of you won't be having toast for breakfast next year. Bread's going to become expensive." Her laugh was low and guttural. "I do hope the fruit harvest in Florida is okay. Beetles love fruit." She put her finger to her gold lips in mock concern, before flinging it up in a dramatic gesture. "I'll bet you haven't ever spent time getting to know the humble beetle. Did you know that beetles are the most successful, resilient, and evolutionarily sophisticated creature on the planet? No? There are more species of beetle on the planet than we can count. They can live in the most hostile of habitats, on land and in water, and they outnumber us considerably." She smiled. "But what they've lacked, until now, is a leader. Well, that's all about to change." The screen behind her showed the once-golden wheat field, now black with beetles. "Today marks the end of the human era and the beginning of a new coleopteran one."

Someone in the silent auditorium laughed.

"Laugh while you can," Lucretia Cutter snarled. "This revolution is already happening, but at such an infinitesimal level that you don't see it. Your crops are failing and your trees are dying. On my order the dung beetles have taken a holiday; your cattle fields are filling with animal excrement that will spread disease. In a few short months you will turn on one another, fighting for the food that remains, and as you starve and people start dying, you'll see that what I'm saying is true." Her voice grew louder to reach over the frightened murmur of the audience. "THE BEETLES ARE RISING!"

Her dress rippled and swayed, catching the light as it broke apart, forming regimented lines of gold scarabs that hovered in the air, revealing Lucretia Cutter's four black beetle legs and black abdomen. She arched forward as two gold elytra flipped up and her two black wings unfolded, vibrating and lifting her off the floor. Her human forearms reached up and lifted her crown, and she shook her head, tossing off her wig and glasses. She placed the crown back on her shiny black scalp, two antennae rising up out of it, her compound eyes shining as she tore her prosthetic chin away to reveal her black mandibles.

"I AM THE BEETLE QUEEN, AND YOU *WILL* ALL BOW DOWN TO ME."

CHAPTER THIRTY-TWO
The Battle of the Ballgowns

D arkus broke his gaze away from the terrifying sight of a hovering Lucretia Cutter. His feet felt like they were welded to the stage, but his body was screaming that he should run. He grabbed Virginia's and Bertolt's hands and they looked at him, their eyes wide with fear. From where they were standing, in the wings of the stage, they couldn't see the audience, but they could hear the confused gasps and suppressed screams. One man, thinking this was part of the show, applauded and called out, "Amazing costume! Look at the prosthetics!" until Mawling fired a warning shot at him.

"It's now or never," Darkus whispered.

"Now," Virginia said, and Bertolt nodded.

"Don't let any of her beetles bite you," Darkus said. "Remember the yellow ladybugs."

And then he was running onto the stage, flanked by his friends.

"NO!" Darkus cried at the top of his voice. "We will NEVER bow down to you!"

Lucretia Cutter turned her head, her black mouth open wide. *"You!"* she spat. "I thought you were dead!"

"Darkus!"

His dad was standing in the middle of the front row of the audience, dressed in a smart blue tuxedo, clean-shaven with slicked-back hair.

"Get away from her!"

"Dad!" Darkus faltered.

"I will just have to kill you again." Lucretia Cutter turned to the audience. "Let this be a warning to you"—to the camera—"to all of you." She threw her head back and made a ghastly scratching noise.

"NO!" Bartholomew Cuttle cried.

Novak screamed as her dress vibrated, exploding into a thousand hovering black beads, leaving her standing in her black catsuit.

Lucretia Cutter made a series of clicking noises that Darkus recognized, and the bombardier beetles who had clothed Novak flew straight at his face.

"Darkus!" he heard his father shout. *"Run!"*

It was too much for the ceremony guests, who'd been pinned to their seats by fear, and they cried out and grabbed one another.

Darkus dropped into a crouch, grabbing the hose strapped to the side of his backpack and flicking a switch as he pointed it at the bombardier beetles zooming toward him.

"Virginia!" he cried. "Bertolt!"

"Here!" they replied in unison, running forward, each with their backpack pooters switched on.

Baxter reared up on Darkus's shoulder, ready to spike any bombardier beetle that made it past Darkus's hose. Within seconds Darkus had sucked up the attacking bombardier beetles and was back on his feet. He turned his head, worried that the beetle's acid would burn through the tank, but once inside, away from the sound of Lucretia Cutter's commands, they calmed down and behaved like ordinary beetles.

"*Security!*" a man shouted. "What are you waiting for? *Get her! Get Lucretia Cutter!*"

A woman screamed and leapt to her feet. It was a famous scream that had been heard in movie theatres all over the globe, and the air above the theatre seats suddenly became thick with shimmering white beetles.

Everybody stared with disbelief at a suddenly stark naked Ruby Hisolo Jr. as a throng of beetles gathered above her head. Her dress had broken apart into a battalion of hovering insects.

Another scream, a deeper, richer voice, sounded, and a menacing throng of emerald-green jewel beetles zoomed up to join the *Cyphochilus*, as Stella Manning stood beside Ruby Hisolo Jr. in nothing but Spanx and a corset, batting the insects away from her face.

The cameras, already trained on the famous actresses to capture their joy or disappointment when the award winner was announced, now broadcast the naked bottom of Ruby Hisolo Jr. and Stella Manning's panic to the world as the swarm of white, green, and gold beetles hovering above the heads of the audience dived down, biting and scratching the stars of stage and screen. A medley of screams, cries, and shouts of alarm were accompanied by the buzzing vibration of a thousand pairs of beetle wings. Darkus saw that the jewel beetles from Stella Manning's dress had the jaws and teeth of tiger beetles, and that their bite drew blood.

"Dad!" Darkus cried, losing sight of his father as people ran, pushing each other and climbing over seats. Some were trying to fight their way forward to the stage to get at Lucretia Cutter, and others were scrambling toward the doors at the back of the theatre, trying to escape. The naked, hysterical Ruby Hisolo Jr. ran up and down the aisle trying to rip clothes off other people's backs to cover her body. She was regretting her decision not to wear underwear to the Film Awards, and several opportunist photographers were falling over each other trying to get pictures.

A woman pulled out a pistol from her garter belt and fired a shot. There was a moment of stunned silence as everyone turned to look at the hovering beetle woman, to see if she'd fallen. The bullet glanced off Lucretia Cutter's exoskeleton, ricocheting backward, severing a wire that held up one side of the massive screen showing the decimated wheat harvest. One corner dropped to the ground and swung forward, revealing a pyramid of gold birdcages filled with exotic parakeets that were squawking and thrashing about their cages, trying to get out.

Lucretia Cutter laughed, a horrible guttural mix of gurgles and hisses, reveling in the mayhem. More shots were fired. One man swung his fist at a swarm of beetles, lost his balance, and hit a famous movie star, who spun round and punched him in the face. Fights broke out all over the theatre. Lucretia Cutter turned to the camera with the red light.

"I demand that your government draw up a charter handing sovereignty to me." She leaned forward. "If they do it quickly, maybe you won't starve to death."

Darkus followed Lucretia Cutter's eyeline and spotted Ling Ling behind the camera. This show was all for the cameras. He had to get Lucretia Cutter off the air, but he also had to stop the beetles attacking people. He looked out into the auditorium and spotted Uncle Max and Motty fighting with Mawling and Dankish. Calista Bloom was standing behind them, taking a picture of herself with all the famous people being attacked by beetles.

His eyes landed on the big spotlights mounted on tripods at the back of the theatre. He waved at Virginia and Bertolt and pointed.

"We've got to stop this," he shouted. "The lights! Use the lights!"

Bertolt frowned, but Virginia's eyes lit up and she nodded. She gave Bertolt a shove and they jumped off the stage, running into the auditorium, sucking up Lucretia Cutter's beetles as they went.

"Baxter," Darkus said, taking the beetle off his shoulder, "can you fly to that camera and find the off switch?" The rhinoceros beetle nodded and leapt into the air. "Novak, get into the wings."

"What are you going to do?"

"Don't worry about me," he replied, jumping to his feet and launching himself off the stage at the deadly chauffeur.

Ling Ling sprang up, her torso flipping and legs scissoring as she twisted in the air. Darkus slid right through the space she'd been standing in and clattered to the floor. Ling Ling landed, one foot on either side of Darkus's head.

"No!" Novak screamed, scrambling to the edge of the stage.

"Hi!" Darkus grinned.

As Ling Ling drew up her leg to kick Darkus in the face, he flicked the switch on his air pump, firing a stream of bombardier beetles back out of the hose of his aspirator, right into Ling Ling's face. She stumbled backward, her hands covering her face as it sizzled and burnt from the acid sprayed by the panicked beetles.

Darkus scrambled away, following the cables that sprouted out of the TV camera to an electrical box.

Lucretia Cutter's antennae flicked and thrashed about as she called the bombardier beetles away from Ling Ling, instructing them to join the army of beetles attacking the humans in the auditorium.

Darkus flipped open two plastic containers strapped into his utility belt, each containing four titan beetles.

"Get into the electrical box," he whispered to the Base Camp beetles, "and eat through the wires. Stop the broadcast."

The titan beetles didn't need to be told twice. They scurried down through the wires and began chewing the cables.

Darkus felt his body suddenly being lifted into the air, and he grabbed onto the camera. Ling Ling ripped off his backpack, tossing it aside. Darkus struggled and kicked, but she was surprisingly strong.

Darkus heard Uncle Max shout, "Get your hands off my nephew!" and saw him running toward them, pushing up his sleeves, but Mawling had spotted him, too, and was charging down the stairs from the stage like a steam train.

Calista Bloom, who was sticking close to Uncle Max for safety, tripped, crying out as she fell to the floor in front of Lucretia Cutter's meathead.

"Mum!" Bertolt howled, jumping onto the spotlight stand and yanking it around to point at Mawling, who was instantly blinded and then attacked by a swarm of beetles who had been drawn to the light.

Calista Bloom scrambled to her feet, skidded on her stiletto heels, and fell backward, doing an accidental bicycle kick right into Mawling's privates.

Mawling hovered for a moment, pulling a face that looked like he'd sucked a lemon, his hands clasping his crown jewels. Uncle Max spun around and punched him. Mawling crumbled to the floor.

Ling Ling's arm swung back, and Darkus thought she was about to strike him, but instead she was defending herself from a microphone stand that was swinging down toward her head. She blocked the blow, grabbed the stand, and spun around. Novak was clutching the other end of it.

Ling Ling pivoted, wrapping her free arm around the shaft of the stand and lifting Novak into the air. Novak let go, launching herself backward, flipping into a reel of cartwheels and a roundoff, landing in an attack stance.

Darkus was stunned. Before he could cheer, Novak was running forward, launching herself into a spinning pirouette of roundhouse kicks, spotting as she spun, never taking her eyes off Ling Ling.

Ling Ling pushed Darkus aside as Novak's foot swiped across her cheek, splitting her already blistered skin and spraying blood across the floor.

Darkus stared at Novak's feet. They were claws. Black chitinous claws like her mother's.

Ling Ling rallied, coming hard at Novak, who blocked her punches and kicks but was no match for the deadly chauffeur. Novak flipped backward. Stumbling, she fell to her knees, and suddenly Ling Ling was standing over her, her face all bloody and blistered.

Darkus scrambled forward and grabbed the discarded microphone stand, sweeping it at Ling Ling's supporting leg, knocking her off balance. "RUN!" he shouted at Novak.

He jumped up onto a theatre seat, where he could see that Virginia and Bertolt were each standing behind one of the enormous chrome spotlights at the back of the theatre, trying to control their movement. He pointed up into the heart of the beetle vortex above people's heads. "SHINE THE LIGHT THERE!" he shouted. "UP THERE!"

Virginia saw him, followed his finger, and nodded, moving the bright light so it pointed into the throng of beetles. She shouted to Bertolt to do the same, and the beams met, creating a concentrated ball of light.

The beetles, unable to help themselves, were drawn to the light. They pulled away from combat with the humans and, hypnotized, flew into, through, and around the light.

CHAPTER THIRTY-THREE
Predator and Prey

*D*arkus, listen, please."

Darkus turned at the sound of Novak's voice and jumped down from the theatre seat.

"You have to help me," Novak blurted out, grabbing his hand. "Mater's going to put me back in the pupator."

"What's a pupator?"

"It hurts, and I'm frightened." Novak was biting her lip so hard he could see blood. "She's going to turn me into a beetle, like her."

"No, Novak, I won't let her." Darkus shook his head.

"Thank you." Novak flung her arms around him. "I knew you'd understand. Thank you, thank you."

"Ow! Let go!" Darkus laughed, pulling away.

"You must stay away from Ling Ling." Novak's eyes were wide with concern. "She kills people, and she doesn't have to try very hard to do it."

Darkus's eyes flickered to a gang of gym-loving actors and stunt men who had encircled the chauffeur. Ling Ling stood in the middle of them, calm and poised to fight.

"Did Hepburn find you?" Novak asked. "Is she okay?"

"Hepburn was amazing." He popped open a pouch on his belt. "Her Morse code is perfect."

"Oh, darling Heppy, there you are," Novak cooed as she lifted the pretty jewel beetle and hugged her.

Darkus looked up. "Hey, why are the spotlights not up in the air?"

He heard cries of alarm behind him. The beetles were attacking again, and more savagely this time. The white beetles' claws sliced and cut faces and necks.

He looked at the stage. Lucretia Cutter was proudly surveying the carnage in the auditorium, and standing beside her was his father.

Darkus was about to shout, but Novak grabbed his arm. "No," she said. "Darkus, he's on her side."

Darkus's guts twisted. He shook his head. "He can't be."

"He knows about the pupator. He's going to let her change me."

"No." Darkus looked at Novak. "He isn't like that."

"Darkus, I heard them talking."

"I won't believe it." He broke away from her. "Where are the security guards?" He looked about angrily. "There are loads of them outside."

"Ling Ling took out everyone inside the building and locked the doors. Maybe the men outside don't know there's anything happening in here."

"Don't they watch TV?" Darkus snapped. "We need to get them inside. Now."

"How?"

Darkus pointed at a glass box on the wall. "Fire alarm."

Between them and the button, Ling Ling was kicking the stuffing out of ten men.

"Baxter!" Darkus called, and the rhinoceros beetle, who'd been on top of the camera, fighting beetles, flew to his hand. "Can you break the glass with your horn and push that button?"

Baxter didn't wait to reply, but spun around, flying up and over the heads of the fighting humans.

"We're losing," Darkus said, looking around in horror. "We need those security men *now*."

"I'll get them in," Novak said, leaping up.

"Novak, your feet!" Darkus looked down at the hooks on the end of her claws. "Why didn't you tell me?"

"Do you hate them?" she asked. "They're ugly, aren't they?"

"Are you kidding?" Darkus looked at her. "They're AWESOME! Can you run up walls and stuff? Like a beetle?"

"I don't know." Novak frowned. "I've never tried."

"What!?" Darkus exclaimed. "If I had beetle feet, that's the first thing I'd do."

Novak looked down at her black feet, pivoted, and ran, her strong claws powering her forward. As she approached the wall she raised one foot and then the other, the sharp serrated edges of her claws cutting into the brick as she ran up to the ceiling and then around the corner to the stage door.

An ear-splitting alarm rang out. Baxter had done it!

Jumping back up onto the chair, Darkus saw that Uncle Max had Dankish up against the wall, his hand around the villain's neck, while Calista Bloom scolded him, but they were both being attacked by beetles now. Darkus scanned the room, but couldn't see Virginia or Bertolt anywhere.

Grabbing up his backpack, he strapped it back on. This fight was far from over. He turned to the stage, a tumult of suspicion, anger, and love churning in his belly as he saw his father in heated conversation with Lucretia Cutter. He wasn't arguing, or fighting her, like he should have been doing. He seemed to be pleading with her.

Darkus glared at Lucretia Cutter, wondering how you hurt someone who was bulletproof.

The greatest weapon you have is knowledge. Dr. Yuki Ishikawa's voice sounded in his head. *Think, Darkus. You know what she is. Every creature has a predator. That is how balance is maintained.*

Darkus looked past the screen, hanging precariously from one wire, to the golden pyramid of cages full of exotic birds, fluttering around and flapping their wings. "Of course!" he gasped, launching himself up the steps on the left side of the stage and running behind Lucretia Cutter.

"It's dinnertime, my feathered friends," he cried out, flinging open the cages and shooing the birds out into the theatre. They rocketed up into the seething torrent of beetles, happily pecking at and swallowing as many as they could. Seven of the bigger birds peeled away from the flock, flying to the front of the stage, where the biggest beetle they'd ever seen was hovering in the air.

Lucretia Cutter shrieked and fell to the ground as the birds pecked at her wings and eyes.

"*Baxter!*" Darkus gasped. In his haste to fight back, he'd endangered his best friend. He spun around, studying the wall beside the fire alarm. There was no sign of him. Darkus couldn't breathe. He felt something knock against his ankle, and looked down: The rhinoceros beetle was head-butting him. He swept the beetle up, kissing his thorax, before placing Baxter on his shoulder. "Stay close, Baxter, I don't want those birds to get you."

Darkus's giant pooter was empty and, he realized, the safest place for the Base Camp beetles. Inside they'd be protected from the hungry birds. He jumped off the edge of the stage, scurrying to the electrical box, which was a mess of copper wires thanks to the titan beetles.

"Quick, guys, I need to suck you up into the pooter, before those birds try to eat you!" He switched on the suction and vacuumed up the titan beetles. "This room is full of birds," he whispered to the hidden battalion of Base Camp beetles in his utility belt. "Don't come out unless I call you."

The Base Camp beetles chittered in reply.

A team of security men burst through the double doors at the back of the theatre, led by Motty. They headed straight for Ling Ling and the ring of fallen actors groaning on the floor. Darkus saw Virginia and Bertolt in the aisle, back to back, vacuuming up Lucretia Cutter's beetles. The tide of the battle was turning. Most of Lucretia Cutter's beetles were in the stomachs of the happy birds, or in Bertolt's and Virginia's pooters.

"Get away from me!" Lucretia Cutter screeched, punching a bird.

Ling Ling was in front of the stage, fighting off the security guards, disarming them as quickly as they drew their weapons. Dankish, wounded and limping, clambered onto the stage, where he met the injured Mawling. Novak rushed onto one side of the stage with the security guards who'd been stationed outside the stage door.

"NO!" Lucretia Cutter swung her head angrily. She was surrounded, and being pecked at by birds. "You cannot stop me." She looked out into the theatre. "IT'S TOO LATE!" She wrapped a beetle leg around Darkus's dad's waist and rose up, lifting Bartholomew Cuttle into the air. "You're fools!" Her human forearms slapped away the last attacking birds. "You can't win. I already have the planet in the palm of my hand!"

"Dad!" Before he had time to think, Darkus was running: through a door, up a flight of stairs, bursting out onto the balcony, into a box overlooking the stage.

As Lucretia Cutter rose, with his dad clasped to her abdomen, Darkus jumped up onto the railing and threw himself off, grabbing her around the neck. The shock of his attack made Lucretia Cutter release Bartholomew Cuttle, who dropped to the stage floor with a sickening thud.

"I'm going to kill you, boy!" she shrieked, whirling around and grabbing him with two arms and two serrated beetle legs, rising higher into the fly tower of the theatre. There were bars with lights and ropes hanging down, attached to pieces of scenery. On a platform high above him, Darkus saw Gerard. He tried to cling to her neck, but Lucretia Cutter pulled him off and brought him around to face her.

"Ever been bitten by a beetle?" she said, stretching her black mouthparts wide, her mandibles reaching out toward him. His face was inches from her razor-sharp teeth, and her breath stank of rotten pear drops.

"BEETLES!" Darkus cried out, kicking his feet violently against Lucretia Cutter's abdomen. Pushing himself backward into the air, he flung his arms over his shoulders as if doing a backward dive into a swimming pool, giving him enough momentum to escape her grasp.

He should have fallen like a dead weight to the ground, but the Base Camp beetles were there with him, exploding out of his backpack and utility belt, zooming out of their pockets, gathering underneath him, flying up as hard as they could. Baxter was in between his shoulder blades, Novak sent up Hepburn, Bertolt sent Newton, and Virginia hurled Marvin into the air. The titan beetles inside the pooter flew upward for all they were worth, pushing against the roof, slowing Darkus's fall and lowering him slowly, and safely, to the ground.

"ENOUGH!" Lucretia Cutter lost her temper, zooming down and shouting orders at her injured henchmen. Dankish and Mawling disappeared into the wings, and Ling Ling ran to the red curtains on the stage. Vaulting up and grasping the drapes between her ankles, she folded the fabric into handholds and climbed to the top, then flipped herself upside down, hooked her feet around a lighting bar, and clambered up into the fly tower.

As Darkus landed, Novak ran toward him, smiling, her arms wide.

"You did it! You won!" she exclaimed as a giant black chitinous leg grabbed her from behind, dragging her backward and up into the air.

Darkus saw the shocked look on Novak's face, and then she screamed, a sound of pure terror as Lucretia Cutter soared upward carrying her daughter.

"No!" He ran forward, but he was too late.

Baxter rocketed up after Novak, the rhinoceros beetle valiantly trying to attack Lucretia Cutter with his horn.

She smashed Baxter out of the air with a claw, and the big black beetle tumbled to the ground at alarming speed.

"BAXTER!" Darkus cried out.

Lucretia Cutter laughed, flying up into the fly tower, and was gone.

Darkus lurched forward. Baxter's wings weren't opening. He was going to hit the ground. Darkus couldn't reach him in time. He sobbed as he threw himself toward his best friend, knowing it was too late.

And suddenly Dad was there, his arms outstretched, catching the rhinoceros beetle and drawing him into his chest, tumbling to the floor with a grunt of pain.

Darkus stumbled to his father.

"Dad? Baxter?" He fell to his knees at his father's side, wiping away tears. "Are you okay?"

Bartholomew Cuttle carefully opened his hands. Sitting on his palm was a stunned but living rhinoceros beetle. Baxter lifted his foreleg and waved at Darkus, weakly, to show he was alive.

"Oh, Baxter! You crazy, brave beetle! I thought I'd lost you." He grabbed the beetle up to his chest, curling his shoulders forward around his cupped hands. "Don't ever do that to me again."

Baxter opened his mouth and smiled up at Darkus.

"Dad, you saved him. You saved Baxter." Darkus beamed at his father. "I knew you were on our side."

"Listen to me, Darkus." Bartholomew Cuttle was getting to his feet. "I have to go with her. I have to go with Lucretia Cutter."

"What? But—but I saved you."

"Yes. And you were amazing. But you've seen what she's going to do. What she's already doing. It's much bigger than this awards ceremony. She won't stop until the world is under her control." Bartholomew Cuttle took his son's hand. "I have to go with her. It's my only chance to stop her, and I have a plan." He paused. "But she'll only trust me if she thinks I've abandoned you. If she thinks I've chosen her over you." He gripped Darkus's hand and looked him in the eyes. "Can you understand? I know it's a lot to ask."

Darkus nodded, and his father put a piece of paper into his pocket. "She has a secret laboratory—it's called the Biome."

"Hidden in the Amazon," Darkus said.

"Yes!" His father looked surprised. "And you were right about Spencer Crips. She has him there. Tell his mother he's alive, being made to work for Lucretia Cutter. These"—he pointed at Darkus's pocket—"are the coordinates. I got them from the butler—he's on our side. You need to tell the world what's going on. Go to the entomologists, they'll help you."

Darkus got to his feet. "Dad, you've got to protect Novak. Don't let Lucretia Cutter put her back in the pupator. She's frightened, and she's my friend."

"I will. I promise." Bartholomew Cuttle nodded. He put his hands on Darkus's shoulders. "That night we argued, I should have listened to you—about the beetles, about everything. I'm sorry. They're amaz-ing. *You* are amazing." He hugged Darkus and Baxter tightly. "I'm going to need you to be brave for a little longer, and if you can bear it, come and save me one last time." He let go. "And then we'll be together again, and nothing will separate us. I promise."

"I'll rescue you as many times as you need me to," Darkus said, his eyes filling with tears. "Me and Baxter will."

"I love you, son," Bartholomew Cuttle said over his shoulder as he turned, hobbling across the stage, following Dankish and Mawling up a ladder into the fly tower.

CHAPTER THIRTY-FOUR

Stowaways

*H*umphrey and Pickering stood on the flat roof of the apartment block adjacent to the Hollywood Theatre. They'd found a fire escape that took them up onto the roof.

"If we can't get into the theatre on the ground floor," Humphrey said, looking at the gap between the two buildings, "then we'll get in from the top."

Ten feet of space marked the separation between the two buildings, and a drop of fourteen stories.

"Look!" Pickering tugged at Humphrey's sleeve. "Lucretia Cutter's helicopter!"

On the theatre rooftop was a helipad and a black helicopter with a gold scarab emblazoned on the side. Sitting in the pilot's seat was the French butler.

"I see it," Humphrey grunted. "I also see the massive gap between us and that rooftop."

"It's not so big." Pickering couldn't take his eyes off the helicopter, and kept licking his lips.

Humphrey pointed at a thick chain strung along the edge of the helipad. "If you could get that chain, tie it around that air-conditioning vent, and throw it back to me, I could swing over and climb up. It looks strong enough to hold my weight."

Pickering's brow creased. "But how will I get over there?"

"I'll throw you," Humphrey said.

Pickering's mouth fell open. "You'll what?"

"You go way back there, to the far edge of the rooftop, and I'll stand here." He rooted his feet against the stumpy wall that kept them from the extreme edge of the roof. "Run as fast as you can toward me and jump, as if you were going to leap across the gap, and as you jump, I'll grab you and fling you."

Pickering's eyebrows lifted so high they touched his thatch of hair.

"No other way to get over there," Humphrey said, wiping his nose with the back of his hand.

"You'll throw me as hard as you can. Right?"

"Right."

"Okay." Pickering trudged off to the other side of the roof. When he got there he squatted down in a sprint start position, his bum in the air and fists on the tarmac.

"Wait!" Humphrey stopped him. "Tuck your skirt into your underwear. We don't want it getting in the way."

Standing up straight, Pickering gathered up the long flowery skirt and stuffed it in his drawers.

"On three," he called out, squatting back down. "One, two, three." And suddenly he was dashing toward Humphrey.

Bending his knees, Humphrey held his hands out, ready.

As Pickering's feet hit the floor to make the jump he let out an almighty shriek. "NOWWWWWWWWWWWWWW!"

"ARGHHHHHHHHHHHH!" Humphrey roared as he hurled Pickering forward as hard as he could, flinging himself backward immediately after letting go, to stop from falling over the edge of the building. As his buttocks hit the floor he wondered if he'd just missed a good opportunity to get rid of his annoying cousin once and for all.

He propped himself up on his bulbous elbows and looked to see if Pickering had made it to the other side. There was no sign of him. He peered down into the alley between the two buildings. There was no splattered Pickering on the ground.

As Humphrey got to his feet, he saw his cousin lying flat on the theatre roof, blood streaming from his beaky nose. It was broken and pointing left, rather than straight down. As Pickering slowly sat up, Humphrey gave a belly-gurgle of a laugh. It had worked!

"Oi, Pickers!" he shouted.

Pickering looked at him and blinked, blood streaming down his chin.

Humphrey pointed. "Get the chain."

Gingerly getting to his feet, Pickering stumbled forward, worked loose a broken brick from the base of a chimney and carried it to the iron post that the chain was welded to. He smashed at it till the chain broke away. Humphrey kept an eye on the butler, but he hadn't noticed them. Pickering unthreaded the long chain from the post, and then he carried it in his arms back to the chimney, looped it around, and tied it in a knot. Then he threw the loose end to Humphrey.

Humphrey tugged on the chain to make sure it would take his weight, and then, before he had a chance to change his mind, he wrapped it around his wrist several times and ran at the roof edge, leaping as far as he could, grabbing up the chain as he began to fall and swinging himself forward. He hit the theatre wall hard, and dropped down a couple of feet. But the chain held firm, and hand over hand, he pulled himself up onto the theatre roof.

Once he'd got his elbows over the lip of the building, Pickering leaned over and grabbed at his belt loops, helping to heave him over.

Humphrey lay on his back, panting. His heart was beating faster than it ever had before.

"The butler's getting out of the helicopter!" Pickering hissed, dropping down onto his belly beside Humphrey. "He's going to that door—it must lead into the theatre." His eyes lit up as he looked down at Humphrey. "We should follow him."

They heard a commotion on the street below. Humphrey peered over the edge of the building, still waiting for his heart to stop hopping about inside his ribs. There were people screaming and running out of the theatre.

"Something's happening in there."

"Let's go inside and find out what it is." Pickering jumped up.

"No!" Humphrey shook his head. "Think about it, dummy." He pointed at the helicopter. "That's how Lucretia Cutter is leaving the building." He grinned at his cousin. "So we don't want to go into the theatre. We want to get onto that helicopter, with her."

"That's a good idea!" Pickering marveled. "I wonder where it's going?"

"Probably to one of her swanky houses on a private island with coconut trees and swimming pools," Humphrey replied.

The cousins scrambled to their feet and dashed over to the helicopter.

"There's nowhere to hide!" Pickering exclaimed, looking into the cabin. He was right. If they got in, they'd be spotted and chucked out immediately.

"Do helicopters have luggage compartments?" Humphrey wondered.

"Here!" Pickering squealed, opening a hatch door. "It's full of bags."

"Quick, pull them out. I'll chuck them over the edge."

Pickering emptied the luggage compartment and scrambled in, while Humphrey dumped all Lucretia Cutter's bags over the side of the building.

"Move up," Humphrey said. He crawled in backward on all fours so he could shut the door.

"Ouch! There isn't enough room. You're too fat."

"Shut up." Humphrey pushed backward, and with a wrench slammed the door shut. He heard his cousin whimper. "What's the matter?" he hissed.

"Your bottom is wedged against my face," Pickering said unhappily. "You'd better not fart."

"Shhhh." Humphrey cocked his head. "I can hear someone coming. Just think, when we get out, we'll be in paradise."

"Alone with Lucretia Cutter," Pickering cooed.

CHAPTER THIRTY-FIVE
Christmas Day

*D*arkus followed Uncle Max down the hospital corridor. There were Christmas decorations hanging from the white ceiling, and as he passed by windows into wards, he realized that there were a lot of people who didn't get to spend Christmas with their family. It wasn't just him.

"Here we are," Uncle Max announced, opening a door and marching through it.

Sitting up in bed, drinking green tea, was Professor Andrew Appleyard.

"A very merry Christmas to you, Andrew," Uncle Max boomed, sitting down on the chair beside the bed.

Darkus shuffled shyly to his side. "Happy Christmas, Professor Appleyard."

"And a merry Christmas to you both." Professor Appleyard lifted his tea. "May your life cycle be longer than a mayfly's." He chuckled.

"I brought you a present," Darkus said, offering the brightly wrapped box he was nervously clutching.

"I'm too old for presents," Professor Appleyard protested. "You didn't need to go and do that."

"I wanted to," Darkus said.

The professor put down his tea and delicately unwrapped the present. When they'd got back from America, Uncle Max had called the hospital to check on Professor Appleyard's condition, and been told that he'd come out of his coma the day before the Film Awards and seemed to be making a full and speedy recovery. Darkus was relieved, but he still felt responsible for Professor Appleyard ending up in the hospital in the first place.

"Are you all better now?" he asked.

"I think so," the professor replied. "It would seem I was bitten by a venomous insect, which is peculiar because the venom they found in my system appears to have been from a black widow spider, but the only insect I saw before I passed out was a yellow ladybug, and black widows are not native to this country." He shook his head. "Luckily I've been bitten by a black widow before, and I appear to have built up some immunity."

"You've been bitten by a black widow?"

"Oh, it was my fault entirely, I scared the poor thing by accident.

Black widows are not aggresive," he said, pulling the paper off his present. "Oh, Darkus, how wonderful! Chocolate-covered crickets. What a treat. Thank you."

"The ladybug was Lucretia Cutter's," Darkus said. "We've been studying them. The ones with eleven spots are deadly."

"Really? How interesting. I'd love to see your work." Professor Appleyard rubbed his eyes. "I must have angered Lucy when I asked the global entomology network to call for citizen invasion monitoring, getting people to keep an eye out for her Frankenstein beetles."

"I thought it was my fault," Darkus said.

"What? Why would you think such a thing?"

"I led the ladybugs to you," Darkus admitted.

"Dear boy, no. I have been worrying about Lucy Johnstone ever since the Fabre Project closed down. You aren't the only one fighting her, you know."

Darkus beamed. "That is good to know."

"I've checked with the doctors," Uncle Max said. "They're happy to discharge you, if you want to go home."

"I would love to go home." Professor Appleyard smiled. "I need to feed my arthropods."

"Then we'll take you. I've got the car in the parking lot."

"We're going to have Christmas dinner at Virginia's," Darkus said, "and you're invited, too. There won't be any bugs to eat, but if you want to come, we can tell you all about Lucretia Cutter."

Professor Appleyard had already thrown back his blanket and was slipping his feet into his shoes. "That sounds wonderful, Darkus. I want to hear all about it. I watched the Film Awards on the television." He pointed up to a screen bolted to the wall. "I've never seen such madness."

Darkus reached up and rang the doorbell.

"Happy Christmas!" Virginia yelled as she yanked the door open. "Where are your uncle and the professor?"

"They're coming. The professor's got a wheelchair until his strength comes back," Darkus said, following Virginia into the Wallace house. "But he's fine."

Serena, Virginia's older sister, was sitting on the stairs talking into her mobile phone, looking bored and picking the nail polish off her neon-yellow fingernails. Virginia led Darkus into the living room. David, her oldest brother, sat in a big armchair, headphones on, eyes glued to a game console. He grunted at them as they entered the room.

"That's David's version of 'Happy Christmas,'" Virginia said.

There was a thundering sound as Sean ran down the stairs, bursting into the room behind them. "Did you bring the rhinoceros beetle?" he asked.

"Where are your manners?" Barbara Wallace waddled in, flicking a tea towel at David. "Offer Darkus your seat, David—he's all alone, with no parents to spend this Christmas Day with."

"I wish *I* had no parents," David muttered.

"I heard that."

"I'm fine, Mrs. Wallace," Darkus said as Keisha and Darnell chased each other in and out of the room, shrieking.

"What can I get you to drink, Darkus? Would you like a mince pie?"

The doorbell rang and Virginia sprinted out of the room.

"An orange juice would be lovely," Darkus replied. "Thank you."

It was Bertolt and his mum, followed by Mrs. Crips carrying a Christmas cake.

"Merry Christmas," Bertolt said, with a wide smile.

"Come in, everyone!" Virginia shouted as they all piled into the living room.

"Thanks for inviting Mrs. Crips," Bertolt whispered to Virginia.

"Of course!" Virginia smiled. "No one should be alone on Christmas Day."

Sean came in with a dinner plate of chopped-up bananas, melon, and sweet potato. "I've brought a snack for the beetles," he announced, setting the plate down on the coffee table beside the Christmas newspapers. The beetles didn't need telling twice. Baxter and Marvin flew down to the plate and began eating. Baxter climbed onto the banana and Marvin hugged the sweet potato.

"Newton doesn't eat much," Bertolt explained apologetically.

"So cool." Sean stared at them in wonder.

Uncle Max wheeled Professor Appleyard's chair in, and it had a bag full of presents hanging off the back, which he placed under the Christmas tree. The three mothers, Mrs. Wallace, Mrs. Crips, and Miss Bloom, sat together on the sofa with glasses of sherry, discussing the newspapers on the coffee table. The front pages were covered in pictures from the Film Awards, mostly of the naked, screaming Ruby Hisolo Jr.

Stories reported that Lucretia Cutter had gone crazy, designing live beetle dresses, and that Novak Cutter was a dreadful actress who should never have even been nominated for an award.

"I don't understand." Bertolt picked up the *Daily News*. "Why is no one talking about the millions of beetles Lucretia Cutter has released into the ecosystem in a bid to take over the world?" He shook his head.

"Because a story about a naked film star sells more papers," Barbara Wallace replied, and the mothers nodded.

"But her beetles *are* out there, wreaking havoc," Uncle Max said. He pointed to a story on page five. "Look. There's a story here about ruined wheat crops in Texas. America's declared a state of national emergency."

"So what do we do now?" Virginia asked.

"First week of January," Darkus said, "there's the International Congress of Entomology in Prague. Uncle Max is going to take me, and Dr. Yuki Ishikawa's coming, too. He saw the Film Awards."

"He is?" Bertolt smiled. "Oh good."

"Me too," Professor Appleyard said. "It'll take more than black widow spider venom to stop me from going to that conference."

"Darkus has an extraordinary collection of beetles to show our fellow scientists," Uncle Max said proudly, "and a story they all need to hear."

"You up for that, Baxter?" Darkus grinned, and Baxter flew to his shoulder, nuzzling his head against the boy's neck.

"After Prague," Uncle Max said, "Motty and I will be leading a rescue mission to the Amazon. We're going to find Barty, Spencer, and Novak and bring them home—and, while we're at it, do a bit of giant insect hunting." He waggled his eyebrows.

"YES!" Virginia leapt to her feet and punched the air. "Another adventure."

"Hush now. Sit down, Virginia," Barbara Wallace said. "I've had enough talk of adventure."

Bertolt got to his feet. "I don't like adventures. Not one bit." He turned to his mum. "But I *have* to help Novak. She needs us."

"Oh c'mon, Mum!" Virginia protested. "You saw Lucretia Cutter on TV. Imagine what she's going to do to Novak for helping us. You've got to let me go."

The flickering firefly and the cherry-red frog-legged leaf beetle rose into the air, hovering above their humans' heads.

"Today is Christmas Day." Barbara Wallace held up her hands. "Why don't you children each open a present?" She gestured to the mound of gifts under the tree. "How about that red one, Virginia? That's for you. Bertolt, Darkus, yours are the ones with stars on them."

Sulkily, Virginia got down on her knees and pulled out the red present from under the stack of gifts stuffed under the heavily decorated tree. She handed Bertolt and Darkus their presents and looked at her mum for permission to open hers. Barbara Wallace nodded, and Virginia halfheartedly ripped off the paper, pulling out a pair of camo trousers and a small bag, in camo fabric, stuffed full of things.

"Oh wow!" She unzipped the bag, emptying onto the floor a compass, a Swiss Army Knife, a mosquito net, a set of waterproof matches, a tiny first aid kit, a reel of string, and water purification tablets. She looked up at her mum. "This is amazing!"

Darkus and Bertolt ripped open their presents to find they each had a small camo bag stuffed with the same things.

"Well, I thought they would be useful," Barbara Wallace said, "if you're going to the Amazon jungle."

"You're going to let me go?" Virginia jumped to her feet, flying at her mother, arms wide. She hugged her tightly.

"The compass is so you can always find your way home," Barbara Wallace said, stroking Virginia's head.

"Oh, thank you, Mum, thank you, thank you." Virginia kissed her mother's forehead and cheeks.

Bertolt turned to his mother, and she nodded. "I saw that Lucretia woman with my own eyes. She needs to be stopped." Calista Bloom smiled proudly. "And I think you'll do better if I *don't* come this time."

"The Amazon!" he whispered breathlessly, looking at Darkus.

Darkus nodded. "It's time someone stood up to Lucretia Cutter and made her realize this world does not belong to her."

An Entomologist's Dictionary

ABDOMEN: The part of the body behind the thorax (human abdomens are usually referred to as the tummy or the belly). It is the largest of the three body segments of an insect (the other parts being the head and the thorax).

ANTENNAE (SINGULAR: ANTENNA): A pair of sensory appendages on the head, sometimes called *feelers*. They are used to sense many things, including odor, taste, heat, wind speed, and direction.

ARTHROPOD: Means *jointed leg* and refers to a group of animals that includes insects (known as hexapods), crustaceans, myriapods (millipedes and centipedes), and chelicerates (spiders, scorpions, horseshoe crabs, and their relatives). Arthropod bodies are usually in segments, and all arthropods have an exoskeleton and are invertebrates.

BEETLE: One type (or *order*) of insect with the front pair of wing cases modified into hardened elytra. There are more different species of beetle than any other animal on the planet.

CHITIN: The material that makes up the exoskeletons of most arthropods, including insects. Chitin is one of the most important substances in nature.

COLEOPTERA: The scientific name for beetles.

COLEOPTERIST: A scientist who studies beetles.

COMPOUND EYES: Can be made up of thousands of individual visual receptors, and are common in arthropods. They enable many arthropods to see very well, but they see the world as a pixelated image—like the pixels on a computer screen.

DNA (DEOXYRIBONUCLEIC ACID): The blueprint for almost every living creature. It is the molecule that carries genetic information. A length of DNA is called a gene.

DOUBLE HELIX: The shape that DNA forms when the individual components of DNA join together. It looks like a twisted ladder.

ELYTRA (SINGULAR: ELYTRON): The hardened forewings of beetles that serve as protective wing cases for the delicate, membranous hind wings underneath, which are used for flying. Some beetles can't fly; their elytra are fused together and they don't have hind wings.

ENTOMOLOGIST: A scientist who studies insects.

EXOSKELETON: An external skeleton—a skeleton on the outside of the body, rather than on the inside, like those of mammals. Insects have exoskeletons made largely from chitin. The exoskeleton is very strong and can be jam-packed with muscles, meaning that insects (especially beetles that have extremely tough exoskeletons) can be very strong for their size.

HABITAT: The area in which an organism lives. This is not the specific location. For example, a stag beetle's habitat is broad-leaved woodland and not London.

INSECT: An organism in the class Insecta, with over 1.8 million different species known and more to discover. Insects have three main body parts: the head, thorax, and abdomen. The head has antennae and a pair of compound eyes. Insects have six legs and many have wings. They have a complex life cycle called metamorphosis.

INVERTEBRATE: An animal that does not have a spine (backbone).

LARVAE (SINGULAR: LARVA): Immature insects. Beetle larvae are sometimes called grubs. Larvae look completely different from adult insects and often feed on different things than their parents, meaning that they don't compete with their parents for food.

MANDIBLES: Beetles' mouthparts. Mandibles can grasp, crush, or cut food, or defend against predators and rivals.

METAMORPHOSIS: Means *change*. It involves a total transformation of the insect between the different life stages (egg, larva, pupa, and adult; or egg, nymph, and adult). For example, imagine a big fat cream-colored grub: It looks nothing like an adult beetle. Many insects (including beetles) metamorphose inside a pupa or cocoon: They enter the pupa as a grub, are blended into beetle soup, re-form as an adult beetle, and break their way out of the pupa. Adult beetles never molt, and because they are encased in a hard exoskeleton that doesn't stretch or grow, they can never grow bigger. Therefore, if you see an adult beetle, it can never grow any bigger than it already is.

PALPS: A pair of sensory appendages near the mouth of an insect. They are used to touch/feel and sense chemicals in the surroundings.

SETAE (SINGULAR: SETA): Tiny hairlike projections covering parts of an insect's body. They may be protective, can be used for defense, camouflage, and adhesion (sticking to things), and can be sensitive to moisture and vibration.

SPECIES: The scientific name for an organism; helps define what type of organism something is, regardless of what language you speak. For example, across the world, Baxter will be known as *Chalcosoma caucasus*. However, depending on what language you speak, you will call him a different common name. The species name is always written with its genus name in front of it and it is always typed in italics, with the genus starting with a capital letter and the species all in lowercase type. If you are writing by hand, it should all be underlined instead of italicized. See Taxonomy.

. . . .

STRIDULATION: A loud squeaking or scratching noise made by an insect rubbing its body parts together to attract a mate, as a territorial sound, or as a warning sign.

. . . .

TAXONOMY: The practice of identifying, describing, and naming organisms. It uses a system called *biological classification*, with similar organisms grouped together. It starts off with a broad grouping (the kingdom) and gets more specific, with the species as the most specific group. No two species names (when combined with their genus) are the same: kingdom → phylum → class → order → family → genus → species. This system avoids the confusion caused by common names, which vary in different languages or even different households. For example, Baxter is a species of rhinoceros beetle: Some people may call him an Atlas beetle, Hercules beetle, or unicorn beetle, and there are lots of different species of rhinoceros beetle. So how do we know what Baxter really is? If you use biological classification, you can classify Baxter as: kingdom = Animalia (animal) → phylum = Arthropoda (arthropod) → class = Insecta (insect) → order = Coleoptera → family = Scarabaeidae → genus = *Chalcosoma* → species = *caucasus*. But all you really need to say is the genus and species, so Baxter is *Chalcosoma caucasus*.

. . . .

THORAX: The part of an insect's body between the head and the abdomen.

....

TRANSGENIC: An animal can be described as transgenic if scientists have added DNA from another species.

Acknowledgments

There is a triumvirate of angels without whom I could not be an author. I want to thank my husband, Sam Sparling, for the personal sacrifices he's made for my writing career. He is my first reader, greatest cheerleader, and trusted partner in crime. Thank you to my dear friend Claire Rakich, beta reader extraordinaire. Her honesty, feedback, and enthusiasm helped steer this story and all my stories. Special thanks to Jane Sparling, my mother-in-law, Nana Jane to my children, and the most generous and kind person I know. Without these three angels, *Revenge of the Beetle Queen* would be sitting on my desktop half-written.

I owe an immeasurable debt of thanks to Dr. Sarah Beynon, scientific consultant for this trilogy of books. She has helped me get over my fear of insects, letting me hold my first beetle, and has become a great friend. If you love beetles you should visit the Bug Farm, Sarah's wonderful visitor attraction in Pembrokeshire, Wales, where you can handle insects and learn all about the little creatures that run the planet. More information here: www.drbeynonsbugfarm.com.

Huge thanks to the National Theatre for granting me a sabbatical, and especially Alice King-Farlow, who has been generous and understanding about every single thing. The year 2016 would have been a different experience without your support, Alice.

I want to thank my awesome agent, Kirsty MacLachlan, and everyone at Chicken House. Jazz, Esther, Laura, Sarah, and Kes, you are all awesome. Elinor Bagenal, I'm secretly in love with you, but you probably knew that. Thank you for sending the beetles out into the world and finding homes in over thirty countries. Thanks to my trusted editor, Rachel Leyshon—I hope you edit every single book I ever write. Thanks to Rachel Hickman for the amazing cover, and artwork for both books, which has made people pick them up and take a risk on an unknown author. I must thank the powerhouse that is Liz Hyder, a truly passionate and wonderful communicator, and a giant thank-you to Nick and Lori at Scholastic USA, Anja at Chicken House Germany, and all the wonderful people working in publishing companies around the globe bringing beetles into young people's lives.

Barry Cunningham, you are the ultimate beetle champion. I never take your generosity for granted. A big heartfelt thank-you for everything you have done, and continue to do, for me and the beetles.

I would like to thank the Royal Entomological Society, and the entomological community, for embracing, celebrating, and supporting *Beetle Boy*, and forgiving me my fear of insects. In particular I would like to thank Peter Smithers, Simon Leather, Luke Tilley, Patrice Bouchard, and Max Barclay for their support and friendship; you are all heroes in my eyes.

My final thanks goes to you, the reader, and anyone who has written blog posts or reviews on Amazon, recommended my books, or given them as gifts, and especially to Michael Morpurgo for the quote on the cover. You are all wonderful.

A heartfelt thank-you, from me and your coleopteran friends.

If you want to do more, go to www.buglife.org.uk and get involved with the only organization in Europe devoted to the conservation of all invertebrates, everything from beetles to bees.

About the Author

M. G. Leonard is a writer of books, poems and screenplays. She works as a freelance digital media producer for clients such as the National Theatre and Harry Potter West End, and previously worked as Senior Digital Producer at the National Theatre, Royal Opera House, and Shakespeare's Globe. Her debut novel, *Beetle Boy*, was a *Publishers Weekly* Best Book of the Year and a New York Public Library Best Book for Kids. She lives in Brighton, England, with her family. You can visit her online at www.mgleonard.com and follow her on Twitter at @MGLnrd.